When Cupid Falls First

APRIL L. MOON

HARLEY HUNT

THIGPEN-
GANDY

ONE

Josie

"NOT A CHANCE IN HELL. DEFINITELY NOT HIM."

Online dating turned me into a horrible person.

I'd always prided myself on never judging a book by its cover—all the more important as yours truly opened her own bookstore. But when it came to men? I was about the worst cover-judge out there.

If it had been up to me, I'd sooner dive into a Dickens novel or dance with Dumas. Instead, I sat hunched over my counter, bathed in the glow from my tablet, scrolling through a dating app, hunting for some poor soul to escort me to my great-grandmother's upcoming hundredth-birthday bash. If you thought it was because I wanted a knight in shining armor to whisk me away from my bookish bliss, you'd be as wrong as Mr. Darcy was about Elizabeth Bennet at their first meeting.

I needed a human shield.

With a date by my side, my family would be more likely to behave—fewer biting remarks, less prying, and maybe even a few *congratulations* on grabbing a man. None of my family has ever said a word about me opening the Bookish Cat just a month ago in the heart of Seattle.

It was the realization of a dream born when I was a little girl. A dream I never thought possible until someone whispered words in my ear that gave me the courage I needed to quit my course in accounting and just go for it.

As far as Saturdays go, it seemed as typical as could be expected at the shop, my sanctuary for bibliophiles. The ambient noise of radio jazz humming softly behind me made for a soothing backdrop. The scent of fresh ink and crisp paper was more comforting to me than any fireplace. This was my refuge and a long figurative distance away from the men of FindYourGuy.com.

The app was a veritable carnival of humanity, including the muscle-bound gym fanatic, whose profile was a sea of sweaty six-pack selfies.

"More brawn than Bronte," I mused, moving on to the next.

The fisherman, all waders and wide smiles, with a bio that read like the collected works of every fishing joke in the world.

"Not exactly my catch of the day."

And then there was the seemingly nice guy who just happened to have a disturbing enthusiasm for taxidermy.

"Norman Bates meets Dr. Doolittle. No, thank you."

How was it possible, I wondered, that in the vast sea of online dating, no one seemed to even remotely resemble the elusive man who had been everything I ever wanted?

But I knew why.

None of them are Caleb.

I found my fingers grazing over the worn, leather-bound journal I kept under the glass counter, the one thing in this shop that would *never* be for sale. It was empty, not a single line written on its many blank pages. Its emptiness mocked me, just like Caleb's sudden departure from my life seven years ago.

He'd been there, and then he wasn't. Vanished as if there hadn't been something incredible growing between us.

It was raining the day he left, which wasn't even poetic—just a daily reality in the Pacific Northwest. We were standing in front of a bookstore I was admiring, just moments after he'd said the words that I've carried with me ever since. I could have sworn he was going to continue on to say something dramatic, something life changing...

And then he was running. Away from me.

Not another word, only a half glance over his shoulder to where I stood, drenched and alone. That was the end of every kiss, every embrace, every moment of true sensual bliss in my life. The journal fell as he went, a piece of him that was now etched into my life, blank pages and all, as I'd never dared to write a word in it.

My heart pinched as I traced my thumb over the cover. The raised leather drew a design that was invisible to the eye, but my fingertips knew it well from the many years of following along its edges. Even though nothing was written in it, the journal was far from new, the pages frayed and bent, the cover no longer the unblemished, rich color of coffee, but scratched and nicked.

I'd tried to pen him out of my life, tried to replace him with chapter after chapter of new men. But each one was less remarkable than the last, and none could compare to the plot twist that had been Caleb. Each passing day only made it more and more obvious.

I sighed and tucked the journal under a receipt book, out of sight and out of mind—or so I hoped. It seemed no matter how many years passed, that book, that man, would always leave me with a bittersweet taste of longing.

I missed him, the human cliffhanger who left me aching for every unwritten word of our story.

The soft jingling of the bell above the door brought me back from the edge of my daydreaming. I looked up to see a man shuffle in, the wind outside hustling him through the door with a cold slap of rain on his coat. The sudden change from the muted blues of jazz and the rustling of pages to the fresh smell of damp wool was jarring.

The man seemed entirely out of place, his posture rigid, his eyes darting around the room as if the books were about to stage a coup. His hands were clamped around a wet baseball cap, twisting it in an anxious rhythm that matched the drumming of rain on the windows.

"Can I help you find something?" I asked, offering what I hoped was a reassuring smile.

He started, as if startled to find someone else in the room. "Yes, uh... I need a book. For my wife," he said, his voice rough, as if he wasn't used to speaking much. It was akin to a timid whisper trying to masquerade as a roar.

"Oh? What kind of books does she like?" I inquired, expecting the usual vague descriptions like "romance," "thrillers," or "those murder mysteries."

He seemed to shrink a little, the cap bearing the brunt of his tight grip. "I, uh, don't rightly know. I thought she'd like the birthday gift I got her. It was a mixer, a very fancy one, but she tossed it out the window." His cheeks flushed a deep shade of crimson.

I stifled a laugh, as this woman sounded just like me. Offering a mixer as a birthday gift to a paramour was like offering Anna Karenina a subscription to a fashion magazine.

And I'd bet he'd run straight out of the lion's den to find her something else. So, here he was, a hapless husband in the wilderness of the written word, trying to make amends through literature. It was romantic—and desperate—in a distinctly Seattle, rain-soaked sort of way.

Yep, this man would likely have been sleeping on the sofa for a month without my help.

And he clearly needed my help. "Describe her to me."

I nodded, tucking a stray lock of hair behind my ear as I listened to the man's account of his wife—a woman who loved gardening, who had a soft spot for animals, who valued memories over material things. He seemed sincere, truly wanting to understand her, to reach out to her.

All the while, I let my fingers wander beneath the counter, ghosting over the familiar, comforting leather of Caleb's journal. It was as if I was trying to draw upon some arcane knowledge that would provide some divine understanding of the man in front of me, the woman he loved, and the unseen strings that connected their hearts.

And I knew I could do it, because of the journal—the one that kept me connected to the man who'd stolen my heart without even trying.

As my skin brushed the raised leather, a small jolt of electricity sparked. It was a sensation I'd felt many times before, a mysterious intuition guiding me, always to the right recommendation. This time was no different. The answer arrived like the final piece of a jigsaw puzzle falling into place, clear as day.

"*Black Beauty*," I announced, with a certainty that startled even me. "She needs *Black Beauty*."

The man looked taken aback, perhaps expecting a more adult title or at least something less... equine. But I was sure of it.

I fetched a copy from the classics section, its glossy black cover reflecting the soft lights of the bookstore. "It's more than a horse's tale, it's a journey back to her childhood. A reminder of simpler times, of purity and innocence. It's about understanding, resilience, and the bond between humans and animals." I cleared my throat to recount my favorite passage. "*'My troubles are all over, and I am at home; and often before I am quite awake, I fancy I am still in the orchard at Birtwick, standing with my friends under the apple trees.'*"

He blinked at me, his lips slightly parted. "That sounds like just the thing."

"Imagine," I continued, my eyes filled with conviction, "her holding this book, these words... It's an apology, an acknowledgment, and an olive branch, all rolled into one."

I held the book out to him, hoping he'd trust my somewhat unorthodox prescription. The way his eyes lingered on the cover told me he was willing to take that leap of faith.

No sooner had the jingling bell heralded the man's exit than a sudden commotion erupted from the adjacent aisle.

"You are uncanny!"

Barb, my part-time employee and full-time agent of chaos, burst from behind a towering box of books, startling me enough to send me stumbling backward.

"Barb!" I yelped, my heart playing a rapid beatnik rhythm as I tried to regain my footing. My glasses skidded down my nose, hanging precariously on the tip. The world was a dizzying blur of colors until I managed to shove the glasses back up into place. As I adjusted them, my multicolored shawl slipped from my shoulder.

My surprise turned into a laugh when I saw Barb standing there, her hair standing on end like she'd been static-shocked, and her apron covered in dust from her hiding place. Her surprise attack had quite literally blown the dust off a box of forgotten '90s thrillers I'd picked up at a trade show.

"Man, Barb, you nearly gave me a heart attack!" I chided, holding a hand over my pounding heart for dramatic effect.

Unperturbed, Barb shot me a mischievous grin. "How do you do that, Josie?" she asked, her eyebrows arched in genuine curiosity. "It's like you've got some literary superpower."

My cheeks warmed at the compliment, and my fingers instinctively touched the cover of Caleb's journal under the counter. "Oh, it's nothing really," I said, attempting nonchalance. "Just a wild guess based on what he told me about his wife."

But even as I tried to brush off my uncanny ability, a secret smile tugged at my lips. *I might have a touch of a superpower*, I thought. But I could never say that out loud, or people might think I'd lost my damn mind.

Like what I thought about Caleb when he told me he was an angel.

TWO

Caleb

THE HUMMING OF AFTERNOON TRAFFIC MIXED WITH
the chatter of diners at Rocksmith Café. I sat at a corner table
reading an L.A. Dobbs mystery book. I'd picked up mystery
books at first to help me better slip into the role of private
investigator, and they'd grown on me.

I found that the more I read, the more invested I became in
whether the characters would solve the mystery.

"You need anything else, Caleb?" Victory, one of my
regular waitresses, asked.

I gave her a friendly smile over the pages of my book and
nodded toward my half-full lemonade. "I'd love a top-up, if
you don't mind."

"Of course. Be right back." She zipped off, weaving
between the café tables and clustered diners with ease.

Most of the patrons and employees here were supes, drawn
by the feeling of safety in numbers. My senses had no trouble
picking them all out for what they were, though quite a few of
them were puzzled by the sight—and scent—of me.

An adorable selkie family with a new pup, a pair of half-human orcs, three tiger shifters having a business lunch, and a lone wolf shifter named Jaime were all seated on the patio. And me, of course. The fallen cupid who haunted the place, with mystery books and a bottomless lemonade. It was one of the small pleasures in my life, but the easy people-watching from my corner table was the real draw. Or it had been, before I'd gotten hooked on the lemonade.

Right now, I was keeping tabs on Amy and David, two star-crossed lovers who'd been separated for going on six years. But the heavenly Host knew that they were meant to be, and unbeknownst to either of them, they were walking down parallel streets, about to meet again.

Today was the day, and I felt it to the tips of my off-limits wings. Amy was in low spirits, grappling with what felt like an impossible decision. David was lost and restless, searching for purpose after losing another love.

They were both low, they were both lonely, and it was all about to change. I turned the page of my book, letting my senses unfurl, keeping precise watch on David's progress down the Ave, and Amy's down 42nd as they drew nearer.

Any second now... Amy reached the critical spot, and I exerted a little magical pressure on the traffic light. It turned early, the walk sign flashing. David huffed but started jogging to reach it rather than having to wait for the next light. He zipped down the sidewalk and made a hard turn into the cross-walk. The seconds were ticking down, but he kept up his pace. And thank goodness, because messing with traffic-light timing could have other unintended consequences.

When he finally reached my side of the street, he stopped, swiping a bead of sweat off his forehead. Amy was looking down, wiping a tear off her cheek as she walked straight into his broad back.

Gotcha.

"Oh, shit! I'm so sorry!" She fumbled, looking up with horror.

He spun, startled by both being run into and the familiar voice. "Amy? Are you okay?"

"David? Wow, it's been... years." She surreptitiously brushed her cheeks again, but the small movement wasn't lost on David. He'd always been attentive. He was the perfect complement for Amy, who always put others first, even to her own detriment. She needed someone caring and unselfish, who wouldn't take advantage but would put her first and treat her with respect. That someone was David.

I'd bet my last damn feather on it.

"Is everything okay? You look like you've been crying." He searched for words as he gazed into her green eyes. "I mean, you look even more gorgeous than I remember, but I hate to see you upset." He settled a gentle hand on her arm, and she shivered under his touch. It was a small reaction, but I couldn't help my grin. She was still into him, and he had never gotten over her.

"It's been a rough week."

Honesty. They were falling back together so beautifully.

David caught his breath, eagerness rolling off him at the chance to be near her again. "Can we go somewhere and talk for a while? I'd love to hear how you've been. Maybe we can work through the rough week together." He squeezed her shoulder lightly, and she nodded, bottom lip between her teeth.

I pushed a gentle suggestion toward him of a quiet coffee shop only a block over, where they wouldn't bump into anyone else to interrupt the conversation.

"I know of a great coffee shop. Is your drink still an Americano, two extra sugars?"

She nodded in shock. "I can't believe you still remember that."

He smiled down at her, genuinely happy. "You're worth remembering."

The two walked off toward the coffee shop, side by side, with the first hints of rekindled attraction flaring around them.

Perfect.

I withdrew my focus, letting the café chatter and occasional horn-blasts from the traffic filter back in. No changes, except a new party of six seated a few tables away. Trolls, wearing a glamour to hide their bluish-gray skin. Victory was approaching with a tray full of drinks—including my fresh lemonade—when it hit me.

Fated mates, and now was their moment.

The lone wolf's eyes were pinned to her, his lip curled in a protective half-snarl as she moved quickly toward the table of rowdy male trolls. I scanned the patio, letting my senses unfurl, assessing the options. The wolf was seated next to the selkie family, their sweet little girl playing happily with a pair of spoons, her back to the wolf.

Destiny could always use a little help.

Two more steps, and I nudged one of the wrought-iron café chairs across the patio into Victory's path. She tripped, her human senses unable to react to the spatial change in time to avoid it. She let out a horrified screech as the tray lifted free of her fingertips, all seven iced drinks tilting forward with her momentum, straight toward the unaware selkie baby.

Jaime moved in a blur of wolf speed, inserting himself between the icy shower and the blissfully unaware toddler.

The drinks hit his chest with a crash, sodas and ice cubes

making a mess of his tight T-shirt, and plenty of it splashing back to soak Victory's white uniform shirt.

"Oh my gosh, oh my gosh, I'm so sorry! Shoot. Shoot, shoot—the boss warned me about one more mistake... I'm going to lose my job!" Panic flared in the air around her, but the wolf was rock steady as he settled his hand on her cheek. His aura was all possession, all heat as he spoke.

"It's fine. Why don't you and I go get cleaned up. Someone else can see to the table."

"My boss—"

"—never needs to hear about this. Come."

"Okay. Yes, let me get you some towels. I'm so sorry, again. I don't know how that even happened."

The wolf followed her silently, but he cast a curious glance around the patio, having caught my interference with his superior senses.

When his eyes landed on me and paused, I couldn't stop the smile and nod, cluing him into the fact that it was me. With a human, I'd never tip my hand, but here, there was no harm. Knowing what I was would only push him to pursue what his wolf knew was right, even though he had been consciously fighting it because Victory was human.

Almost.

My senses didn't lie, and somewhere decades back, she'd had a wolf ancestor. It was probably why she was drawn to this place, even though she couldn't have had more than a drop or two of werewolf blood in her veins.

I left a few bills under my empty lemonade cup to cover the club sandwich plus a generous tip and then hit the sidewalk. My office was a few blocks away, and I was eager to tick Amy and David off my list of couples.

Victory and her wolf hadn't been on the list, but fallen or

no, I couldn't resist the pull of new love. My cupid instincts wouldn't let me.

I let myself into my silent sanctuary, the familiar tang of old linoleum and a hint of dust soothing after all this time. The lights flickered overhead, revealing my well-worn desk and cracked green Naugahyde chair, with a visitor kicked back in it.

"Gabriel. What are you doing here?"

"Don't sound so thrilled to see me, now." He grinned, not bothering to do more than oscillate back and forth in my chair. I dropped my messenger bag into the client chair and propped my hands on my hips.

"I'm always thrilled to see one of my brothers, you know that. Just concerned. Is everything okay... upstairs?"

He snorted. "Fine, fine. Same old. Harmony, peace, and more gold than Fort Knox ever dreamed of. I'm here to see how things are with your mission. I had a feeling we'd reached a pivotal moment."

That gave me pause. Pivotal moment? Each couple on my list was pivotal, in my opinion. They'd made their way on it because I'd screwed up, a fact I could never take lightly. So what could be so pivotal about Amy and David. Unless—

"Ah, I did give a wolf a little push this afternoon, but they were fated, and he was spiraling."

He nodded, grin growing wider, as if he had one of those pies and I was the unsuspecting asshole about to get whipped cream up my nose.

"You know the Host is pro-love, whatever form it takes. Supes don't usually make our list because they don't need help, but if you think they did, I'm not one to argue."

He could argue, though. My instincts? They had proven more than once to be wildly off base. And he was right that supernaturals didn't make the list, only humans. If I was

13

wrong, and it hadn't been the moment for Jaime and Victory, I could have just set off a terrible chain reaction. Lead pooled in my stomach. What had seemed so right a few minutes ago was suddenly seeming very, very dangerous.

"Hey, don't start second guessing yourself." Gabriel rose from my chair and came around the desk to put his hand on my shoulder. "Your instincts were always good, and you've spent seven years now making up for past mistakes. That couple you matched today was solid. That's why I'm here, to give you an extra set of names."

I was floored. Stunned. "You want to give me an assignment? But I haven't finished the list. I'm close, but—"

"This couple is time sensitive, and the Host says you're the only cupid for the job. Consider it... a turning point."

Resolve flooded my chest. This opportunity to prove myself was priceless, and I would not mess it up, not this time. "Consider it done."

Gabriel smiled, the expression broad, making me feel that I was missing something, like an inside joke. With a snap, he poofed out of my office before I could ask.

I sighed and dropped into my comfortable old green chair. There, on my desk, were two new headshots with names written on the back.

My new assignment.

So, what was I missing? I drummed my fingers idly on the desk as I focused on their faces and let my senses soar out, feeling for their locations.

There.

With Gabriel involved, I couldn't say I was surprised to find them both a block away, in one of the shops on the Ave.

Instinct demanded I grab my bag and go check them out. Were they already a couple, or was it pure coincidence that they were together in a shop right now, just when Gabriel visited? Either way, it was too good an opportunity to miss.

I walked down the busy streets, minivans with too many bumper stickers getting honked at by cussing cabbies as people walked every which way, their heads down with eyes locked on phone screens. I didn't see the appeal, but I had a leg up on the average person. I could sense everyone around me—their moods, their emotions. It might have been overwhelming, but I was wired to handle it. I tried to respect people's privacy and only use my powers when I could intervene for good.

And right now, I was getting close to two people, both in interesting moods inside the... what was this place? I'd never come across it before. It must be new. I'd spent years walking up and down the Ave to and from my private investigation office, but never before had I seen that sign on the awning.

The Bookish Cat.

It was forest green, which matched the ivy crawling up the outside of the red brick building perfectly. The windows were clean, no writing on them, simply the spines of hundreds of books, stacked enticingly. And sure enough, there was a calico cat curled up inside the display window, eyes flicking with bored judgment over every person walking past on the sidewalk.

I paused, considering my match, both of them inside. They were in opposite parts of the store. The woman was closest, near the windows. In fact, if I ducked a little, I could see her through the shelves in the display window. She was a petite redhead with a dusting of freckles over her button nose.

She was sad, though. A ripple of grief floated around her, and her raincoat was belted tightly, as if to ward off more than the light drizzle of a Seattle afternoon.

I stretched farther, finding the man toward the very back of the store, hidden behind one of the bookcases. He was filled with intense longing, and I didn't think it was for a book. It had clearly been a while since this man had gotten laid.

Welcome to the club, man.

Done assessing, I stepped inside. A bell chimed merrily overhead, but I ignored it. I was intensely focused on the couple. I needed to see the man, see if anything about him gave me a clue.

I strode past two stacks, not paying attention to anything else in the shop, until a signature I hadn't sensed in years stopped me dead in my tracks. I scanned the shop quickly, and the world seemed to disappear under my feet when I spotted her behind the cash register.

Was I flying? No, that wasn't possible. I hadn't had my wings since the day I left her.

Josephine.

Holy Shit.

THREE

Josie

THE SOFT TINKLE OF THE DOORBELL ANNOUNCED
another visitor, but my eyes remained glued to the chapter in
Seattle's bylaws entitled "Tenant Rights Regarding Pets."
Nestled under my hand, Gatsby purred with leisurely content-
ment. He was a fluffy white Persian and one of the three unoffi-
cial residents of the Bookish Cat.

He was also wholly undisturbed by the prospect of
eviction.

"There's got to be a loophole here somewhere, Gatsby." I
traced over the legalese with a slightly smudged fingertip. My
nose scrunched up as I squinted at the paragraphs of unfamiliar
terms and subclauses. "I mean, it's not like I invited you in. You
heard the name of the shop and took it literally. You're part of
the store's charm now."

Gatsby simply purred louder, his jade eyes half-closed as he
pushed his head into my palm. He didn't seem concerned in
the least about the consequences of his unauthorized tenancy.

Above us, nestled in a second-story nook with a clear
view of the street outside, Matilda lazily stretched out a paw.

A playful calico, her claws briefly glinted in the dappled afternoon sunlight streaming through the book-lined windows.

The third trespasser, Heathcliff, a sleek black cat, was mysteriously absent from his usual perch atop the tallest book-shelf. I'd only discovered his hiding spot last week when a customer squealed with delight, pointing upward and exclaiming, "Look, it's like he's the king of books!"

Indeed, the Bookish Cat was a haven for bibliophiles and feline enthusiasts alike, our shared love of quiet corners and cozy atmospheres bringing us all together. The idea of disrupting this peace with cease-and-desist notices was a damn disaster, and yet the landlord's decree was clear—the cats had to go.

But these four-legged interlopers were more than mere strays. They'd swiftly become part of the Bookish Cat's soul, its identity. And I was determined to keep it that way.

It didn't hurt that they were freaking cute. I was instantly attached.

Damn landlord.

I felt the new patron hovering in the entry of the shop, so I cleared my throat and closed the spiral-bound book of bylaws.

"Welcome to the Bookish Cat, can I..."

My heart abruptly caught in my throat, the words dying on my lips as my breath hitched. There he stood, like a ghost from the past.

Caleb.

The same Caleb who, with his devastatingly handsome features, was my first real love. The same Caleb who had vanished from my life seven years ago, leaving nothing but a mysterious blank book and a cavernous void in my heart.

How utterly strange and surreal to see him standing there

in the doorway of my bookstore, like a character from a well-worn page had suddenly stepped into reality.

"What the—"

I didn't know what to do, so I covered my face with the bylaws, fake reading while I tried to figure out what was going on.

As Caleb strolled toward the counter, each step echoing against the worn hardwood floors, my mind was tugged into the past, to the whirlwind that was our romance. The rows of books blurred into a kaleidoscope of color as I traveled seven years back, finding myself in the middle of laughter and stolen kisses in the forests of Federal Way, Washington. Our whispered promises and shared dreams. The warmth of his palms as he cupped my breasts like he never wanted to let go. It had been intoxicating and intense, but it had also been fleeting. Painfully so.

He had said he couldn't have a "normal" relationship—words that tumbled out of his mouth in a rush, as if they were well-rehearsed lines from a script. He had spun me tales of a life too complicated, too involved. He tried to hide behind clichés, hollow excuses that couldn't possibly encapsulate the true depth of his reasons.

The thought had made me bristle then the way it still did now. How could anything as profound and complex as love ever be "normal"? I'd pleaded for him to share the real reasons, but I never got a real answer before he left me for good.

Until today.

"'Time, which sees all things, has found you out,'" I quoted to the bylaws I hid behind.

"You always did love *Tess of the D'Urbervilles*," he replied, as if it was entirely normal that he'd appear out of nowhere after breaking my poor, naïve heart all those years ago.

Stealing a glance over the top of the bylaws book, I studied Caleb. It was as if the last seven years had barely grazed him. His hair, still that unique shade of sandy chestnut, was longer and slightly tousled, giving him an irresistibly boyish charm. His firm jawline was shadowed with a day's worth of stubble, adding a rugged touch to his features, and reminding me he was all man. I had to hold myself back from caressing his cheek.

His striking blue eyes, though, were the same as I remembered—deep and intense, mirroring the vast expanse of the Pacific Ocean that lapped the shores of my hometown. They twinkled with a warmth that made my heart flutter like it used to. But that warm exterior lit a spark of hunger in me, a craving from deep within that wouldn't be satisfied until he held me in his arms.

His attire had remained unaltered as well, a mix of casual and professional—a well-fitted charcoal-gray blazer over a simple white T-shirt, paired with dark jeans that sat perfectly on his hips. In spite of myself, I felt a rush of familiarity, a jolt of attraction that was just as potent now as it had been then. It was a testament to the kind of man Caleb was—irresistible, frustrating, and yet wholly unforgettable.

Damn it.

A sigh escaped my lips before I could contain it. There he was, Caleb, unchanged and somehow hotter than any man had any right to be.

If he could even be called a "man," given his particular status on Earth.

"Can I help you find anything in particular?" I asked, feigning ignorance, my tone as casual as I could manage, given my racing heart.

"It's been a while," he said, his voice as smooth as velvet and equally disarming.

I stubbornly stuck to my role. "In that case, welcome back to the world of books." I gestured toward the towering shelves, lined with everything from modern prose to ancient poetry. "Our fiction section is quite extensive, if that's what you're after."

He chuckled, the sound resonating in the quiet store, bouncing off the stacks of books and knick-knacks. "Josie..."

My heart somersaulted at the sound of his voice so close. His unwavering gaze broke my resolve. With a small laugh that didn't quite reach my eyes, I put down my pretense. "Caleb. Wow, it's been a long time. Welcome to my bookstore, the Bookish Cat."

He just walked in—obviously he knows its name. Why am I such a mess at the sight of him?

He looked around, his eyes reflecting genuine pleasure. "Your store?"

"Yes, all mine," I said, my voice echoing with a hint of pride in spite of myself.

"That's wonderful. Really." His tone was laced with sincerity.

"So..." I struggled to keep my voice steady. "What brings you here, Caleb?"

"Just a little bit of detective work," he replied casually, as if he hadn't just dropped a bombshell.

"A detective? You?" The word slipped from my lips, wrapped in surprise and a touch of disbelief. "Like, a private eye?"

Since when are angels private eyes?

Caleb nodded, a smug smirk curling at the corner of his mouth. "Yes. Just like the ones in your mystery novels. Some things have changed since the last time we saw each other."

It was hard not to let my curiosity get the better of me, but

I fought it, tamping it down. It wasn't my right to know anymore. I left Caleb behind when he walked out on me. Or so I told myself.

"And what's your case today, *detective*?"

"As a matter of fact, there are two people in here," he began, nodding toward a man browsing the contemporary fiction section and a woman engrossed in a book of sonnets, "who need to discover each other."

The statement was as perplexing as it was unexpected. I stole a glance at the pair he was referring to, the wheels in my head beginning to spin. They were as different as night and day — one a casual browser, the other lost in the rhythm of verses.

"So, you're playing matchmaker in a bookstore? What's next? A game of Clue in the self-help section?"

He shot me a million-dollar smile and said, "I'm serious. Any ideas on what might help them out?" He remained sincere, perhaps remembering my passion for all things story.

Subconsciously, my hand reached under the counter, fingertips brushing against the worn leather of Caleb's journal, now my tool, my secret source of wisdom and intuition. The pages fluttered under my touch, whispering ideas and insights.

I felt a shiver of energy, a familiar tingling sensation that made the hairs on the back of my neck stand on end. I knew. I knew just what these two needed. I knew the books that would bridge the gap between two souls unknown to each other.

I went to the shelves and pulled a copy of Murakami's *Norwegian Wood* for the man, Anais Nin's *Delta of Venus* for the woman. I couldn't explain how I knew, but the ink on the pages was insistent. I glanced at Caleb, my smile wry. "Trust me, they'll thank us later."

The look on Caleb's face was a priceless blend of skepticism and intrigue. "Those books for those two?" His brow furrowed in disbelief. I merely shrugged. Guilt niggled at me for not mentioning his book, but now was hardly the time to talk about what he'd left behind.

"Do you trust me?"

He tilted his head in reluctant agreement.

I approached the first member of the unsuspecting couple, my hands carefully cradling the books as if they were fragile birds. "You'll love this," I assured the man. "It'll take you on an adventure you didn't even know you were looking for." Then I strutted to the woman. "You really need to give this a try. If I'm wrong, you can bring it back."

Her smile widened. "That sounds like an excellent deal." She cocked her head. "Do you do this for all your customers?"

"You'd be surprised," I said with a wink.

The two approached the counter to pay at the same time, speaking low about the recommendations. They handed each other their book, both eliciting initial surprise that was soon replaced by intrigue as they looked over the covers. As they chatted at the counter, purchases in hand, I couldn't help but send a triumphant glance toward Caleb.

One point for Josie and the Bookish Cat.

"Miss Ray! I have told you a hundred times already, these cats are a scourge on my property!"

There, framed in the doorway like some gloom-bringing thundercloud, stood Mr. Anderson, my asshole landlord. His watery, squinted eyes immediately fell on Matilda, now lounging nonchalantly on top of a stack of romance novels. "This will not do!" His voice echoed through the store, punctuated by a thunderous sneeze.

Before I could think of a response, Caleb twisted his hand in the air, his fingers tapping out an inaudible rhythm. Almost immediately, Mr. Anderson's gruff exterior softened, a puzzled look stealing over his features.

"Actually, I think I forgot something. I need to attend to it." His words trailed off as he hurried out the door, leaving me staring after him in a wake of bewilderment.

I gawked at Caleb, who lifted an eyebrow in return.

"I tried to explain this to you years ago."

FOUR

Caleb

"But you just... and he just..." Josie waved toward the door, where her landlord had just abruptly exited, her mouth hanging open like a fish.

She's incredibly sexy when she's all cute and flustered.

"Yes," I said gently, hoping she wasn't about to react badly. Again.

When I'd told her the truth of what I was seven years ago, she'd pushed me away in disbelief. Refused to see me for nearly a week before she agreed to talk again. After that, I hadn't had time to prove things, not really, before I'd been called back to the Host for correction.

A correction I'd *more* than *deserved*. Josie had been the perfect distraction, one that had led to too many slip-ups. A dozen couples, two dozen fates, knocked off course, all because I thought I'd found my Chosen. An angel finding his Chosen was a big deal—a once-in-eternity kind of thing—but there was one big problem. Josie was human. Despite that, I'd let myself get carried away with the belief that she could be the one, at the expense of those who relied on me for their fates.

It was egregious. Too much, and even a loving heavenly Host had to do something to right my wrongs. So they had. My wings were stripped and my other couples reassigned until I'd corrected the matches I'd messed up.

Seven long years of being earthbound, fallen from grace, and I was finally down to the last few names on my list. All I had left to do was match my last three couples, and I could get my wings back. Be *whole* again.

But what would that mean for Josie? A human Chosen... I didn't know. It had never before in the history of angels happened—an angel having a human Chosen. I wasn't even sure it was divinely possible to *have* a human Chosen. Only that I felt that pull in my chest, always to her.

She was doing fine without me, my presence back in her life seeming to throw her off more than anything. She still didn't believe what I was. So maybe I was wrong. A Chosen should *need* her other half, and Josie didn't seem to need anything from me. I'd been wrong about so many things.

I resisted the urge to shake my head to clear it. She was still staring at me like I'd grown a third eyeball. I needed to say something to set her back at ease, prove that she wasn't losing it.

Of course, being a cupid *specifically* was a bit harder to prove than for most supernatural species. Wolves could shift, vampires had fangs and super speed, and trolls had blue skin.

But cupids?

Well, we helped true loves find each other. It was a very precise art, and it wasn't easy to explain or show at the drop of a hat. So I couldn't blame her for her reaction.

Granted, bringing couples together wasn't my only divine trick, hence our current predicament. The flick of my hand that sent the angry landlord away had gotten her unstuck from her current predicament, but had also made her head spin.

As for the landlord, he would get back to his desk and make his very important phone call—a need I'd plucked out of the cloud of stress hanging over the man—and be distracted for a while. But eventually, he'd be back, trying to toss out her cats. He was allergic, so the instinct was understandable. But perhaps there was something I could do to fix the problem permanently?

I needed to change the topic of conversation, but it was hard to think straight. Josie was exactly as I remembered, only slightly older, slightly wiser, and even more gorgeous. She wore a simple sweater, her hair pulled halfway up, the bottom spilling over with a waterfall of soft curls. She'd also filled out a little, and the extra curves looked phenomenal on her.

A stretchy neon book cover would look phenomenal on her. It's Josie.

"Your landlord doesn't like the cats? They seem quite content here." I threw out the first thing that came to mind, even though I already knew the answer. Anything had to be better than the thought of her curves and how badly I wanted to touch them. *Needed* to touch them.

Josie had always brought out un-angelic urges in me. She was my downfall and my addiction—one I needed to steer clear of.

She finally snapped out of it, focusing on what I'd said.

"Yes, they are quite content, given the fact that they each showed up and made themselves at home."

"They're strays?"

She lifted her chin in challenge. "Not anymore. They belong here. They're part of the Bookish Cat family."

I smiled, impressed with Josie as usual. She was never one

to back down from a challenge. "You've always had a big heart. It's one of the first things I admired about you, way back when."

She cocked her head. "Well, thank you. Do you often run away from people you *admire*, without ever looking back? Or saying goodbye? Or explaining?" Her aura turned sour, almost bitter. She leveled me with an accusing glare and picked up the fluffiest of the cats.

She missed me?

She'd always held a special place in my heart, but she'd moved on. I knew because I had come back for her. It was only a few human weeks after I'd been called up to give an account to the Host, and I'd used my powers to trace her as soon as my feet were back on mortal ground.

I remembered it like it was yesterday. It was raining—like always in Seattle—and I was drenched through my soggy, squelching shoes by the time I found her at the edge of her college's football field. She was huddled under an enormous maple tree, snuggled up to a college guy in one of those brightly-colored leather jackets. Josie never knew I was there, but I saw the whole thing—his arm around her shoulders, the two of them tucked together, studying. When he leaned in to kiss her, I walked away.

I was too late, had left too abruptly, been detained by the heavens for too long, and I had to let her go. So I did, keeping myself busy for seven long years, patching up failed matches and ignoring the constant pull in my chest toward her.

"You know, everybody told me working at a bookshop would be boring, but I have to say, you sure keep it exciting." A woman appeared out of nowhere at my side. "Is he part of the decor now? I approve." She ambled away again, a stack of

Highlander romance books tottering with each step, but not falling.

"I'm sorry about my employee. She's, well, Barb." Josie's cheeks colored, a beautiful peach flush tinting her skin, taunting my fingers with the desire to touch. To taste.

"Don't apologize. I love everything about what you've built here, truly. I knew if you decided to follow your dreams, you'd make it spectacular."

She looked down, sinking her nose into the cat's ruff and taking a beat before responding. "It was thanks to you, you know. What you said back then gave me what I needed. Do you remember?"

"Of course I do."

"'*The future you seek is seeking you.*' Everyone else told me it was crazy, that I should do something *secure*." Her eyes were fiery when she looked back up. "You know what's secure? Trusting my instincts. Leaning into what I believe in. Knowing what I can do. That's my security."

Pride for her accomplishments swelled in my chest, the feeling surprising. I had no claim on her, no horse in this race, and yet... I wanted this for her. I wanted her to be living the life of her dreams. Except, I sensed no trace of the football player. No leftover wisps of his essence, nothing changed about her, or her signature, to indicate they were still together. Nor that she was with anyone else, as far as I could tell.

Was she single again?

It shouldn't matter. It really shouldn't. I'd tried to get closer to her before, and it hadn't turned out well *at all*. Clearly, she hadn't believed me when I told her what I was, based on her reaction to my distracting her landlord a few minutes ago.

"Why are you looking at me like that?" she prodded, shifting back and forth nervously on her feet.

"Like what?" I asked, curious about her thoughts. She'd always had a unique read on every situation.

"Like..." She let one hand drop from the cat, disappearing under the counter. It was like watching a light bulb turn on, her expression suddenly clear. "You're here for a romance? For yourself?"

That had me rocking back on my heels. "What? Why would you say that?"

"Just a hunch. You *did* come in here for a couple, after all."

Heavens help me. *The couple.* They'd left ages ago, and I'd been so distracted with Josie, I completely forgot to follow them. She'd recommended two completely off-the-wall books, they'd paid, and I hadn't batted an eye as they left.

And here I was, still enraptured by the sight of her instead of doing my job.

Again, damn it.

This was a mistake I couldn't afford to repeat, though. I needed a perfect record to get my wings back, and this was the only extra couple I'd been assigned in *seven years.* I couldn't screw this up, even if every fiber of my being was screaming to stay, to spend time with Josie, to bask in her achingly familiar presence a little longer.

"I have to go," I said, unable to hide the regret in my voice.

"I'd say I'm surprised, but that would be a lie."

Yeah, she wasn't going to forgive me any time soon. Her acidic tone told me everything I needed to know, and then some.

"It was good seeing you again, Josie. I'd love to catch up if you'd be open to the idea."

She bit her lip, both hands sinking into the cat's white fur once more, but she didn't answer right away. I had to go, but I somehow couldn't uproot myself until she answered me. There was no part of me that would leave.

"Oh, for cripe's sake," Barb interjected, hands on hips in the aisle. "She'd love to, Caleb. Call the shop any time. Don't look at me like that, Josie!" She wagged a motherly finger. "You know it's not going to work out with any of those wannabe fishermen on your app. This hunk of a man right here is what you need to wow your mom's socks off."

I looked back at Josie, hoping she'd confirm that I could call and maybe even tell me what Barb was talking about.

Fishermen?

Wowing her mom's socks?

"Fine! He can call, just *please* stop talking!" She made the universal cutting motion for Barb to be quiet, but the woman only grinned, looking pleased as she surveyed the two of us.

Josie was reluctant at best, but it was more than I'd dared hope for when I first walked in, and I'd take it. But now, I had to go track down my couple and see what I had to do to get them together.

"I'll call you tomorrow morning," I said as I walked out the door.

"But will you?" she whispered, a question I was very sure wasn't meant for me but which sent pain spiraling through me just the same.

I FOUND them a little over a mile away and slowed my pace as I realized they were still together and lingering in Gas Works Park. It was a unique piece of Seattle history—what used to be a coal gasification plant had been turned into a park where people and geese alike enjoyed the view of Lake Union.

My couple, however, was ignoring both the water and the Seattle skyline. I spotted them leaning against a fence, elbow to elbow, and... arguing?

No, that wasn't right. They were loud, and they were gesturing animatedly, but they both *glowed* with happiness, not frustration. I walked slowly, gazing out over the water, then back to the gasworks where they stood, keeping my surveillance subtle.

"It's not about the sex. If that's what you think, you're missing the point," he argued.

She threw up her hands, a glint of playful exaggeration in her aura, but no real heat. "Really, then? Enlighten me. What *is* it about?"

"The journey. The *adventure*. Taking a risk, putting yourself out there! Haven't you ever wondered what might happen if you just let go, gave in to the possibilities?" His chest heaved as he stared into her eyes far too intensely for a near-stranger. He looked like he wanted to tear her clothes off.

"Yes, yes I have." The words were soft, so subtle the evening breeze would have carried them away from anyone without supernatural hearing.

Something wordless and wild passed between them, and then she was kissing him, and he was kissing her right back, his hands cupping her jaw and tipping her head up. Heat spiraled upward toward the night sky, and a smile split my lips.

New love. Passion that burned so brightly, the heavens couldn't help but take notice.

They were meant to be, and everything inside me reveled in joy at the sight of a perfect match coming together for the first time.

Josie had known exactly what they needed to spark the flame. I felt that same rush of heat in my own veins, the couple's desire thick in the air affecting me, making me think back to the time Josie and I spent wrapped up in each other like that.

I sped up, leaving the couple alone to see where the night took them. My hand fell to my pocket, grabbing the cell phone I kept there for clients. In seconds, I had pulled up the shop phone number for the Bookish Cat, but my thumb hesitated over the call button.

I needed time to think, to say the exact right thing. If I wanted any shot with Josie at all, I couldn't mess it up a second time.

FIVE

Josie

AS EVENING FELL, I NESTLED INTO MY READING NOOK. The inviting warmth of my apartment, a charming two-bedroom on the fifth floor of a classic Seattle brownstone, surrounded me. It wasn't overly extravagant, but it was cozy and had a glorious view of the city skyline.

The place smelled perpetually of aged paper and a faint whiff of fresh coffee, scents that seemed to linger even when I couldn't find their sources.

One of my great joys was snuggling in my favorite cat-print pajamas that had seen better days. To add to the symphony of comfort, Gatsby, the youngest of the Bookish Cat's feline entourage, had followed me home and was now snoozing peacefully at my sock-clad feet, his soft purring lulling me into a sense of deceptive tranquility.

Because today had been anything but tranquil.

I tried to calm my mind by settling into my reading nook, tucked away in a corner of the living room—my treasured tomes piled haphazardly on vintage bookshelves, spilling out onto small side tables, and even stacked like literary skyscrapers on the floor. These books had been my solace during a childhood when I felt I had no choices, no freedom, no future of my own.

Tonight, however, even my favorite Krista Street book couldn't stop the whirl of turmoil in my head. The day's events replayed in my mind like a stubborn earworm—the sudden reappearance of Caleb with his enigmatic eyes, his casual charm, and the unresolved past that echoed in the hollow spaces of our conversation. The twist of his hand, which sent Mr. Anderson on his way.

As I dwelled on the sight of him, my heart palpitated at the speed of a hummingbird's wings. But every time I imagined him taking me in his arms the way he'd done when we were younger, surrounding me and making me feel like the most important woman in the world, a wiser voice thundered into my mind as if over a loudspeaker.

Don't get your hopes up. He probably won't be back.

He'd been there and then he'd been gone. He'd come back... and he'd likely go again. Tomorrow, the day after? Who knew, but I wasn't going to wait to find out. Barb was wrong—expecting that Caleb would be my date was a bad idea all around. And I absolutely could *not* get attached to the idea of him as a fixture in my life, permanent or otherwise.

In a bid to anchor my wavering thoughts, I turned my attention to the more urgent matter at hand.

My great-grandmother's hundredth-birthday party was nearing, and there was no way I could go without a date, for my own sanity. In a sudden fit of desperation, I set my novel on the antique side table and grabbed my laptop. I settled back into my throne, an oversized plush armchair with an eclectic mix of throw pillows, and logged back into FindYourGuy.com. There had to be at least one man who could fit the bill. To ask

Caleb—even if I did see him again—would be asking too much.

The glow from my laptop screen illuminated the room as I scanned through profile after profile, my mouse hovering over the "Chat Now" button. Forget about the man whose entire profile was in rhyme... no, not the taxidermist again... hmm, a rock collector?

Rock collector is a good contender...

I took a deep breath and clicked on his profile, determined to plunge in headfirst and find myself a date.

> Josie: Hi there. I saw you're into rock collecting! That's really interesting! ☺

> RockCollector89: Hi, yes! I do have a fondness for lithology. My buddies like to joke that I'm always between a rock and a hard place. 😅

> Josie: Haha, that's a good one!

> Josie: So, I'm going to be straight with you. How do you feel about family events?

> RockCollector89: Family events? I usually dig those! 😄 They can be quite fun, much like unearthing a rare mineral.

> Josie: Great! Because I have one coming up soon, and I'm debating whether to bring a plus one.

> RockCollector89: Oh, really? That sounds exciting. Where will it be?

Josie: My great-grandmother's house in Snoqualmie. It's her 100th birthday.

RockCollector89: Snoqualmie, you say? Isn't that near the foothills of the Cascade Range? I might get to see some classic metamorphic rock formations there.

Josie: Uh, I'm not sure. I was more focused on the birthday cake aspect.

RockCollector89: Haha, cake is good too! I suppose I can always eat my slice on a slab of gneiss.

Josie: A slab of what now?

RockCollector89: Gneiss! It's a common and widely distributed type of rock formed by high-grade regional metamorphic processes. The layering of minerals gives it a unique appearance!

Josie: Oh, you're... really into the rock thing, aren't you?

RockCollector89: Absolutely! All rocks, all the time. 🌏

Josie: Well, I would need you to promise not to replace the birthday candles with stalagmites.

RockCollector89: Can't make any promises! 😄 But I would do my best.

Josie: Noted. I'll keep you posted.

I told myself this was a normal exchange, that he was *probably* a normal guy who would talk about rocks. A lot. And maybe that was okay because then he could occupy my mother with various drab tales of quartz and who knew what else while I got some time with my distant cousins, who were the only fun members of the family.

As I drifted off, I tried to think of the rock collector, his mussed blond hair under a baseball cap, the way it was in his profile picture. But no matter how hard I tried, it was Caleb's face that reappeared like a beacon and stayed with me while I slept.

THE NEXT DAY, as I was lost in thought amid the towering bookshelves, the familiar jingle of the shop's entrance bell made me stop.

It can't be him.

Before I could turn around, a voice came from behind me, the voice that still sent the butterflies in my stomach into a frenzy, even after all these years.

"Josie," Caleb said, making my name sound like a sacred incantation.

"Oh, hello." I wished that sounded more natural.

"You did something remarkable yesterday."

I scrambled to stifle the grin that threatened to bloom across my face. Playing it cool was never my forte, but now was as good a time as any to try. I responded with a nonchalant, "Oh, did I?"

His laugh echoed through the room. He looked at me with newfound respect, a sparkle of excitement in his eyes that lit something in the center of my chest, a wave of heat licking across my skin, and I had to hold myself back from doing something I'd regret. Like jumping into his arms and wrapping my legs around him the way I used to do.

"Those books you recommended—they were exactly what the couple needed. And you must have known they would be. You have an uncanny ability."

"Well, that's part of the bookseller's job description, isn't it?" I tried to keep my tone light, even as I fought off waves of desire.

"No, it's more than that," he insisted, stepping closer. "You've... you've really got something."

Does he know about the journal? Does he think I'm a fraud?

He took another step closer, invading my personal space and testing my resolve not to get closer to him. Why was he so damn magnetic? I never had this problem with other men, only Caleb. He was under my skin, with seemingly no effort at all.

"I could use your instincts for my mission. The one I told you about when we first met."

His words hung in the air between us, creating a potent mix of disbelief and anticipation. I blinked once, twice, waiting for his words to sink in, trying to figure out how to respond. The silence of the bookstore only magnified the moment, making it feel as monumental as it was unexpected.

My silence must have worried Caleb because he swiftly added, "And of course I'll return the favor. You help me with my mission, and I help you with... whatever you need. Deal?" His eyes searched mine, looking for an answer.

My mind began to whirl, and I glanced down at the worn rug beneath my feet, biting my lip. His offer was tempting, very tempting, but was I willing to put my heart on the line again? The situation with my family was a hot mess, one that had only grown more convoluted and painful over time. And then there was Nana Geraldine's birthday bash. The stress over my great-grandmother's upcoming party and the whole plus-one expectation was just making it worse. But to get tangled up with Caleb was like signing up to have my heart broken.

"Well," I began, my lips moving before my brain could stop them. "There is something..." I took a deep breath and quickly spilled out the rest. "I've got a family event coming up—a hundredth-birthday party for my great-grandmother—and it could be... well, complicated."

"Why's that?" Caleb asked, his tone soft, inviting. Like my own personal catnip, he was always drawing me in. How I longed to nestle my face into his neck and tell him everything. But I stayed in place.

"You remember how things were with my family," I said, my voice barely above a whisper. I told him as much as I could bear at that moment. How since we'd had a blow up in my first year of university, we hadn't seen eye to eye. How their thinly-veiled remarks about being irresponsible still stung, and therefore how I avoided seeing them as much as possible. How our relationship only grew more toxic with time. Except with my great-grandmother. She and I had managed to stay as close as we ever were—maybe because she was a weirdo herself, though she had earned the right by being on the planet for nearly a century.

He stood listening, eyes wide in empathy and the occasional murmur of "I'm sorry to hear that" and a much quieter mutter of *"Piece of shit"* that I don't think I was meant to hear.

I finished with a sigh, anxious to hear his answer about the birthday party.

"So, you need a date to run interference. Be your arm candy for a day and keep the family occupied and satisfied." He stood taller, and his look of determination brought to mind images of *me* being the one satisfied, not my family. Hot damn, this man was dangerous. "Josie, I told you years ago that love is my job, and an event like this, patching up old grudges, well, it's practically my calling," he said with a chuckle. "I'm in."

The relief that washed over me was immense, like a whole shelf of books being lifted off my shoulders. I let out a breath, and for the first time in a long while, the prospect Nana Geraldine's birthday didn't seem quite so daunting... even if it was going to make things more complicated with the first—and only—love of my life.

I was just going to ignore that last part for now. I always did prefer to be an ostrich with my head in the sand.

SIX

Caleb

I SPENT THREE DAYS CHASING MY LAST FEW COUPLES all over town, but none of them were ever in the same place at the same time. Which was probably why they were the last ones on my list. They posed a real challenge, even for someone with my abilities. And now that Josie had entered my life again, it felt all the more important to remain focused on this goal.

After all, she was a big reason I found myself without my wings.

And so I sat, frustrated and no further along, back at Rocksmith Café for a club sandwich and a bottomless lemonade.

I was distracted, my senses stretched out to follow the easiest match left on the list, when Victory dropped off my sandwich.

"Look okay?" she asked, a little quieter than usual.

"Looks great, as always." My power reached out on instinct to inspect her aura, and I was immediately hit by a deluge of turmoil. "Are *you* okay, Victory?"

She bit her bottom lip, hesitating.

"Would you like to sit with me and talk about it?" I pulled the typical angel move, glad to focus on any problem besides my own. I was fallen, earthbound and wingless, and yet I'd still rather embroil myself with human imperfections than face my own sins.

Victory glanced quickly around the otherwise empty patio, then sank into the wrought-iron seat across from me. "It'll sound crazy."

"I promise I won't judge."

"Do you believe in the... *supernatural*?" she whispered, as if someone was going to jump out screaming at the word.

I smiled. If only she knew. "I do, actually. Why do you ask?"

"I've just recently found out—no, I've recently *seen* some things I didn't know were possible. And I'm not sure how to deal with it."

Going from mundane human to "I've got a wolf-shifter fated mate" overnight was probably overwhelming. "Ah. That can be confusing."

"Very." She fidgeted with the bottom of her half-apron, not meeting my eyes.

"And frightening, if you're not expecting it," I coaxed, sensing the true issue underneath.

Her gaze whipped up, and she nodded.

"I'm sorry to hear that something scared you. Was it Jaime? He seems like a nice guy."

Victory was shaking her head before I finished the sentence. "It's not that he scared me. He's been treating me... almost *too* well. Like I'm made of glass. Something precious."

"And that's a bad thing?" I asked, genuinely confused.

Wolf shifters always treated their mates with the utmost care; they believed their fated mates carried the other halves of their own souls. Unless I was missing something, Jaime would treat her like a queen for the rest of her days.

Although the whole biting-to-bond thing would probably come as a shock to a human.

"No, it's not. But I'm not anything special, Caleb. I'm a regular woman. I work a dead-end job for tips, my family disowned me, and I didn't even finish college. He's wise and rich and... *special*," she whispered again, and I had to hold in a laugh. It was cute, the way she tiptoed around the issue, but I knew she wouldn't see the humor, not yet.

"You don't have to be special to be special *to him*. Shifters take their fated mates very seriously. They only get one, their whole lives."

"You know? You know what he is?"

I nodded.

"Are you a wolf, too? Or something else? He told me there are tons of types of shifters, but—"

"No, I'm not a wolf. Just someone who can sense things."

Best to keep it simple. She's already overwhelmed with what she's learned.

"Wow. And here I've been bringing you lemonades for a year now, and I never knew. We're going to have to develop a system, you know. Blink twice if my table is something besides human." She sank her head into her hands, not looking pleased by the prospect.

If I had to blink twice every time a supe came in, she was going to think I had a problem.

"Do you not want to be his fated mate?" I leaned forward, more invested in her answer than I should have been. Victory was human. Josie was human. And they both found themselves wrapped up in supernatural relationships.

This is not about Josie.

44

This is not about Josie.

This is not about—

"No, it's not that. I think I might actually *really* like him. It's just bizarre. We've barely met, and he says I'm the one. How can he know?" She raked her hand through her hair, and I could read her genuine distress from her aura.

"He knows." I thought about my feelings the first time I saw Josie. The way the earth itself shifted under my feet, the way my wings burned with the power surge that shot through me the first time our hands brushed together, skin on skin. The taste of her lips, the first time I'd stolen a kiss. "You'll just have to trust him on that and give yourselves some time to get to know each other better. See how *you* feel." I cleared my throat, trying to remove the gravel that had lodged itself there at the memory of my first meeting with the woman I thought was my own Chosen.

Who wouldn't look at me twice now.

Desire pulsed through me like it was yesterday, and not seven years ago. I was never going to get over her, just like Jaime was never going to get over Vic.

"You sound so certain, just like him." She looked sad, sinking back against her chair.

Her pungent fear washed over me, and I debated whether to ask or wait.

I gave it a minute, letting the moment stretch between us, nothing but the tempting smell of French fries and an afternoon breeze to distract her from her heavy thoughts.

"I'll think about it. What about you? What's got you so distracted this afternoon?"

I saw the subject change a mile away, but I wouldn't pry if she wasn't ready.

"Ah, this and that. Investigations. You know, the usual."

"I'm not buying that. Come on, penny for your thoughts."

I considered her demand for a moment, tempted to give an excuse about work, when an idea came to me. "Actually, I *could* use your help with something."

"Whatcha got?" She was visibly relieved at moving the focus off herself.

"I was invited to be a plus-one at a family birthday party, one where I need to be on top of my game... except I've never done this before. Any tips on being the best birthday party companion around?"

She tapped her fingers on her chin, squinting at me. "Do you like this girl?"

"Yes."

"Good. Okay, so, here's what you need to do. When you pick her up, you need gifts for the birthday person. Nothing too show-off-y, but nothing cheap. Think classy. Then you also need something for her. Flowers, chocolates—that stuff's okay, but it's better if you can get something *she* loves. It can be small if the relationship is new."

"What if the relationship started seven years ago, and I royally screwed it up and haven't seen her again until last week?"

She winced.

I sighed. "Yeah, that's what I thought."

"No, it's okay. If she's giving you another chance, there's still hope. You must have left some kind of good impression if she invited you to the party, right?"

"I hope so." Damn, I hoped so.

"Think slightly bigger on the gift, but again, not showing off. Thoughtful. Meaningful. And you need to put in the effort. Is this a family party or a friend party?"

"Family. Her great-grandma is turning a hundred."

"Whoa. Big one, then. Okay, you need to study up. Know everybody's name from great-grandma down and at least one to two things about each person. The more personal, the better. Somebody's allergic to dairy? You know it. Somebody owns a sailboat and loves to talk travel? You better know every knot and every sailing term."

I leaned back in the chair, surprised. "I'm not sure memorizing facts will be enough to impress her. Not after I left last time. She's still keeping me at arm's length."

She frowned, weighing my words. "It might not be enough, but you have to start somewhere. Plus, it gives you an excuse to spend time with her again. When's the party?"

"In a week."

"Good. That gives you time to keep showing up, to prove that you're not just here to leave again. She's afraid, most likely. You're a great guy. I'm sure she doesn't want you to slip away again."

I wasn't so sure. Would it be best for her if I let her keep me at a distance? What could I promise her, after all?

And yet, something deep inside me couldn't bear the idea of losing her again. She was mine. No matter how hard I fought it, the truth was immutable, unchanging. There would never be another woman for me.

"You've got your homework now, cowboy." Victory winked and looked away but didn't leave.

Her frown turned into a grimace, and I knew she was thinking about her own fears. She was hesitant when she spoke again. "What if he changes his mind, Caleb? Everyone else in my life has. If I give it time, let him get to know me, he might realize that he can do so much better."

I reached across the gap between us, resting my hand over hers. "Victory, that's not going to happen."

"It might. You don't know. And if I get to know him, fall in love with him, too, and then he leaves..."

"That's never going to happen." Jaime's words startled her, and she jumped, snatching her hand from under mine.

"Jaime! I didn't see you there. I thought we were going to meet up later, after my shift."

"We are, but I felt that you needed me." He gestured to his chest, where their bond was anchored.

"I—we were just talking. Everything's fine."

He turned a questioning look on me, and I bobbed my head slightly. It was theirs to work out, but it wasn't in my nature to leave a couple on the precipice and in pain.

"Can you take a break?" Jaime's eyes were on fire for her, a look I knew well.

She cast a worried glance at me, but I waved her off. "I'm good. I need to eat this and get on the road." I picked up a triangle of sandwich and took a too-big bite to illustrate my point.

Victory rolled her eyes at my immaturity but allowed Jaime to lead her off, his hand gentle on hers.

My mind wandered back over the conversation, seeing things about Josie in a new light. Was she afraid I would leave again, too? Get bored of her, or think she wasn't special?

That couldn't be further from the truth, but if that was why she was pushing me away...

No. I wanted to repair our friendship, but I couldn't afford to do anything more. I had to repair my mistakes, regain my wings, and move forward. No matter how much I cared for Josie, I couldn't go back.

The last time was disastrous enough.

SEVEN

Josie

I HAD ALWAYS DREAMED OF HOSTING A BOOK SIGNING at the Bookish Cat, to turn the little haven of books into a bustling hub for authors and readers alike. With my shop finally gaining a foothold in the local community, here was my chance. Never mind that it was a great excuse to get my thoughts off of *other* subjects.

As I scrolled through a colorful article aptly entitled "How to Host Your First Book Signing Event," I was grinning like I used to on Christmas morning. My eyes drank in the vibrant photos of cozy, crowded bookshops, authors signing books with broad smiles, and readers clutching their newly signed copies like precious jewels.

My mind was abuzz with ideas. Creating an atmosphere with soft music and warm lighting, setting up a cozy corner for the author, preparing little gifts for the attendees. The anticipation of the event was as delightful as the novels that lined the shelves of the shop. The prospect of meeting an author, of watching them interact with their fans, filled me with the same thrill that had been the reason for the bookstore in the first place—creating new relationships between the mind, the heart, and the imagination.

And then my phone pinged. Something about it was more foreboding than the high-pitched ding let on.

It was from my brother.

> Frederick: Grandma is hitting the big one-zero-zero, Jos. It's shaping up to be quite the family reunion. You should try showing up for this one. A little time off from your fancy new bookstore wouldn't hurt. It might actually be interesting for the family to catch a glimpse of the elusive 'real world' Josie Ray.

The words on the screen knocked the breath out of me, echoing in my mind with a bitterness that twisted my stomach. I could almost hear his voice, laced with the same old criticisms, comparisons, and underestimations.

For as long as I could remember, Fred and the rest of the family had viewed my passion for literature with a bemusement bordering on scorn. His text was nothing more than a modern-day, digital version of Mrs. Bennet's complaints from *Pride and Prejudice*.

Fred's words weren't about concern, they were about control. My love for books was never the issue. Their intolerance of it was a reflection of their inability to accept that I didn't want to follow the family way like Fred did.

Try as I might to get back into the article on book signings, I couldn't. Fred's message had a funny effect on me, like the strange dreams that come during a fever. I found myself staring into the distance, the soft hum of the bookstore fading into the background. There it was again, the faint shadow of an alternate life I'd left behind—a life where I was an accountant, working tirelessly in the business that my parents had built from the ground up, just like I had done with the Bookish Cat.

My family's accounting firm, Ray & Co, was the product of my parents' shared ambition, a symbol of their hard work and determination. They had labored over it for years, tending to it with the kind of love and passion that people usually reserve for their children. And, in many ways, the firm was like a third child to them—only, it was the golden child, the one that could do no wrong.

They had hoped I'd take it over someday with Fred, keep the family business going with new life. And for a while, I thought I would do exactly that. But it didn't take long before I realized I couldn't ignore my calling. I wanted to create a world of words, not figures. I wanted to introduce people to new stories, not new tax laws.

For them, my decision to open a bookstore was a rejection, a refusal to continue their legacy. And their disappointment was like a cold wind, chilling our relationship to the core. Some harsh words between us didn't help. In the end, I had to make a choice. I couldn't sacrifice my own dreams in order to carry on the family tradition.

It was hard to disappoint my family, but in the end, not as hard as it was to disappoint myself.

My conscience, my soul, belonged in the quiet aisles of a bookstore, nestled among the endless worlds captured within the pages of books. After all, as Atticus Finch in *To Kill a Mockingbird* said, "The one thing that doesn't abide by majority rule is a person's conscience." And so I would abide by my own conscience.

It was a choice I had made, and one I'd never regret, no matter how much my family wished otherwise. And trying to stay close to them while I did it had proven too toxic for my own good.

A part of me believed that one day they would come around. After all, *they* opened their own business, and I followed in those footsteps—just in a slightly different direction. But it was as though my love for the written word, for stories and escapism, was a foreign language they simply couldn't comprehend. I wished to my very core that they would see the magic of books, the way stories molded us, how they breathed color into black and white.

Nana Geraldine's birthday felt like an opportunity on the horizon, a chance to start building again. I knew that was her wish. It tore her apart to see us divided, and she'd do anything so we didn't end up like *The Dutch House*, where Ann Patchett wrote that five generations passed before anything that resembled reconciliation in the family began to take hold.

The familiar jingle of the doorbell snapped me out of my thoughts. I looked up, half-expecting to see Caleb, but a little girl walked in. She couldn't have been more than seven, clutching three dollar bills tightly in her hand.

Quit the Caleb-yearn, Josie.

I had no business expecting him to show up. Feelings like that would never improve anything. Still, I couldn't stop the heat that flowed through my veins at the thought of him.

The little girl stepped in farther, her eyes wide with curiosity as she looked around at the tall bookshelves, the comfortable corners filled with cushions and blankets, and the cats lazily napping here and there. The sight of her, so small in the place I'd built, made my heart soften. I watched as she took in the magic of the Bookish Cat, the disappointment of Caleb's absence receding. This was why I was here, doing what

I did. For the stories, for the magic, and for moments like this one.

"Can I help you find something?" I asked, making my way over to the little girl who was still absorbing the surroundings of the bookstore as I kneeled down to her eye level.

"I got three dollars for candy," she replied, holding up the crumpled bills for me to see. "But I wanna buy a book instead."

My heart warmed at her words, a vivid echo of a younger version of myself. All the books in my store cost more than three dollars, but looking at her eager eyes, I couldn't bear to let her down.

"What kind of book are you looking for?" I asked, leaning closer.

"I like trains," she said with a shy smile.

Guiding her over to the children's section, I pulled out a colorful tome about trains. "This one's a favorite of mine," I told her, handing her the book.

She took it reverently, thumbing through the pages with wide-eyed fascination. "Does it cost three dollars?" she murmured, while admiring a nineteenth-century locomotive.

"As a matter of fact, it does," I said, smiling at her. "It's a special deal today, just for you."

She looked at me in disbelief before breaking out in a beaming smile. "Really?"

"Really."

The girl's eyes lit up as she held the book tight, her joy as visible as a glowing light. Just then, the bell over the door chimed again, and in walked a woman, who by her resemblance was unmistakably the girl's mother. As she caught sight of her daughter cradling the book like a cherished treasure, her face broke into a warm smile.

"You got a book, sweetheart?" the mother asked, a note of surprise and pride in her voice. "With your candy money?"

"I bought it with my own money, Mom! And it's about *trains!*" The girl waved the book around, her happiness contagious.

"I'm so proud of you." The mother bent down and hugged her daughter, whispering something in her ear that made the girl beam even brighter. Watching this scene, my heart twisted with a pang of longing for such a beautiful relationship.

"She's a lucky girl," I said, turning to the mother, my voice heavy with unspoken emotions. "Not all mothers are so supportive."

She looked at me, her eyes soft with understanding. "We all need someone who believes in us, don't we?" She glanced at her daughter who was engulfed in images of engines, and her head cocked to the side. "But this book costs more than—"

"It was meant for her," I interrupted and winked.

The girl clutched the book to her chest, her happiness infusing the room with a warmth that could rival any fireplace before she and her mother waved goodbye on their way out of the shop, the mother mouthing *thank you* as she went.

Yes, this moment was worth everything.

Spinning back toward the counter, I almost collided with the very muscled chest that had made my heart race since I first laid eyes on it. Caleb.

"You haven't changed a bit. You've still got the biggest heart in the Pacific West Coast."

"You!" I said for the sake of the obvious, poking that tempting chest to give myself some distance. "You saw that?" Once again with the obvious.

His warm gaze held mine. He wasn't grinning, wasn't

joking around; he looked at me with a softness I didn't expect and wasn't ready for.

"That girl doesn't realize all she's got, having a mother like that. Maybe she will, when she's older," I said.

He held my eyes, not letting me breathe as he took a half-step closer. His voice was gentle when he asked, "Josie, how did things fall apart so badly with your family? It wasn't like this before."

His question hung in the air between us. It wasn't prying, and I wanted to tell him, to share the burden. Something about Caleb's steady gaze made me feel safe.

"Well," I started, the words tasting unfamiliar on my tongue. "You know I never wanted to be an accountant like the rest of them. But it all came to a head when I had to enroll for a second semester of..."

My voice trailed off as Caleb's focus abruptly shifted. His eyes looked past me, his expression hard to read. His whole demeanor changed in an instant, the moment of intimacy suddenly left suspended.

His entire body seemed to tense, as if he was listening to something I couldn't hear. His smile faded, replaced by a look of concentration that hinted at something urgent, something important.

"What is it?" I wanted to know, but I also didn't. I could already tell this meant our moment was ending before it really began.

He blinked back into focus, turning toward me again. His face was alight with an excitement I hadn't seen before. "Josie," he breathed out. "One of my matches... they're so close. And they are a hard one. I hate to go, but—"

"Of course," I said, against my desire to demand he stay right where he was. "It's okay."

With that, he was already moving, heading toward the door. But just as he reached it, he turned back. In two quick strides, he was in front of me. Before I could react, he leaned in, pressing a quick, tender kiss to my cheek. It was over before it registered in my brain that it was happening, leaving a trail of warmth that spread down to parts of me I'd forgotten existed.

"See you soon, Josie," he called over his shoulder, his voice full of promises. I touched my cheek where his lips had been, my heart pounding in my chest as I watched him disappear into the Seattle afternoon.

But those promises? He'd made many of them, and they didn't fade so easily.

EIGHT

Caleb

AFTER A FRUSTRATING AFTERNOON OF TRYING unsuccessfully to pair the most stubborn of my matches, the next day dawned to find me at Alki Beach. I was following Marigold, the female half of said match. She and Axel were ordained by the heavens, and yet I'd tried and failed to get them together no fewer than a dozen times. Having him accidentally deliver her flowers. Causing a minor fender bender between them. Having them run into each other at a nature conservation conference... I'd tried it all.

And each time, they reacted with more firecrackers and napalm than sparks of joy.

So, here I was, dreaming of Josie while tramping through wet, sticky sand. I didn't see the appeal of the beach now that I no longer had wings, but it wasn't optional. If I couldn't get this couple matched, and soon, they might miss their chance at forever, and *that* was irreparable. The dominoes that would fall the wrong way were irreversible, and they impacted untold generations.

It was not a screwup the Host would overlook, especially

not for me. After all, I was the angel whose own transgression was unforgivable. The one where I had fallen myself—right into Josie's arms.

That was specifically why I was sent back, to put these couples back on the right track, prove my worth, and save love-meant-to-be from going down the drain.

Axel and Marigold were not making it easy.

Marigold was blithely unaware of my struggle to give her the gift of true love, contentedly following her daily routine of picking up trash from the beach as she walked. They were both very dedicated to the environment, and I knew I needed to use that, but I'd tried and failed with that tactic already.

No, what I needed was something new, something fresh. Something like Josie's perfect insight with the books yesterday. Damn, she was stunning. And she didn't even seem to realize it. Probably because her family didn't appreciate her, which pissed me off. But at least that was something I could help her with, and the thought excited me.

Not as much as the excuse to get and stay close to her again, but it was hard to match that level of need. Josie called to me. Every second I spent in her presence lit a fire inside me that drove me to touch her, claim her. Bind her to my light. But the claiming required a Chosen, not to mention wings, and mine were gone.

I still felt them, sometimes, ghostly beats against my back, the ruffle of wind that wasn't there in my hair. It was a constant reminder of my failings, and the sting brought me back to the here and now.

The couple.

Could I send Marigold and Axel to the Bookish Cat, or would they somehow object to the use of so much paper?

It was an endless back and forth. Maybe I'd just go back

and ask Josie what she thought. I'd need to bone up on what her family was up to lately as Victory had suggested, and Josie could help me with the perfect fix-up for a pair of Earth-conscious lovers.

It definitely wasn't just so I could get another whiff of her shampoo. She hadn't changed it, all these years later. And the scent brought back memories. Memories of us tangled up together in her sheets the first time. Memories of kissing her forehead before I walked away, sucking in a lungful of that uniquely *her* scent as if I could memorize it.

Watching Marigold pick up trash certainly wasn't sparking anything for me, except for the fact that she was lonely and could pick up twice as much with Axel by her side.

I tried not to let the comparison sink too close to home, but it was hard not to think about how much happier I had been once with Josie at my side. I left the beach, no more able to shake the regret from my heart than I could all the sand from my shoes.

THE BOOKISH CAT was already growing familiar, and the happy jingle of a bell overhead made me smile as I scanned the cozy scene for Josie. She wasn't at the checkout counter, though the glass surface glistened, free of fingerprints. Her pride in the shop was palpable, folded into every nook and cranny.

But where was she? I let my senses unfurl and located her tucked together with Barb in the back right corner. A purr reverberated up my leg, and I looked down to find a fluffy

Calico cat circling my left ankle. I let my power brush up against it gently and discovered she was a girl.

"Well, hello there. You're friendly. Can I give you a scratch?" I murmured, and offered her my fingertips to sniff.

Some animals didn't like supernaturals—wolf shifters particularly got a bad rap with the animal kingdom—but this little feline was as bold as brass. The purring intensified, and she rubbed her face against my hand, scent-marking me.

"You little hussy!" Barb's voice made me jump, startling the little cat into hissing. "That's Josie's man—you can't steal him after she gave you a roof over your head." The cat looked up at me as if to confirm this, so I shrugged. She strutted away, tail flicking her annoyance overhead as she left. Barb tutted and left me standing there like an idiot as she went into the back room.

"Barb, who are you talking to?" Josie's voice sounded funny, and curiosity dragged me into the aisle so I could see her better. She was on top of a round stool, books overflowing beneath one arm, one under her chin, and her other hand adjusting the ones already on the top shelf in front of her.

She saw me and started, dropping the book under her chin. She flailed briefly, and I sped behind her, steadying her with my hands on her waist. I couldn't reach the book, but I snapped it up with a tendril of power, not letting it hit the ground. It floated back up to where she could reach it, and her hand shook as she plucked it from seemingly thin air.

"I'm still not used to that," she murmured, setting the book on the shelf. "I'm steady now, thank you."

I reluctantly removed my hands, the soft warmth of her branded onto my skin. Skin that I'd tasted before, nibbled before, knowing well the soft gasp she'd make each time. I was instantly fighting a hard-on, and had to clear my throat before I could answer. "You're welcome. Can I lend you a hand?"

"Here, Romeo. Juliet needs these on that shelf over there," Barb said, shoving a stack of books into my hands. "I'm going to take my fifteen. If you two get up to anything naughty, I expect a full report." She waved over her shoulder and didn't waste any time disappearing into the back again.

I shook my head at the retreating store clerk. "She's like a modern-day ninja. I haven't heard her coming once, and people usually can't sneak up on me."

Josie hummed a noise of agreement. "She's quirky, but she's an amazing employee."

"The quirkiest people are often the most interesting to be around," I offered as I crossed to the shelf Barb had indicated and began carefully shelving the old books. I seemed to be in the psychology section and handled with great care a first-edition of *The Interpretation of Dreams* by Sigmund Freud. We worked in companionable silence for a few moments before Josie spoke.

"I know you didn't come here to be bossed around by my helper and shelve books. Is there something you want to talk about?"

"Yes, actually." I placed the last book carefully onto the shelf and turned to watch her climb down from the step stool, feeling guilty for letting my gaze linger longer than I should have on her perfect ass. She dusted off her hands and propped them on her hips, not giving me an inch or an invitation to hang around.

I have a lot of making up to do. She agreed to help me, but she's not comfortable yet.

I was oddly nervous when I proposed my idea. "I was hoping we could get together tonight, maybe over dinner, and talk about both of our projects."

"Uhm, is that necessary?"

I straightened, taking a step closer, irrevocably drawn to her. "If I'm going to play your boyfriend, I want to be convincing. I need to know current news about your family, and I'd love to get your opinion on the couples I need to match. I can't bring them *all* here for a book match, so we'll have to think of something else."

"I hadn't considered that," she admitted, fidgeting with the hem of her fitted T-shirt. It was cute, a cat wearing glasses and reading a book of Voltaire's poetry. I could feel the reluctance rolling off her, but it was deeply important to me for reasons I wouldn't examine that she *not* say no.

"Come on, Josie. Nothing untoward; just two old friends catching up. You've got your mission, and I've got mine. We can be friends, right?" I waggled my eyebrows, hoping the silliness would loosen her up.

She snorted at my juvenile attempt at humor. "Yes, we can have dinner and discuss things."

Score one for the angel.

"But just this once, okay? It would be easier for both of us if you knew what's what with Nana Geraldine's birthday ahead of time, but I don't want you getting the wrong idea."

And what exactly is the wrong idea, sweet Josephine? I longed to ask it, but I couldn't, not now.

"Deal. I won't take up too much of your time, I promise." I reached up, lifting a loose strand of hair and tucking it behind her ear. Her skin was so soft, and she caught her breath at the brief contact.

"Okay." She leaned toward me, wavering in her stiff posture. I longed to close the distance and touch her again, no matter how briefly.

Her mind was telling her to push me away, but her body was as drawn to mine as ever.

"And I'll be the best centennial-birthday companion you've ever had."

She rolled her eyes at me but took a half-step closer. Her tantalizing curves were nearly brushing my chest now.

One more step, sweetness. That's all we need.

"You're the *only* centennial-birthday companion I'll ever have."

"So, it won't be hard to smoke the competition." I grinned, loving the light banter but feeling like I was walking a razor's edge between desire and flirtation. Too much, and she'd run. Not enough, and I'd lose this chance.

I didn't deserve another chance.

Despite the attraction sizzling between us, sadness stole in, poisoning the moment with painful memories.

Like that time on the beach. The memory flooded my mind...

"I have powers that help me do my job. Only for good, I promise, if that's why you're looking at me funny."

"Wait, go back. Never mind powers and whatnot. Did you really just say you're an angel?" She shook her head as if she saw an apparition. "What kind of job does an angel have? Don't they just... float around and play harps all day?"

I snorted, amused by her innocence, her curiosity. "Not exactly. There are guardian angels, messenger angels, and then the more specialty types. I'm a cupid."

"Hold up." She sat bolt upright. "You're serious? You expect me to believe that you, an average twenty-year-old native of Federal Way, Washington, are not only a real-live angel, but a cupid of all things? The little naked guy who flies around with the bow and heart arrows?" Her voice went up angrily the longer she spoke, and I cringed back from the fury and disbelief turning her aura an unusual shade of burgundy.

"It's the truth, Josie. I need to be honest with you. We've gotten closer, and I can't hide my nature anymore."

"Right. Is this your move? The thing you tell girls to get them to—"

Horror washed over me as I realized what she was insinuating. "Josie, no. I've never told anyone on Earth this before. We're not allowed to tell humans."

"Are you even twenty years old? Or are you actually an immortal, alive since the dawn of time?"

"Not quite that long." I ran a hand awkwardly over the back of my neck. This was going terribly, but I had no idea how to fix it.

Her eyes widened. "I was joking! This can't be happening. You must think I'm the most gullible girl in town to believe this kind of bullshit."

"Never. If you're willing, I can show you—"

"Stop. Just stop right there." She pushed herself up off the picnic blanket, shaking her head. "This is too much, Caleb. Really. I need some space."

"Josie, please. I can prove it. Let me show you."

"If you think some five-dollar magic trick is going to fool me, you're dead wrong." She walked away with a look of disdain, leaving a gaping hole in my chest where she was supposed to be.

I shook my head, dissolving the painful memory. It had only gotten worse from there, with the clarion call coming a week later, and all that followed.

No, I couldn't go back, and I couldn't make those mistakes again. We were only friends, and that would have to be enough.

"I'll pick you up at seven?"

"It's a date."

Everything in me longed to stay. But I walked out the door.

NINE
Josie

As I sat on the edge of my bed, fussing with the hem of my skirt, Gatsby padded over to me, purring softly.

"You like the outfit?" I reached down, running my fingers through his soft fur, and he nuzzled into my ankle. "Don't worry, it's not even a real date, Gatsby."

Unless we happen to find ourselves in a compromising position, bodies crashing into each other as he goes deeper with every thrust...

I smacked my own forehead to banish the vision.

"We're just two friends hanging out. Nothing to get worked up about."

I was trying to convince myself more than the cat, but the bundle of nerves in my stomach disagreed. Matilda and Heathcliff screeched in a game of tag, knocking over my mug of chamomile tea and taking down a lamp by the cable. Poor things weren't yet adapted to apartment life, but could I blame them? They'd been uprooted from the shop—the place they'd called home—and had to adapt from ruling the dominion to fitting into my one-bedroom apartment.

I sighed, standing up to look at my reflection in the full-length mirror in the corner of my living room. There I was, dressed up in a stylish skirt and a casual top, trying to look laid-back, put together, and sexy as sin, but awash in a flood of chaotic emotions at the same time. The physical appearance completely incongruous to how I felt. I had to appear chill and confident, even though my insides screamed I was anything but.

I met my own eyes in the mirror, a mix of apprehension and determination staring back.

"Come on, Josie," I whispered to my reflection as I started to put on my mascara, "You can spend an evening with Caleb and not let the old feelings take over." But as my image nodded back at me, dread mingled with nervous energy at the idea of seeing him again. How was I supposed to keep my feelings in check around Caleb when even the mere thought of him made me want to tear his clothes off?

My phone rang, resulting in a line of mascara down my cheek. "Sugar kitties! No offense, Gatsby." He cocked his head as I washed my cheek and reached for the phone at the same time.

A video call from Nana Geraldine. I accepted it and was greeted by her lively voice. "Josie, darling!" At ninety-nine, Nana was more vivacious than most people in their sixties, and was one of the few family members I felt at ease with.

She had always been my biggest fan, whether it was a hard-earned B in gym class or the "Most Likely to Write a Book" prize in high school.

"Well, if it isn't Nana Geraldine," I greeted her, a smile forming at the sight of her frizzy white hair that glowed in front of the vibrant hues of art hanging behind her in the log house she called home.

"Oh, you won't believe the plans for the party!" She clapped her hands together, a twinkle in her eye. "Do you remember the photos from my fiftieth?" Her wide grin suggested a fond, mischievous memory. My mind immediately went to an old photo album. The fiftieth was infamous in our family lore; there was laughter, dancing, too much wine, and rumors of skinny-dipping in the moonlight.

I laughed nervously. "Nana, you're not planning anything... erm... *illicit*, are you?"

She winked conspiratorially at me. "Now wouldn't that be something? Might shake up the old codgers a bit!" We both laughed, the warmth and familiarity of our conversation easing the lingering nerves from my upcoming not-date.

Her log house, nestled in the small town of Snoqualmie, was a living, breathing art piece itself. The walls were adorned with her vibrant oil paintings—landscapes of the lush valley, abstract interpretations of her dreams, and the occasional bold self-portrait. Her creativity breathed life into the wooden bones of the house, and the picture windows captured the majesty of the mountains, framing them like nature's own artwork.

"You know, I want the house to feel just like it did way back then. Full of laughter and love," she continued, a wistful note creeping into her voice. "You remember the stories I told you, right? There was so much mischief in those days."

"Yeah, Nana, I remember." I chuckled, fondly recalling the tales of the wild escapades she used to tell me.

As the laughter subsided, she tilted her head and looked at me keenly. "So, are you coming to the grand event alone, sweetheart?"

Something in her voice... The way she asked, it was almost as if she already knew about my conundrum.

"As a matter of fact, I have a date," I replied, as nonchalantly as possible.

Nana Geraldine's eyes sparkled as she squealed, "I knew it! Is that why you're putting on all that face paint? I felt it, felt it in my bones, I did. That's why I called—there was something going on with you. Oh, do tell me more, dear."

"Nana, it's... it's complicated," I admitted, my nerves spiking again at the thought of my upcoming rendezvous.

With her knowing grin and conspiratorial chuckle, she said, "Oh, sweetheart, it's always complicated. Love is a tricky thing." Her voice grew tender, her eyes soft. "Don't force it. Don't rush it. Let it find you when it's meant to."

Her words had a calming effect, reminding me to stay grounded. After all, this non-date wasn't a declaration of love. It was just a friendly get-together to discuss our shared objective of surviving a party with my family. That was it.

"Sure, Nana. Thank you."

"Must go, darling. The local coyote is back, and I'm determined that this time I'll capture him with my paintbrush. Got to go."

"Love you, Nana," I said, but the screen had already gone black.

As I finished cleaning the errant mascara, Nana Geraldine's words were still ringing in my ears. "Let it find you..." *If only it were that easy, Nana. If only...*

"All right, Josie, you got this," I whispered to myself, checking my reflection one last time. "It's just like Bilbo leaving the Shire. Big, scary world out there, but you're ready."

I took a deep breath and turned to find the three cats lined up to say their farewells.

"Ciao, hobbit kitties. Don't wait up. Actually, do. That will give me a reason to be back early." I blew them a kiss and closed the door. Immediately, I heard something crash inside the apartment, and it seemed like a great reason to cancel everything with Caleb...

But I didn't.

I stepped outside, the Seattle summer air wrapping around me like a comforting blanket. As I walked, I tried to lose myself in the sights and sounds of the city. The distant rumble of cars, the clamor of people, the enticing scent of coffee, and eventually the sight of the glistening waterfront. But my mind kept circling back to Caleb, a moth to a flame.

How much has he changed in these past seven years? What exactly has brought him back here and back into my life?

Maybe Caleb *had* changed. And maybe he'd changed for the better. I certainly had.

"Nope. Nope, not going there," I muttered, shaking my head and resolutely turning around. I started to walk back home, telling myself that I could call it off, that I could avoid this emotional disaster waiting to happen.

But as I reached the next intersection, my feet just stopped. I sighed, shaking my head at my own ridiculousness.

"Come on. Even Harry Potter could make himself go into the Forbidden Forest."

I spun on my heel and started back toward the waterfront, a voice in my head—perhaps my mother's—telling me I was crazy. As the distance to the meeting point shrank, my doubts surged again. Could I do this? Could I face Caleb, not as the love of my life, but as a friend?

Not possible, the voice rang through me. *You've always known he's the only man for you.*

"Get out of here," I said to the voice, and a person walking past gave me a funny look. "Sorry, not you."

As I turned the corner, the setting sun cast long shadows,

and the waterfront opened up before me. There he was, leaning against the railing, gazing out at the water. Caleb. His sandy hair was tousled, catching the dying sunlight, glowing like a halo.

An angel.

I caught my breath as I took him in. He was the same Caleb I knew, yet everything seemed to be magnified.

The casual way he watched the water, the quiet confidence in his stance, the way his shirt hugged every muscle—everything about him was disarmingly charming and overwhelmingly irresistible.

The sensation was back, a tingling that set me on fire and put everything into hyper-focus. Wetness grew between my legs, though I tried to tell myself it's only because of the memories and not because of the man in front of me now. Except that my body knew better. I was filled with an undeniable longing, a longing I was fighting to keep under control. A fight I feared I was going to lose.

Remember—friends don't rip each other's clothes off. And we were just friends.

I wasn't prepared to face him yet, to deal with the rush of desire that surged at the sight of him. Ducking behind a nearby streetlamp, I closed my eyes and took a deep breath. I needed to find the strength within myself to face him as a friend, nothing more.

It was as if I'd walked into a scene from *Pride and Prejudice* and he was my Mr. Darcy.

"No, bad analogy, bad analogy," I chastised myself. I took a few more deep breaths, clutching the edge of the lamppost for support. My palms were sweaty. This was not a classic love story. This was just a platonic meeting. Right?

Even as I bolstered myself, every nerve ending, every fiber

of my being, screamed otherwise. *We were always meant to be something more, much more than just friends.*

It was a deafening thought, and ignoring it was going to kill me. But I had to try.

With one last steadying breath, I peeked around the streetlamp. Caleb was still there, oblivious to my inner turmoil. But the sight of him made my resolution waver again.

"Get it together, Josie." I stepped out from behind my hiding place, frozen in indecision between stepping toward him and darting back toward the safety of my apartment.

I steeled my nerves, my great-grandmother's advice echoing in my mind. *Don't force it, don't rush it. Let it find you when it's meant to.*

But how could I tell when it was meant to find me? What if I was just holding on to a memory, a desperate wish never meant to be fulfilled?

TEN

Caleb

JOSIE'S INDECISION WAS TEARING ME IN TWO. I'D sensed her slow approach before she ever made it to the corner, every bit of me on high alert, anticipating our time together that evening. But while I was hyped up, she was moving slowly. Unsure? Changing her mind?

I stared out over the water, keeping my pose relaxed as I waited for her. I wished desperately in that moment that I still had my wings, still had the ability to scoop her up and fly her away from the noise and the clutter of the city, into the clouds, where it was just the two of us. *Angel and Chosen.* Lovers written in the stars. Where I could stare into her eyes, surrounded by the heavens, without all the pressure that came with human life.

But I didn't, and I couldn't. Her being my Chosen was nothing but a dream, one that could never come to be.

And we were just friends, a reality I was struggling by the second to remember as I spent more time in her orbit. Time had dampened the memories of the pull I felt toward her, but the second I'd stepped into her bookshop, it had all come raging back to the surface. I needed her, *wanted her*, with a desire that burned in my blood. I could no more shake off that desire than I could my own nose.

Wanting her was part of me.

Yet here I was, pretending I didn't know she hid behind a lamppost a few feet away, neither coming toward me nor running away.

Please don't run away. Plea or prayer, I didn't know.

I tried my hardest not to pry into her emotions, to let the steady rippling of the water lull me into patience. It wasn't easy, though, and I let out a sigh of relief when she took the first step my way.

A grin split my face as I turned toward her, and then I was sucking in a breath for different reasons. She was stunning in the sun's last rays, bathed in golden light that highlighted her every tantalizing curve. Her chestnut hair gleamed, kissing the top of her breasts, and I had the very un-angelic desire to skim my palms over them and pull her against my chest. Feel her melt and mold against me in the way she used to.

To see, once and for all, if her heart beat in time with my own.

She wore one of her usual quirky T-shirts, paired tonight with a beautiful skirt, which brushed the tops of her knees, setting off the shape of her calves. Every bit of her was perfection, a Greek goddess worthy to be painted by one of the masters. But I'd never let her be hung in a gallery for the faceless hordes to ogle. She was mine, the shy smile she wore only for me.

Something inside me fractured when I realized yet again that it wasn't true.

She couldn't be mine, not to cherish, not to touch. There

was no way an angel could claim a human as his Chosen. I had tried to ignore the fact before, and look where that got me.

Josie and I were companions of convenience. Temporary. Set to be blown away with the wind, erased from the pages of history. Not a love written in the stars, but impermanent names scrawled in the sand. One day, she would move on, find her own love, and I would be left to watch from the heavens, living out eternity without her.

It was more than I could bear and yet no less than the truth. A cupid, an angel of love and desire, destined to never have it for his own.

"Caleb, hi."

"Josie." I stepped forward, wrapping her in a hug. Her head fit perfectly under my chin, and I took the moment to close my eyes, compose myself.

Douse the searing pain of our reality.

I blinked and pulled back, letting my hands linger on her upper arms, starved for the feel of her soft, perfect skin. I itched to slip my hands up, caress the bare hollow of her throat. Follow my fingertips with my lips, and hear her moan out my name. But that would spook her. I had to take it slow, not push beyond what she was willing to share after I'd broken her heart the first time.

If we only have a little while, I'll take whatever I can get.

"Are you hungry? The restaurant gets rave reviews. I hear the ceviche will change your life." I gave her a wink.

She snorted, and I couldn't help but smile at the cute little noise. She could never hold back her opinions, and it was one of the many things I found irresistible about her.

"Raw fish will change my life, all right. Because it will *scar me for life*. No thank you."

I tsked, teasing her. "I bet your cats would love it. Be brave for them." I offered Josie my arm as we turned toward the restaurant, and she took it absently. Absent or no, I reveled in the victory.

That's it, Josie. Trust me. Lean into my side.

"They're *cats*, Caleb. That's not even a little bit of a valid point." She sank into my side, distracted by the silly conversation, and I relished the feel of her chest against my arm, breasts soft and perfectly tempting. *Focus, Caleb, or you're going to get an erection in the middle of the damn sidewalk.*

"Fine, but don't blame me when you go home smelling like fish and they're disappointed in you."

"If you're that worried about it, you can bring them some ceviche on your own time." She shuddered as if the mere idea of ceviche was horrific, her reaction all delicate disgust as I held open the door to the restaurant. It was lovely, with dim lighting and views of the water. Soft jazz played in the background.

"Maybe I will." I smiled down at her as I gave the host our name. Reservations were hard to come by here, but I'd pulled some strings with a lynx shifter friend who knew the owner. People found it handy to have an angel owe them a favor.

"Right this way." The maître d' quietly led us to our table with a flourish of his arm. We were seated at the back of the restaurant, in a private booth right next to a window with a stunning view.

"Oh, it's gorgeous!" Her eyes lit with excitement. She leaned forward, nearly pressing her nose against the window. "How did you get us a spot?"

"I have my ways."

"You didn't... *influence* anyone, did you?" She cocked an eyebrow at me, clearly not pleased by the idea of me using my powers to score us a table. It sent a frisson of pleasure through me, the smallest hint of her acceptance.

"No. I'll have you know I pulled strings with a friend, like any other man with a lovely lady to impress."

She looked skeptical but swallowed the question when our waitress appeared to take our drink orders.

When the waitress left, Josie cocked her head at me. "Lemonade, huh? You still love it, after all this time?"

"What's not to love? It's delicious, like the woman who introduced me to it."

She blushed at the memory, then drummed her fingertips on the table, a different question brewing this time.

"Go ahead, ask."

"Do you actually need food? Or is it a cover thing, like you eat so nobody knows you're not human?"

The ease with which she asked the question made me wonder. *Had* she started to accept what I was? "I don't need it, no. But I do enjoy it. It's a very... human experience. It's a way of connecting, understanding. Humans pour a lot of love into their cuisine. Anywhere you go in the world, there is something unique on a plate. It's history, culture, and that personal touch rolled into one."

She hummed, a crease forming between her eyebrows as she considered it from my perspective. "I wondered about that after you left."

I nodded. "I'm sure you wondered a lot of things. Is that all you wanted to know? You can ask me anything."

"I... I'm not sure. Maybe we should stick to why we're here." She tucked a bouncy curl behind her ear, ducking her head to avoid my eyes as the waitress approached with our drinks.

Don't push, Caleb.

We ordered, and I ignored the waitress's lingering glances. As she walked away, Josie looked back up.

"I bet you get that a lot, don't you?"

"Get what a lot?"

"Checked out. By every woman who has eyes and a pulse. And maybe some who don't."

There was an edge of bite to her tone, and it thrilled me to know she *cared*. I knew from the couples I matched that jealousy could be rooted in a lot of emotions, but none of those emotions were indifference.

"I can't say I've noticed. There is only one woman who has ever caught my eye." I knew that longing was pouring out of me, and I made no attempt to hide it.

She blushed furiously, fiddling with the cloth napkin in her lap, her aura a rosy pink. Pleasure, desire, curiosity...

Addictive. Everything about her drew me in.

"But as you said, the task at hand. Tell me about your family. What do I need to know?" I asked, easing the sexual tension that was steadily building between us. I shifted in my seat while she considered her answer, trying not to stare and glad that, inside the restaurant, I at least had the table to cover my straining dick.

"So many things. I'm not even sure where to start." Her aura bled from a sizzling-red sexual curiosity into deep-navy frustration. "It's been both a whirlwind and tumbleweeds all at once, and even though I'm in the middle of it, I can't see how to possibly fix it."

I reached across the table and stopped her from fidgeting with a soup spoon by entwining my fingers with hers.

She froze like a rabbit scenting a predator.

I squeezed her fingers.

"Hey, it's okay. I'm here to help, remember? Pick *one* family member, and tell me what I need to know about her— or him. We're in no rush tonight, and we've got a week. I'd be happy to take you out again as many times as it takes." I shot her a wicked grin, unable to hold it back.

"That won't be necessary," she said, squinting at me with no small suspicion. "But..." She bit her lip, her eyes tracing down to our joined fingertips then quickly away, as if worried I'd catch her peeking. "How about my brother, Fred?"

"I'd love to hear about your brother, Fred."

"No, you wouldn't. He's more of an ass than Mr. Collins."

"Worse than *Collins*? Surely, that's not possible."

"Collins at least made one woman happy at the end of *Pride and Prejudice*. Fred hasn't managed that much."

I couldn't help it; I laughed. Head back, inappropriately loud for the quiet restaurant, *guffawed*. I felt dirty looks rolling in from nearby diners and sent them all the suggestion to look deeply into their dining companions' eyes or out at the view.

"Tell me how you really feel," I teased, once I could control myself again.

"That's probably rude, isn't it? And I don't want you to hate him or anything. It's just... he's always antagonized me. Nothing I do is ever right with him."

"Ah. And do we care what he thinks?"

"*No*," she insisted. "But he's always in my father's ear, telling him how I should be part of the family business." Josie raked a hand through her hair, mussing the perfect curls slightly. I liked it. It made her seem more real, touchable. Less off-limits.

She has to stay off-limits, Caleb.

No amount of self-chiding made me wish even a fraction

less that it was my hands running through her hair. My fingers weaving into the silken strands, pulling her to my lips for a kiss.

I cleared my throat. "You have your own business, though, and it's incredible."

"I know. And I always thought..." She shook her head, dropping her eyes back to her lap. "I always thought that would be enough, when I got to this point. But it wasn't." The words were so small, yet the pain in them made me ache. Her parents' acceptance of her business was incredibly important to her.

Surely, they knew that?

I let my thumb trace over the back of hers, gently soothing while she composed herself. "I'm sorry they haven't been able to give you what you need. But it doesn't mean they won't come around."

Especially if I have anything to do with it.

"You don't know my parents."

"I—"

"Look at you two, such a beautiful couple!" A man in an elegant suit arrived at our table, completely destroying our deep conversation. "We are always pleased to host young love."

Josie snatched her hand from mine, looking horrified. "We're not a couple. Just friends. Having a very *friendly* dinner." Her smile was tight and didn't reach her eyes as she spoke.

"Ah, my apologies." He shifted uncomfortably. "You are indeed two lovely friends. Has everything been satisfactory so far this evening?"

"Yes, excellent." She glared at him.

"Magnificent. If you need anything at all, just let us know." He half-bowed and then left, crossing to check on another table. But the mood was broken, and both of Josie's hands were planted firmly back in her lap.

They stayed that way until the food came a few minutes later.

She was two bites into her chicken piccata when she dropped the bomb on me.

ELEVEN
Josie

"WHAT EXACTLY IS YOUR DEAL?"

The words escaped my lips in a rush, and his startling blue eyes widened as he was stunned into silence. My heart pounded in my chest, a frenzied rhythm that echoed the turmoil of everything I'd felt since he'd reappeared.

Caleb's face paled, his golden curls shimmering under the elegant chandelier's light. His fingers traced patterns on the white tablecloth.

"Josie," he began, his voice unsteady. "It's... it's not that simple. My existence isn't like yours." His gaze dropped to the tabletop, his long fingers nervously rubbing his forehead as he continued. "There are restrictions, rules that bind me."

"*Restrictions?*" I echoed, my mind spinning as I tried to understand what he was saying.

His hands stilled, and he met my gaze once again. "Yes, restrictions. As an angel, I have duties, *obligations*, that I can't simply shrug off." His voice dropped lower, barely above a whisper as he added, "There are limitations to what I can and can't do. To what I can and can't feel, and for whom."

But his explanations, his roundabout way of addressing the issue, did nothing to calm me. He may have been trying to explain, but he only ignited my anger further.

"*Limitations?*" I shot back, memories of our past cascading through my mind. "What about at Steel Lake Park?"

"Please," he pleaded, as if the memory caused him physical pain.

"Remember?" I started, my voice breaking slightly as I forced myself to face the memory. "It was so hot that day," I continued, a ghost of a smile playing on my lips as the image danced in front of my eyes. "You loosened the buttons on your shirt, and I tucked my tee into my bra to brave the heat. It was the first time I caught you staring at my breasts, and you stuttered an excuse before I took your hand and led it to my waist. You caressed my cheek with the back of your fingers." I closed my eyes as the sensation came alive again, the sweetness of it, though I'd felt the desire in his fingertips even then. He nodded, his expression softening as he, too, seemed to drift into the past.

"And then the stars started to appear, one by one. It was so clear, so beautiful. That's when we said that one day we would hike Mount Rainier together." My voice dropped to a whisper, my eyes still fixed on his. "We had that old flannel blanket from my parents' place spread out on the sand. Your hand floated along the curve of my neck and down—"

"Josie..."

But the memory had a hold on me. "You drew circles along my hips, across my stomach, gently pulling the elastic and letting it slap back down on me as you looked into my eyes, and I smiled at you with a challenge to go further." I sucked in a breath, the anticipation I felt that day creating a wetness between my legs in the present. "And you did. You slipped your whole hand down. This hand."

I took his hand in mine, inspecting it as if to see if it really did happen. Like those memories branded into my own skin would be right there branded into his, too. I heard him moan, low and quiet, only enough for me to hear, and the sound sent a thrill of heat shimmering through me.

He remembers.

"These fingers reached down, caressed the place that no one else had touched—"

"You weren't wearing any underwear." His eyes burned into me, but I wasn't going to release him now. I knew his cock was growing hard under the table, didn't have to see it to know it. I always knew when Caleb was in the throes of desire.

"You slid your finger between my folds, teasing, even as my body demanded more."

He closed his eyes as I still held his hand between us. "You were soaking wet for me."

"I was desperate for you," I corrected him, a little breathless at the way his voice sounded strained as he fell into the memory right along with me. "And you brought me to the brink of explosion before you even spread my lips. You tortured me, and you loved every second of it."

His eyes snapped open again, holding mine with burning heat as he spoke.

"I gave you such a reward though, didn't I? I knew you were ready, when I found that throbbing little clit of yours. One press. That was all it took. You screamed louder into my ear with each circle." He drew those same circles on my palm, and the shudder that tore through me felt like I was reliving every second of that night seven years ago. "I found you open and ready for me, dripping, but I stayed focused on you. You were so sweet under my touch as I pressed harder into that spot, lifting its cover, making you moan until your voice was rough with satisfaction."

Waves of heat rose up my neck, not because the conversation made me blush, but because I would have done anything for him to climb across the table with its fancy linens, toss the crystal aside, and shove his hand down my skirt the way he'd done then. I was playing with fire, and it was burning me up with need.

But I can't forget that our love story ends with him taking off on me.

I dropped his hand. "And when you had taken every ounce of my energy as I'd screamed and moaned and begged you to stop and start again... we lay there for an hour, talking about the stars, the great beyond, the heavens above—like it was all a mystery. Only for you, it wasn't."

His gaze was steady on mine despite the accusations in my tone, his lips pressed into a tight line as he nodded silently yet again.

"And after that..."

"Please, Josie," he tried again, but I couldn't stop now.

"That swim," I rushed on. "I remember looking over at you, your skin glowing in the moonlight, and I thought I'd never be happier than I was in that moment. I was right." I paused, my breathing shallow as a combination of anger and sadness cascaded through me. "We sat on the edge of the dock, our feet dangling in the water, your arm around me, holding me like you were going to hold me forever. You pointed to Mount Rainier and said that one day we would be at the top, and the world below would be a distant memory." My eyes burned as I held his gaze. "You had no *limitations* then, Caleb.

We had nothing but *promises*. It was just us, and we were perfect."

He swallowed hard, but I couldn't let him off the hook.

"Why was it so different then?"

He dropped his face into his hands, and my heart twisted at the sight of him struggling. But there was one more thing he needed to hear.

"You seemed very human when we fell in love."

Caleb looked up, silent, his eyes reflecting a deep turmoil. His lips parted as if to say something, but no words came out.

"I know it was a long time ago," I whispered. "But I've been carrying all of that with me ever since you left."

"I'm sorry." He looked me straight in the eye, and there was no doubt he meant it. Two little words that left one big chink in the armor I'd built around my heart. A crack I felt all the way down to the marrow of who I was.

"Excuse me." The fancy maître d' returned. "But can I interest you in some dessert?"

"No," we both said in unison. I snapped, but he just sounded sad.

"I didn't want to hurt you," Caleb said. "You have to know I would never want that."

The maître d' cleared his throat. "I'll leave you to your conversation then."

"So, angels just have a bit of a cruel streak, then?" My sarcasm was hardly veiled.

"Of course not. But I had crossed a line I was never supposed to. That was on me, not you, and it set off a chain of events, along with my already faltering performance, that tore me away from here. I've been in Seattle ever since I was sent back down to fix what I got wrong. I would have loved to see you sooner, but..." He bit his lip before answering. "But I was sure you had moved on, and I didn't see you in the city, not once before now. I don't know what I would have done if we *had* crossed paths, since I can't be to you all I wanted to be back then."

Back then. Meaning he didn't want to be more to me now? It stung like a bitch, proving that the lies I'd been telling myself about keeping him at arm's length for the sake of this party were just that—lies. He was so far under my skin, I would never get him out.

But that wasn't all, was it? There was more there he wasn't saying.

"Let me get this straight," I said, but my tone was already softening, the realization of his condition coming clearer now as I moved past my own hurt feelings. "Your life is devoted to love, but you're never allowed to have it? You're just always on the outside, watching?"

Caleb, taken aback, fell silent. He stared at me, his ocean-blue eyes clouded with an emotion I couldn't decipher. It seemed like my words had struck him more deeply than I'd intended.

Finally, after what felt like an eternity, he exhaled a sigh that seemed to carry the weight of centuries. His voice was soft when he responded, laden with an ache that was probably a lot like my own.

"I never thought about it that way before, Josie," he admitted, an undercurrent of sorrow threading through his words. His gaze fell to his hands, clasped tightly in his lap. "That I'm always on the periphery. I write the love story—I don't live it. But you have to know, Josie... you're human."

"Newsflash!" I couldn't stop myself from tossing some sarcasm his way. "Josephine Ray is indeed one-hundred percent human."

He tilted his head, smiling at my childish outburst, but reached out, his hand hovering over mine—so gently that the heat emanating off it was the only sign it was there. "It's never been done before, an angel having a human Chosen."

His voice trailed off as his hand retreated, the depth of his loneliness resonating in the silence that followed. We sat there, suspended in the hush of the fancy restaurant, enveloped by the soft clinks of cutlery and hushed conversations from the surrounding tables. The pain in Caleb's voice, raw and unfiltered, hung heavy in the air between us.

Chosen. A shiver came over me as the sensation of pins and needles left me breathless. Something in that word, the power of the single word—Chosen—froze me in place.

But it couldn't be that simple, not just plain old soul mates like Caleb matched. Not even the 'meant-to-be' of the romance novels that filled the shelves of the Bookish Cat. Caleb inhaled deeply before continuing.

"I thought you and I were different, meant to be. I was *so certain.* I hope you know I would have never crossed those lines if I'd known."

"Known what?" I pressed, needing to hear it, even though every word was cutting me open, slowly killing me inside.

"Known that I *couldn't* be with you. You deserve better than a broken man, half of what he should be. One who can't even give you what you deserve, a lifetime commitment. I can't ever be with a human, no matter how it feels. *Felt.*" The correction was just another blow, piled on top of the dozens before it. "Josie, they took my wings. I got called back to the Host, and they stripped me of the very thing that made me an angel. I'm fallen now, broken. I'm not worthy to take *any* Chosen, let alone you."

His confession left me yearning to reach across the table

and soothe the pain in his eyes. Instead, all I could do was squeeze my hands under the table, my nails digging into my palms, while I swallowed down the urge to comfort him. He really thought that? That he was somehow worth less or unlovable because they'd taken his wings?

There were no words that could capture what I wanted him to hear. That I'd felt all those things, too, but the difference was I still felt them now. We held our eyes on each other—me waiting for him, him waiting for me—yet the silence spoke loudly of all we wished we could say, and couldn't.

Because there was only one choice left for us—leave behind the past seven years of anguish, and accept that we couldn't be *that way* together... ever. But now that we both knew, maybe there could still be a place for each other in our lives.

"Coffee?" The maître d' reappeared. *Again*.

A part of me really wanted to smack that customer-service grin right off his face, but at the same time, we could finally breathe. There was nothing more to say on that topic, not now.

"Maybe some dessert isn't such a bad idea after all," I said, giving a half-smile as a peace offering to Caleb.

"Yes." He nodded slowly, taking in my expression as if he were reading me somehow. "Dessert is a great idea."

The maître d' bowed his departure as if he knew all along, leaving Caleb and me in what had become a very awkward silence. We both started to speak at the same time.

"We don't have to talk about that."

"I wish there was something I could say."

We smiled meekly at each other, a new understanding growing between us. We were who we were at that moment, *not* who we were seven years ago. The surety was palpable inside me. We could do this. We could be friends.

I folded my napkin and dramatically set it on the table to set a new mood. "Mr. Caleb Cupid, I believe we have some other unfinished business involving my immediate and extended family."

He caught onto my tone and straightened his collar with a grin. "Yes, ma'am, we definitely do. I believe you were going to tell me more about this stubborn brother of yours."

"Oh, if you think he's stubborn, wait until I tell you about what my father said to me the last time we spoke five months ago."

Caleb narrowed his eyes. "I'm ready, but fair warning, I have a feeling 'stubborn' just might run in the family."

I sighed. "I wish you were wrong."

And that was how our evening continued, with a few laughs, a lot of sighs, and more stories of family drama than I thought I could tell over *three* pieces of cake.

TWELVE

Caleb

THE WEEK FLEW BY, BETWEEN ME FOLLOWING MY matches and two more meetings with Josie at the Bookish Cat to go over her family specifics, not to mention the little *side project* I'd taken on after my conversation with Victory about the perfect gift. Moroseness warred with anticipation as I got ready for the birthday party.

My nights were filled with visions of her. Both current, her smiling with Gatsby intertwined around her ankles, and older, gilded memories of her. Bare skin resplendent in the moon-light, her hair floating like a dark cloud around her in the lake. The taste of her lips, the way she gasped out my name as she came on my fingers. The electric heat between us every time our skin brushed. Blinding power surged through me at just that one memory of her passion. She was a thing of beauty; a masterpiece I'd stolen for a little while.

I cherished each day, each second of time I had etched into my memory with her.

Because it really did feel like stealing. Like I was hoarding precious moments that didn't belong to me. I knew we didn't have a future together, and yet I couldn't pull back. Couldn't be anything less than fully invested, though I knew how bad the fall would be once we'd finished our little bargain, and I was back with the heavenly Host.

I'd seen it in her aura, the wave of acceptance that we could never be together again. Even as I knew it had to be that way, it broke that last shred of will power I'd been pretending I still had.

I slid my arms into my jacket sleeves, pulling on the cuffs of my button-down shirt, and looked in the entryway mirror. We'd agreed to semi-casual attire, so I was sporting jeans with a blazer, a freshly-shaven face, and styled waves. Slipping into my party outfit was like stepping into the role, and it was too good of a fit.

Boyfriend.

I craved it, that forbidden thread between us. Anything that tied us together, pulled us closer.

I had no right, but I still wanted her. I wanted her with an unholy need, one that wouldn't die no matter how hard I tried to kill it with the cruel reality of our situation. I was an angel, she was a human. I could never have her.

The soft *pop* of air pressure changing behind me had me spinning to find Gabriel, who had poofed himself into existence on my sofa. He was already reclined, fingers laced behind his head, a cocky grin on his face.

"So, big plans tonight?"

Satan's asshole, he is too perceptive. Do I tell him about Josie's great-grandmother's party?

"Sort of. I've got a friend who's helping me with my last few matches in exchange for my attendance at a family event."

"A human friend?" He cocked an eyebrow.

"Yes, she's human."

"A *pretty* human?" he asked, leaning forward onto his elbows, studying me with a wicked gleam in his eyes.

"She's..." *Stunning. Intelligent. Gorgeous. Vivacious. Hilarious. Sexy enough to send me straight to hell.* "Very pretty."

"Pretty enough to catch a cupid, do you think?" He was smiling now, but all the arrogance was gone. Was he worried? Worried that I'd flub up my chance at ever regaining my full power? An emotion I couldn't name settled into my gut, heavier than a stone.

"No, Gabriel. I've learned my lesson. I won't be making the same mistake twice."

She's not a mistake, not even a little bit. She's just off-limits, a little voice inside me whispered, but I ignored it. *Had to* ignore it.

"Ah, I see."

Was he disappointed, or was I imagining things? I did up the buttons on my coat, trying to get a read on him. It was pointless, though. He'd kicked back again, loafer-clad feet propped on my coffee table as if he didn't have a care in the world. As an archangel he could shield his aura from others of his kind, so I couldn't tell if he didn't let me, and as usual Gabriel was a firmly closed book.

I crossed the small distance, bumping his feet off the table before settling into the chair across from him.

"I'm sure you didn't come just to check on my afternoon plans. Is everything okay? I matched that couple you sent, and so far, they seem to be falling in love smoothly."

"Yes, they're doing fine. Right on schedule," he agreed, not taking offense to me keeping his—admittedly pristine—shoes off my furniture. Archangel or no, there were *boundaries.* "How did you get them together so quickly, anyway? Bookish folks can be a challenge. Introverts are usually hesitant to take the first step."

"Ah, it was all Josie. The friend I'm helping today. She's got this sixth sense about what book a person needs. Uncanny, really. She gave them each a book, and voila."

I waved vaguely in the air, not sure what else to say, nervous that he'd remember her from all those years ago. Though the Host hadn't named her specifically during my punishment, she had left an unforgettable impression on me, and it was hard to imagine her having any less of an impact on those around me.

"The plot thickens," he murmured. "Are you sure she's human?"

"One hundred percent." Well, ninety-nine percent. I felt I should make that qualifier for myself. How *did* she know the exact right books that would bring those two together?

He shrugged, seemingly not remembering her after all. "Well, we don't complain when it's easy, right? There is one other thing I need to remind you about."

I tensed but tried to stay calm. Was he going to warn me off getting too close to her? If he gave me a direct order from the Host...

"The angelic seals. The book needs to be found in order for your wings to be restored. I've got a sense that it's here in Seattle. The bookshop owner is perfect—she loves rare books. Maybe she can help you hunt down whoever's got it."

"I... hadn't thought of that." The admission felt like an enormous, stupid oversight, but it was true. The book of angelic seals was powerful, nothing like an ordinary book, though it looked plain to the human eye. Only those with angelic blood could read the script inside, and no mortal ink could stain its pages. "I'm not sure how I'll explain the importance of a blank leather journal to her, but I can ask."

I shoved down the thrill I felt at having another reason to visit the bookstore *after* her great-grandma's birthday was over. I shouldn't want it, but I did with every cell in my celestial body.

"I'm sure you'll come up with something." He grinned again, as a knock on my front door startled me off the chair and into motion.

"This is probably her. I should—"

"I'd love to meet her, this mysterious friend with uncanny beauty." Gabriel rose, smoothing back his perfect blond hair in a practiced move and pasting on a devil-may-care smile.

"No!"

He froze, giving me an incredulous look. You didn't tell an *archangel* no. It just wasn't done.

Shit!

"I don't want to confuse her or introduce any more supernatural influence into her life. I've already been enough of a disruption."

"Well—"

Another knock, impatient this time. Josie was very punctual, and I was officially one minute late for our agreed pickup time.

"Please, Gabe," I pleaded shamelessly.

"Fine, fine." He waved, the motion bored, and then popped out of existence a second before I twisted the doorknob.

"Hey, Josie. Do you want to come in?"

Josie looked lovely, a light-pink skirt made out of something frothy—tulle, maybe?—paired with a classic, off-the-shoulder black sweater. It left the wide expanse of her collarbone completely bare. All it took was one look, and the temptation was there.

She had a displeased look on her face. Was she trying not to be put out at my lateness? I resisted the urge to smirk. She was predictable in the best possible way. Her bottom lip poked out in an adorable pout, and I was overcome with the sudden urge to kiss it, taste it. See how she responded if I sucked it between my own, let my fingers skim over the delicate line of her clavicle.

I wanted to peel that sweater over her head, toss it on my floor, and trace that little indent with my tongue. Peel off her bra, and then—

Shit. I had to stop. I *had* to stop.

I stepped forward, but the intent in my eyes must have cued her to my thoughts because her eyes widened, and she dropped the pout.

"Um, no. We should get on the road. Don't want to be late, or early, for that matter. Right on time is best. We don't want to turn into the White Rabbit in Wonderland, do we?" She smiled, and I sensed her frantic pulse slowing a bit as she allowed herself to slide into her comfort zone, books.

"We *do* have a very important date. Let me grab my keys and we can go."

"Excellent." She did a little spin, the motion all awkward exuberance which caused her tulle skirt to flare out like a flower around her. The soft floral perfume she wore bloomed into the air, and I adjusted the collar of my shirt as I snagged my keys off the hook, trying to turn the dial down on my very physical response to the increased time together.

It was going to be a *long* day if I didn't get myself under control, and quick.

WE RODE in Josie's car, the first part of the drive passing in companionable silence. The familiar streets of Seattle gave way to more nature as we headed for Snoqualmie, a gentle drizzle dampening the roads and prompting drivers to turn on their headlights.

"Are you ready for this?" she asked, breaking the silence. Her knuckles were white with her grip on the steering wheel, and her aura was all prickly edges from the nerves.

"I'm ready. I know that Fred reports everything back to your father. I know that Emily and Lena are your actual friends, not just cousins. I know about Uncle Jim's cancer and prosthetic leg and to avoid all topics of hiking—even though Nana Geraldine's house is perfectly located for it. Every single thing you've shared, I remember."

"That's... impressive. Do you have some sort of angelic super-memory?"

"Something like that." I winked, and she swerved a little but quickly pulled the car back into the center of the one-lane road we'd pulled onto.

I shouldn't have found it satisfying to know I affected her that much, but I did. I was a masochistic bastard, because I loved every second of the pain.

"Well, we're going to put it to use tonight. And I hope you're ready because we're here."

She put on her blinker and turned onto a curving gravel driveway. A lovely log home came into view a few seconds later, its large frame casting a cheerful glow out into the gloomy weather. She parked off to the right side of the porch, at least a dozen other cars already taking up the prime parking spots.

"I haven't said it yet, but thank you. Thank you for doing this, for pretending. I'm sure it probably violates some angelic code. Limitation? Whatever you call it. I appreciate you being here. And I'm sorry in advance, for anything awkward my family may say—"

I pressed a finger to her lips, gently stopping her. "You don't owe me any apologies, not for anything today, or any day. I'm the one with all the making up to do in this relationship, and I'm more than happy to be here. I promise."

I let my finger drop, gently tracing the edge of her mouth down to her chin before completely dropping the contact. Her aura turned a deep plum, desire lighting her up. Her eyes were wide, pupils blown as she stared up at me in the dim car interior. We swayed together, drawn like moths to the flame that would surely burn us both up. So why was I hell-bent on making that leap anyway?

"Well, well, well. What do we have here?" A cocky male voice had us springing apart like shrapnel, and I pushed out my senses to see who it was.

Fred. Right off the bat, we were in the deep end.

She sucked in a fortifying breath, shot me one last look, and cracked open the car door. I hurried to follow suit.

"So, your boyfriend is real after all." His condescending tone made me bristle as he brushed past Josie, circling the car to extend his hand.

I shook it, using the contact to get a more in-depth read on the man.

What I found shocked me.

Jealousy, hot and prickling.

Suddenly, everything she'd told me about him clicked into place. He wasn't antagonistic because she *wasn't* in the family business. It was because he *was.*

"Fred, I've heard so much about you. It feels like we've known each other for years."

He looked surprised, casting a glance quickly at Josie before homing back in on me. "Is that so? Well, I can't say the same. My dear baby sister hasn't told me a thing about you, besides your name. I can't *wait* to catch up."

His smile was half-predatory, and if I hadn't sensed his one-hundred percent humanity, I'd have sworn he was a shifter. But no, just a run-of-the-mill overbearing brother. Those were feral enough, apparently.

I looped my arm around Josie's shoulders, reveling in the heat of her as we ascended the wide, sawn steps of the porch, doing my best to read the inhabitants quickly, in case anything else jumped out at me that would be useful in easing the way for her.

It was a wicked tangle of emotions, and as Fred threw the door wide, I knew one thing for certain—these people needed me, desperately.

THIRTEEN

Josie

NAVIGATING THE GRAVEL DRIVEWAY OF NANA
Geraldine's log house, I gripped Caleb's hand, steeling myself
for the inevitable awkward encounters. Fred was only the
beginning, and I knew it.

The house was a veritable hive of activity, the chatter and
laughter of around seventy-five people spilling out onto the
lawn. Despite the drizzly weather, people huddled under the
shelter of gazebos erected especially for the event. A harpist was
playing, and given the sheer number of wrinkles on her face,
she must have been one of Nana's schoolmates.

The scent of damp earth and the subtle perfume of ever-
greens mixed with the fragrant aroma of home-cooked food.
The large log house, with its stone chimney billowing smoke
and windows aglow with warmth, was a picturesque backdrop
to the gathering.

And then I saw them.

Caleb squeezed my hand reassuringly as we approached my
parents. They were standing near one of the long, food-laden

tables under a banquet tent, deep in conversation. When they saw me, their expressions shifted into smiles that didn't quite reach their eyes. It was going to be as awkward as I'd expected. My mother's gaze flitted between me and Caleb, her curious scrutiny unhidden. Dad was a bit more subtle, but the slight crease of his forehead gave him away.

"So glad you came," Mom greeted me with a tilt of the head. Dad gave me a curt nod, his attention shifting to Caleb.

I could tell exactly what was coming next. The good ol' Mom and Dad act of butter us up, chew us up, and then spit us back out again. We hadn't been there for two minutes, and I already wanted to crawl into a hole.

"Of course I'd be here." The knot of tension in my stomach grew tighter. Who was I fooling, thinking this might be a chance to mend bridges?

"I tried to tell her not to come." Nana Geraldine's voice cut through us. "Because I am just *over the moon* about her new bookstore." She winked at me. "But she insisted she didn't want to be anywhere else."

"It's true." I smiled at her. "And it's so wonderful to see you, Nana." I wrapped my arms around her, certain she'd grown smaller since the last time I came to Snoqualmie.

She broke from my embrace. "Wait just a minute now. You haven't introduced us to this *fine* example of a young man. You must be Caleb."

"Indeed I am." Caleb extended his hand, a jovial grin splitting his handsome face. "Pleasure to meet you, and happy birthday, ma'am."

Nana shimmied her shoulders and took his hand. As soon as they touched, Nana's face changed. Her brow furrowed, and she cocked her head to the side, looking deeply into his eyes. "Caleb, you say? I could swear..."

Her voice trailed off, and all of us stood waiting for something to happen, Caleb included. He returned her intent look, and I knew he was using his powers to scrutinize her.

Nana shook her head, as if coming out of a fog. "Never mind me. You seemed so familiar for a moment there, but that must only be because Josie has told me so many wonderful things about you."

Thank you, Nana, for not outing me in the first five minutes.

"At least that's one of us," Dad grumbled.

"Champagne!" Nana shouted as a server came by with a tray. "Thank you, Michelle. Michelle here is the daughter of the neighbor down the road. Isn't she delightful? I thought perhaps she and Fred might enjoy spending time together. He's always so huffy, so a *real lady* might help him loosen up, don't you think?" She clucked her tongue.

"Nana!"

"Mom!"

"Mrs. Ray!"

We were all equally horrified, which seemed to be exactly Nana's intent. She cackled as she took a glass of champagne from Michelle's tray. "To young love!"

She gave us no choice but to toast to it.

"Young love," we muttered with *much* less enthusiasm in reply. Except Caleb, who was full of gusto. Given his cupid status, loving love seemed to come with the territory.

"That's the spirit!" She twisted quickly, smacking straight into Michelle and her tray of full champagne glasses.

"Nana!" I cried, being the closest and desperate to catch her before she toppled. Horrible visions of glass-shard-related injuries and ambulances and a broken hip briefly blinded me, but with a blink—

Everything was fine. I sucked in a startled breath, blinking in shock as I tried to process what I'd just seen.

The tray was righted, and the tipping glasses tinkled on the tray as they settled back in place.

But most shocking of all, Nana remained upright. *Like magic.*

The rest of us had frozen in a tableau of nervous wreck—arms outstretched, horror on our faces. The only movement was our eyes as mine briefly met Mom's with mutual panic rushing through our veins.

But everything was fine. The music continued, and we all slowly relaxed back into a normal standing position.

"That was a close one," Dad whispered, his chest heaving up and down as the tension subsided.

"You can say that again." Michelle took a step back, and we watched Nana continue her social rounds. "I was sure we were both going down."

"Me, too," I said and looked at Caleb... who did not look the least bit surprised. Of course he wasn't surprised. It was just like the floating book and the landlord. Catastrophe once again averted thanks to my not-boyfriend-nor-lover-but-only-a-friend.

He caught me watching him and immediately his expression changed. "What luck, right?" He smiled widely. "I think I'll have a glass of champagne myself." He downed the whole glass in one great big gulp.

Smooth move, angel boy.

"Caleb, you must tell us more about yourself," Mom said, her tone overly sweet as she leaned in, a ploy to make the interrogation seem casual.

Within the beat of a butterfly's wings, they bombarded Caleb with an array of irrelevant questions—everything from his thoughts on the latest economic developments to his opinions on some obscure painting they'd seen at a gallery—when a hand wrapped around my arm and tugged me backward.

With a wicked grin, my cousin Lena announced, "Josie, I have to borrow you for a moment." I knew that tone of voice, the one that said she was about to grill me for all kinds of dirty details.

As we moved away from the crowd, I cast a backward glance at Caleb, who was deep in a discussion about trade tariffs with my dad. His eyes met mine for a brief second, and he flashed me a reassuring smile.

Despite the strange situation, I couldn't help but marvel at how effortlessly he seemed to navigate the minefield that was my family. Perhaps it was his angelic patience, or maybe he really was that good at holding his own. Whatever it was, it lit me up inside. As much as I loved Lena, all I wanted was to be at his side.

"Josiiie," Lena began, her voice a teasing sing-song, "I have to hand it to you. This one is a stunner!" She tilted her head toward Caleb, who was humorously impersonating some historical figure to the amusement of my parents. The twinkling lights in the tent accentuated his angelic features, the soft glow making him more striking than usual, if that was even possible.

I must have him.

Lena was still making faces at me, so I rolled my eyes, offering a lighthearted shrug in response. "Yeah, he's pretty easy on the eyes, right?"

"Wait, wait." My cousin Emily joined us, her high ponytail bobbing in the air as she was more than six feet tall and built like Superwoman. "Are we talking about the prize Josie snagged?"

"Stop it!" I hissed. "He's just a guy, a great guy."

"Great guy? *Come on,*" Emily continued, her eyebrows rising suggestively. "Have you *seen* the muscles on this dude? And in the sack?" She wiggled her eyebrows. "You can't tell me he doesn't make you scream six ways from Sunday." I gasped— not in surprise, because Emily has always loved locker-room talk, but because it was loud enough to be heard by any of Nana's geriatric guests walking by. Fortunately, no one did. "You've got to admit, he is quite the step up from... Well, every other lame-ass guy you've ever dated."

"Hey!" I nudged her playfully, feigning offense. "I'll have you know my past boyfriends were perfectly—um—adequate."

Emily snorted with laughter, slapping a hand over her mouth to stifle the sound. "Adequate? Josie, you can't even call them boyfriends. What about the one who would only let you undress in total darkness? Or the one who sent you a letter in the mail with a relationship contract? Thank goodness they rarely lasted a rotation of the moon. Speaking of which, your last *boyfriend* thought that the moon landing was a hoax!"

Despite the jest, her words stung a little. I was a serial dater, it was true. No one could make good conversation, enjoy quality book time, or frankly, just be normal. Making love had become a check-box exercise that left me reaching for a vibrator the second they were out the door.

But most of all, none of them were Caleb.

"Adequate or not," I said, forcing a smile and attempting to steer the conversation away from the rocky terrain of my past relationships, "I'll be thrilled if Caleb survives the raking over the coals."

"Looks like he's doing just fine." Emily tipped her head toward the conversation Caleb continued with my parents, a mischievous glint in her eyes.

But I was not so confident.

My father's eyes were pulled half-shut, and I knew that meant he wasn't buying it. And Mom was looking off in the distance, barely listening. Perhaps their initial tactics had failed, but the battle wasn't won. Tension rolled over me like a weighted blanket. Caleb cast me a glance, and I could tell even he was feeling on uncertain ground.

And just like that, the weather cleared.

As the last of the raindrops fell, a cheer erupted from the crowd, a collective sigh of relief. The clouds parted, revealing a brilliant blue sky, bathing the log house in a glorious afternoon light. The guests spilled onto the lawn, their chatter and laughter filling the air as sunshine injected a dose of warmth and optimism. Kids ran around the sprawling garden, their joyous squeals echoing off the tall trees surrounding us as their shoes got damp in the grass. The adults moved tables adorned with bright floral arrangements out from under the tents, their glasses clinking together in celebration. It was as if the party had suddenly burst into life, the sunshine injecting a dose of warmth and optimism that permeated everything. It was, in every sense, a real celebration now.

"I told you all we were going to have a great day!" Nana declared, and we applauded her taking the credit for the weather.

I glanced at Caleb, who seemed to be intentionally avoiding my gaze.

"Little sis," Fred began as he sidled up to me, his tone sharpened by his characteristic dry wit. "You, the bookstore owner. Quite the far cry from your old Wall Street dreams, isn't it?"

I smirked, used to his teasing. I tried to give it right back to him with an overly dramatic reply. "I've got books about Wall Street. Maybe you should come check them out."

"Maybe I should."

"Yeah, maybe."

Were we still taking jabs? Or was he actually saying he would stop by? With Fred, it was hard to tell.

"You know you're welcome anytime." I extended an olive branch. "I'd love to show you around."

He shrugged, a quick up-down of his shoulders that would've seemed indifferent if not for the glint of... was that respect in his eyes? "You know I'm more spreadsheets than Shakespeare, but I'll keep the invitation in mind."

Before I could decipher his intentions, he strolled away, leaving me both irked and confused by his response.

It was my father who brought Caleb over to me by the arm, guiding him like a lost pet. "Caleb, what did you say you do again? Ah yes, independent contractor. Rather vague, isn't it? And awfully convenient," he said, glancing at my mother who had a poorly concealed accusation on her face.

"Yes, I've heard of these independent contractors," my mother chimed in, leaning in closer to Caleb, wine sloshing in her glass. "You know, *independent contractors* who help at family gatherings, work functions, or to make exes jealous. Quite the novel concept, isn't it?"

"Or," my dad continued, "he's a real date and doesn't yet know that Josie doesn't do *serious* relationships."

I felt a surge of anger bubble up inside me. They'd managed to insult both of us in a single go.

"No, no." Mom shook her head. "Josie wouldn't *dare* bring an online date to her great-grandmother's one-hundredth-birthday party." She glared accusingly in my direction. "Tell us the truth, dear." Her nostrils flared, and the child inside me felt like she'd been discovered with her hand in the cookie jar. "Just who is this man, anyway?"

"He's... he's..."

I didn't know how to finish the sentence, scared and panicked and ashamed all at once.

But Caleb stepped in, and I didn't have to say a word.

FOURTEEN

Caleb

JOSIE'S PARENTS WERE LIKE BLOODHOUNDS ON A HOT trail. Everything I said, they questioned, and both of their auras screamed distrust. It was a bit insulting, really, given I had *actually dated* Josie in the past and had feelings for her now. Granted, not ones I could act on, but they were real. I couldn't pin down why they were so sure we weren't a real couple.

It wasn't until they were dragging me across a damp lawn and accusing her of bringing a fake date that I realized how acutely they didn't believe us. Her panic was so thick in the air, I could practically taste it.

"He's... he's..."

In that moment, watching Josie splutter, I knew exactly what I had to do. Call it angelic powers, call it intuition, call it basic male instinct. They were all in alignment, and I couldn't let her finish the damning sentence.

I crossed the distance separating us in two long strides, sank my hands into her artfully-pinned curls, and slanted my lips across hers. Her eyes fluttered shut as electricity billowed out from the touch, lighting every sense I had on fire. How could I need her this badly and not be meant to have her?

There it was again, that phantom ache in the wings I no longer had.

She was everything perfect, and I was instantly addicted like it was the first time. To her touch, taste, scent. I tilted her chin up with my hands and her lips parted, our tongues tangling in a timeless dance, right there on the lawn in front of the heavens and her entire family.

But even knowing what she did now, she didn't pull away, didn't shy back. Instead, she looped her arms around my neck, her fingers teasing the short hair at my nape, and I had to bite back a low moan at the delicious sensations that sparked through me. It was like every cell in my body sang, and if I'd had any doubts about why I'd thought she was my Chosen, they dissipated like the morning dew.

The sudden flare of heat between us turned achingly tender, as I felt the buffeting shock of all those watching, their auras mingling in a distracting cloud around us. The kiss softened, our movements slowing, and finished with me planting a gentle kiss at the corner of her now-puffy lips. I dropped my forehead to hers, hesitant as I met her eyes. They were wide, but I didn't sense a hint of regret in them.

Until her mother spluttered in shock, barely a foot away. Josie winced, and I let my hands trace down her neck lightly to her shoulders, then pulled her tightly into my side. I wasn't throwing her to these wolves, even if they were related.

"Well, hot dog. I'd say we've got a live one!" Nana Geraldine whooped with glee and started tapping her spoon on the side of her champagne glass a little harder than was truly necessary. Josie tried to burrow into my side as the crowd of family and friends grew silent, and for a moment, it was as if they were all holding their breath.

"Here, here! For Josie and her hot-to-trot fella!" Nana Geraldine shouted.

A raucous cheer went up from every corner of the lawn, and Josie buried her face in my shoulder. I cupped the back of her head, suddenly questioning my choices.

The distrust had fled from her parents' auras, though, with their signatures now reading sour but *curious* rather than accusatory. It was a baby step in the right direction.

Lena rushed up to Josie's side and latched on to her other arm. "Come on, we're taking a cousins photo down by the fountain. You'll have to be parted from your lover boy for just a minute or two."

Her father huffed his disgust at me being called his daughter's *lover boy* and walked off, dragging Josie's mother along with him. Nana Geraldine just laughed and went back to chatting with nearby birthday well-wishers.

"Will you be okay here for a minute?" Josie asked, turning to me with a gorgeous flush in her cheeks.

"Absolutely." I trailed a fingertip lightly over her rosy cheekbone and gave her a reassuring smile. I loved seeing her flush with need. That was something I'd never question.

"I'll be *right* back."

"I mean, it might take *two* minutes," Lena mused as she dragged her away. Josie cast me a last, worried look, but her cousin was relentless, and in a few seconds, she was swallowed up by the crowd of partygoers.

I was still following her signature down the hill when Nana Geraldine appeared back at my side, her face serious.

"You and I need to talk. Come with me." She spun on her

heel and marched toward the house with the stately vigor of a war general. Damn respectable for a hundred years old.

Once we were inside, she pulled me into a quiet alcove—or was it a laundry room?

"Don't go snooping in here. I don't need a handsome young thing like you seeing my dowdy old unmentionables!" she chided but didn't look in the least shy about her *unmentionables.*

I definitely stopped looking around, though. *There were things I couldn't unsee.*

"Now, I've asked you here because I sense there's something *more* about you. Am I right?"

I scuffed my palm over the back of my neck, unsure what to say. She was a hundred and lively, but if I gave her too much of a shock… Better to stick to the safe side.

"Well, I—"

"Ah-ha! I can smell a lie brewing. I've lived a long time, and you're not my first run-in with the paranormal, boy, so don't try it." She leveled a pointed gaze down her nose at me, which was incredible because I was at *least* a foot taller than her.

"The only thing that matters to me is this—does Josie know what you are?"

"Yes, she does."

She nodded her approval at my answer.

"And are you serious about my great-granddaughter? Or is this a passing fling? She's been hurt before, and I don't care what kind of myth in a *scrumptious* package you are, if you plan to hurt her, I'll toss you out on your ear, God as my witness."

Somehow, I doubted even God would mess with Nana Geraldine. Especially not if she called *him* scrumptious. I felt dirty.

"I have no intentions of hurting her, ma'am." I made that

111

mistake once already, and I swore to myself that I wouldn't repeat it. Even if I was going to be waking up in twisted sheets, thinking about that kiss and how her lips tasted every night for the next month.

"Excellent. She could use somebody like you. I think you'll be good for her." She patted me lightly on the chest, as if I were a puppy or a kitten and not an angel with the power to flatten everything within a hundred-yard radius with a snap.

But how could I explain to Nana that this was all just an agreement, a deal Josie and I made since we couldn't be what we were before?

"Nana! Are you in here? It's time to cut the cake."

"Duty calls, young man." She paused, one foot through the arched doorway. "You do right by my great-granddaughter, or me and the dancercise posse will swoop down into that big city and show you what for."

"Yes, ma'am. Oh, wait! I have something for you."

I reached into my jacket pocket and held out the bow-adorned package. It was a set of watercolor paints, made by a master artist in Italy. I'd come up with the idea while working on Josie's gift, though I hadn't found the right moment to give it to her yet. The delicate first edition warmed my breast pocket, safe and sound until I could slip it into Josie's hands.

"Oh, these look lovely. Won't you blow on them?" It was an odd request but easy enough for me to fulfill. "Thank you, dear. I always did appreciate a bit of heavenly good luck." She patted me again with a twinkle in her eyes and then zipped off with surprising speed for someone her age.

"Caleb? What are you doing in my nana's laundry room?" Josie peeked her head through the door, looking at me quizzically.

"Your nana wanted a private chat. She sensed that something was up with that kiss."

"Ah. And I suspect she saw your"—she waved her hand up in a spiral—"magical fix-er-oo on the champagne glasses. She's sharp, and she wouldn't let something like that just go by without a question."

"Does it make you uncomfortable when I... *fix-er-oo* things? Or rather, your family members?" I tried hard not to laugh at the term, but I was so relieved that she seemed to be coming to grips with who I was and what I could do, I didn't dare do anything to jeopardize it.

"I'm getting used to it. It still knocks me back a step because it's not something you see every day. But... look, Caleb, I've had time to get used to the idea that you're not like the rest of us. I think so long as I know that you only use your powers to *help*... I'm okay with it. I trust you." She furrowed her brow and looked away briefly, a sense of guilt rolling across her aura for reasons I couldn't figure out.

I trust you. The words were sweet poison, yet I drank them down just the same, relishing the rush they gave me.

"I'm glad to hear it." I took a step closer, letting my hand slip around her waist. We were alone for the first time since that kiss, and it was still fresh on my mind, despite it needing to be *fake*.

"Actually, there's something I should probably tell you about the last few years—" The words died on her lips as I reached up and cupped her cheek, running my thumb lightly over her soft skin.

The back door burst open. Emily pushed through, juggling half a dozen tiny plates with brightly colored cake on them. "Josie! Need your help. So much cake, so little time. Also, you already got one hella-good kiss in tonight, so sneaking off to make out in the laundry room is really just rubbing it in."

Josie jumped to help her cousin, taking half the plates and tossing a guilty look over her shoulder at me. "We were *not* making out."

"Uh-huh. I'm not saying I blame you, because *hello sailor*." Emily tossed a saucy wink at me, and Josie elbowed her in the side. "But seriously, there's so much cake. We need your help."

"I'll help, too," I offered, but put a hand on Josie's arm to stall her. "We'll be out in just a moment."

"*Sure,*" Emily said with another wink before slipping back outside.

"What is it?" Josie asked.

"Just a little something I didn't get a chance to give you before Fred interrupted us in your car." I slipped the first English edition of *Dante's Paradiso* out of my blazer pocket, nothing but a bright red ribbon for adornment, and pressed it into her hands.

"Oh." She breathed the word so softly, it was barely audible. "This is... phenomenal. Where did you find this, Caleb?"

She slid the red ribbon off, carefully cracking the front cover so she could look at the copyright page.

"Italy, a private collector."

"Eighteen-oh-two! This could be in a museum. It's so beautiful." She reverently closed the cover, letting her fingers lovingly dance over the stamped spine. "Thank you, Caleb. I'll treasure it always."

"I'm glad. A special book for a special woman." I couldn't resist. I let my finger trace the inside of her wrist. It was a selfish indulgence, but the more time we spent together, the more I needed to touch her. Everywhere. There was a flash of heat in her eyes that made me want to push her against the closed laundry room door, kiss her until her lips turned pink and swollen, and strip her right out of that skirt. We'd have to be quiet, with her whole family on the other side of the door, but I could swallow her screams with a kiss.

She tasted way better than cake frosting.

But we were here to do a job, and this was a *fake* date, I reminded myself with no joy whatsoever.

"We should get back out there and help Emily with the cake," I said, the words full of quiet regret.

The last time we'd had cake together, she'd been telling me all those dirty memories. Memories about her coming on my fingers, about her screaming my name. At this rate, I was never going to be able to look at cake without thinking of Josie and getting hard again.

"Right! Oh, shoot. Can you keep this safe for me until we get back home?" She pressed the book carefully back into my hands. The heat of her touch was a brand, promising that however this ended, I'd always feel her soft fingertips.

She was everything soft and perfect and good in life, and my time with her was running out, faster and faster. One day soon, all I'd have left to hold on to would be the memories.

"Of course," I murmured and then followed her back outside into the exuberance of the party, my devastating thoughts a cruel juxtaposition.

THE REST of the night passed in an uneventful blur of smiling faces and raucous laughter. Nana Geraldine knew how to party, and I used the free-flowing champagne as cover to pull as many strings as I could, gently starting conversations and mending old fences, one by one. Now that I had her blessing, I didn't hold back. It was small in the grand scheme of things, but it was a start toward healing in Josie's family. By the end of the night, Josie was practically dead on her feet.

As we ambled to the door together, Fred stopped us.

"Wait up!"

We stopped and turned toward him. He ran a hand through his wind-swept hair, the flawless style from a few hours ago long gone. He opened his mouth, then closed it. The tension was already building between the two of them again, and I could sense he wanted to say something. So, I sent him a gentle suggestion to take the leap.

"I just wanted to say... I'm happy for you, about your shop. It seems to be the perfect thing for you."

Josie's mouth dropped open, and she cast a surprised glance at me, as if to say, *are you hearing this*?

I gave her a soft smile and a pointed glance back at Fred, reminding her that she should say something.

"Uh, thank you. It's a wonderful place. Especially if you like cats, and I know you do. I was serious, earlier. If you ever want to stop by..."

"I'm not in the city often, but maybe. I might even bring Mom and Dad along. Maybe one of these days, we'll turn up and surprise you."

"That would be great, Fred. Any time."

They smiled at each other, the first genuine warmth I'd seen between the two of them all night.

"Great. You two drive safe." He shoved his hands in his pockets and turned to leave but then stopped. "I'm really happy for you, sis."

"Thanks, Fred. That means a lot." She nodded and leaned heavily into my side as Fred continued to stroll back inside.

Josie trembled in my arms as we walked to the car. Today felt like so much more than just a party for family reconciliation, more even than a fake relationship to appease the parents. So much more than a deal between friends to help each other out.

I squeezed Josie tighter, and she squeezed me right back. There was something far too fulfilling, far too *right* about having her in my arms.

FIFTEEN

Josie

MORNING SUNBEAMS PLAYED TAG WITH THE weathered sign of the Bookish Cat as I unlocked the door. The scent of musky paper from this week's still-unopened delivery of new books from England, laced with a hint of vanilla from the incense I kept in the back, rolled out to greet me.

And so did three cats.

"What are you doing here? How did you get in?" I had left them snoozing in the morning sun at home, but sure as day, they were lounging on various shelves, indifferent to my arrival.

The question of how they managed that magic trick couldn't distract me from the real issue weighing on my mind.

An intoxicating memory clung to my senses—the taste of last night's fateful change of direction...

Caleb's kiss.

Just the thought of it brought wetness to the lace panties I'd picked with care this morning. I had zero plans of showing them to anyone—least of all, Caleb—but something about yesterday reminded me that I was a woman. I needed to feel that sensation on my skin, in my veins—my pussy was crying out for more attention than I'd given it in years.

My fingers wandered down, slipping beneath the waistband of my jeans. Just the slightest of touches was all I would allow. I was on the clock, after all. And I wasn't afraid to admit that I kind of *liked* the torture.

I navigated through the maze of towering bookshelves with practiced ease, since I set up every single part of the store. Each book was a world unto itself, humming with stories untold. That kiss awoke a part of me I'd forgotten about, the part where I got my *own* love story. I found myself echoed in the books that surrounded me—in heroines who dared to love, in heroes who left, in plot twists that unraveled in the wake of a single, fateful kiss.

God, it had felt like fate. Over the last seven years, I'd let myself forget how he did that to me. But being around him changed something inside of me, too. I was damn proud of everything I'd built since he left, but his presence made me want more out of life.

I ran my hand over *Little Women* because I'd been bold like Jo, who dared to defy societal norms and love freely. A few shelves away, I tapped *The Book Thief*, where Rudy Steiner's steadfastness reflected the essence of Caleb. The wrenching plot twists and single fateful kisses in *The History of Love* were a perfect fit for what was happening between Caleb and me. Alma Singer definitely knew what she was talking about when she wrote that.

The shop had been my escape, but now I saw our love story reflected in books from left to right, from classics to philosophy, fantasy to romance. As for the stack of Highlander steamy romances? I flipped through the pages a little too long this morning.

Behind the counter, I lingered, the weight of my thoughts pressing against the silent anticipation of opening the store in five minutes. My fingers found the power button on the tablet, but my mind was lost in the labyrinth of last night.

The vivid taste of that kiss lingered—taking me back to our love affair in Federal Way seven years ago, when I was sure of my future and the fact that he was it.

His touch, the smell of his skin, the sound of his whispered affections all surged back as if carried on a rogue wave crashing into the shore of my quiet life.

And there goes my pussy throbbing for him again.

But beyond this inexplicable physical reaction I had at the mere thought of him, his touch ignited questions that I had buried deep within the corners of my heart.

Why now? Why here? Why did every fiber of my being lean into him despite the chasm of years spent apart? One kiss shouldn't be able to do so much.

Stories from the past and present tangled together, long-forgotten love letters and stolen kisses resurfacing from the depths of my guarded heart. Lovemaking that had lasted for hours and days as if the world were ending. The past had strolled into my present, uninvited, through a door I thought I'd bolted shut.

The soft ping of my tablet pulled me out of my illicit thoughts.

"Nana Geraldine" flashed across the screen, and I composed myself before swiping to answer the video call. Her beaming face framed by a wide-brimmed sunflower hat was there waiting for me.

"Nana, you're up early after the big party!"

"I'll have plenty of time to sleep when I'm dead," she scoffed.

"Nana!"

"I know you don't like it when I talk that way, but that's why I'm living it up in the meantime."

Sometimes, Nana's humor was a kick to the gut. "So, did you love the party?" I asked, settling into the plush reading chair. I could open the shop a couple minutes late. There was no one at the door.

"Oh, it was just delightful, dear. You wouldn't believe the shenanigans we got up to after you young'uns left. Why, Mabel and I whipped out our dancing shoes and cut the rug until the wee hours, singing at the top of our lungs. And we just might have wrapped the neighbor's fir tree with toilet paper. I haven't done that in at least ten years! What a thrill!"

"Nana!" I exclaimed, both scandalized and amused. She was never going to change, and thank goodness for that.

Nana's hearty laughter rang through the tablet again, her eyes filled with feigned innocence. "What? I'm just a harmless old lady having fun," she said, fluttering her eyelashes in pretend bashfulness, her eccentric hat bobbing with the movement. I couldn't help but join in her laughter, the image of Nana and her geriatric crew partying into the early hours of the morning bringing a much-needed lightness to the emotionally heavy start of my day.

"And you? Recovered yet?" she asked, her eyes twinkling with her signature mischief. "And you know I mean recovered from that history-making kiss from your beau."

"Oh, that." I waved my hand. "It was nothing."

Nana sighed and tensed her lips, her tone turning serious. "It wasn't nothing. And we need to talk about this." Her eyes were still twinkling, but it was as if they held secrets now, secrets that were waiting to break free. "It's time you knew. It matters now."

I blinked at her sudden change, my smile faltering. "Knew what, Nana?" I wasn't sure I wanted to know.

Nana wasn't one for secrets, or so I'd thought.

She leaned toward the camera, the brim of her sunflower hat falling out of view. There was an excitement there, a mischievous glint that hinted at tales of yore and adventures untold. It was a look that I'd seen in my customers' eyes when they picked up a book they couldn't wait to dive into.

"Once upon a time," she began, a playful grin breaking across her face. "When I was about your age, a little older maybe, I met someone." She held my gaze, her eyes intense.

I leaned in closer, curiosity piqued. "Okay, I'll bite. Who was it?"

She held up a hand, wagging her finger at me. "Nuh-uh. Patience, dear. I'm getting to that. This wasn't an ordinary someone. This person... couldn't even truly be called that." She paused dramatically, her eyes gleaming with excitement. I had a sense that whatever she was about to reveal was something big.

"Couldn't be called a person?" I asked, now genuinely intrigued. The store opening could wait.

"He was celestial," she said, her voice just above a whisper.

Did she just say what I think she said?

"Celestial?" I echoed, my voice catching in my throat. I waited for her to break into laughter, to tell me she was just pulling my leg, but she remained serious. She nodded solemnly. "Yes, celestial, dear. Not too unlike the 'fictional' characters you're so fond of in your books."

I stared at her, unblinking. Was Nana suggesting that she'd experienced something like what I'd experienced? No, she couldn't be.

But the knowing look in her eyes told a different story. I felt the color drain from my face as I grappled with the implications of her revelation. My mind spun, questions ricocheting around my head.

Nana met an angel? Does she know what Caleb is?

"I know, dear. It's a lot to take in," she said softly, a hint of compassion in her eyes. "But it's true. And now that you've met one too, I thought it was high time I shared this with you."

The way she said "met one too" with such nonchalance, as if meeting celestial beings was as normal as running into an old friend at the grocery store, made my head spin.

I didn't know whether to laugh or cry. I had so many questions. I needed answers. And it seemed like Nana was the only one who could provide them.

"You know about Caleb..." I began, my voice barely a whisper.

Nana just smiled, her eyes filled with understanding and maybe... relief?

"Indeed, dear," she murmured. "Indeed."

We sat like that, looking at each other and not knowing what to say, until there was a knock at the bookshop door.

"There will be time for us to talk, Josie dear. In the meantime, just know that this love is unlike anything else you will ever experience."

The screen went black.

Another polite knock on the door and I rushed off my chair, eager for the distraction.

The small bell above the door heralded the customer's entrance after I unlocked it. A middle-aged woman stepped inside, her eyes wide with delight as she glanced around. She was a new customer, taking it all in.

"Morning," I greeted her, forcing a smile despite the turmoil inside.

"Good morning," she replied with a wide smile. "I wonder

if you could help me. I'm looking for a family saga to read on my vacation. Something that will keep me hooked," she said, squeezing her hands in anticipation.

"I've got a whole section of family sagas." I led her to the far corner where those hefty books were shelved. "What sort of dynamics are you interested in?" I asked, turning back to her.

"Oh, I love a meddling grandmother character. The matriarch of the family who has her fingers in every pie." The woman laughed.

A chuckle escaped my lips. "Well, I certainly know about that character type. The kind that phones you up out of the blue and gets straight into the middle of a mess," I said, my mind flitting back to Nana.

The woman hooted, a hearty sound that echoed around the shop. "Exactly!"

"Any other character types you're fond of?" I asked, pulling out a few books I thought she might like.

"Hmm... How about some sibling rivalry?" she suggested.

"Oh, that's a common one," I agreed, a wry smile pulling at my lips. "The kind where one sibling has followed family tradition, but the other has become a black sheep."

"Yes!"

"But then there's this undercurrent of love and respect beneath it all. Even if one of them returns after seven years with a mysterious secret," I added. Fred and I had a complex relationship, but yesterday felt like something new was happening between us.

The woman nodded enthusiastically. "Yes, yes! That's exactly it!"

"Anything else?" I asked, eager to see where this conversation would lead.

"Perhaps a childhood sweetheart who comes back to town,

reigniting old feelings and stirring up drama?" she proposed, an impish grin on her face.

My heart skipped a beat. "I know that one, too," I said, swallowing hard. "The kind that shows up unannounced, his return sending shockwaves through the protagonist's life. They share a kiss that's a mix of old memories and new feelings. And suddenly, all those old wounds are reopened, the past coming back to haunt the present," I added, my voice a soft murmur.

"And always a happily ever after." She sighed.

"Always." I let out a tight sigh. Happily ever after, my ass. More like make do with the best I could get. Even *Nana* had gone through the turmoil of a love that didn't last forever with one of these celestial cads. Just who did they think they were, anyway?

Angel-shaped Don Juan dickwads.

She cocked her head. "Or else the love interest could die. That always does well in a family saga."

Yikes. "No!" That would be going a little *too* far.

"Oh, okay." The woman's eyes were wide with interest. "Then he lives and causes incredible chaos in an already complicated family. That's the kind of drama I live for."

"Let me cull the options for you." I was getting fearful of what she might come up with next.

I helped her narrow her selection to an excellent series that could keep her going all summer.

"I know you're going to love these," I said as I rang her up on the register.

She placed a fifty-dollar bill on the counter but then reached out and took my hand. The contact surprised me. Her grasp was unusually hot, hotter than any skin I'd ever touched, as though if I wasn't careful, I'd get burned. It was as if she...

And then I knew.

She isn't human.

The woman squeezed my hand. "You'll get your happy ending, darling."

And she was gone, the books she'd selected poofing out of existence right along with her.

The air was electric as I stood there in the silence, a buzzing energy that hummed beneath my skin and jolted through my veins. She had been standing there, as real as I was, but these days, as I became more and more aware of the not-so-human beings around, I knew that woman could have been anything.

And that made her message all the more important. My heart pounded an erratic beat against the backdrop of hushed whispers from the old, worn books. The realization hit me like a lightning bolt.

Caleb is the man for me.

Gatsby appeared, purring at my feet.

I saw it then, as clear as the sun's first light breaking the dawn, as undeniable as the constellations adorning the night sky. He wasn't just another character in the complex web of my existence. No, he was the plot twist, the climax, the denouement, all rolled into one.

I'd been trying to map out my life's narrative without its protagonist, the key character around whom everything revolved. It was Caleb. It had *always* been Caleb.

I could see it in the way his name resounded in my mind, an echo reverberating off the walls of my heart, leaving a trail of warmth. I could see it in the way the universe seemed to be aligning itself in a strange, inexplicable pattern, leading me back to him.

Even the fact that it had been seven years... there was something powerful in that number.

Everything inside me filled with a cocktail of emotions so potent it threatened to spill over.

Fear. Excitement. Longing. Hope. Desperate need. Each one vied for dominance, but one stood out, stronger, bolder.

Courage.

I would not be held back by fear or uncertainty anymore. I was ready to face Caleb, to lay everything out on the line. To tell him that despite the chaos, the turmoil, the celestial complications, he was the one.

My heart's compass pointed toward him, as certain as true north.

This was bigger than us. It was a saga written in the stars, etched into the universe's grand design. It was our love story, and I was ready to turn the page and start the next chapter.

Gatsby jumped onto the counter, and I'd be damned if he didn't just push my keys at me ever so slightly with a wink just as Barb walked in.

"Barb, I've got to go!"

"Nice to see you too—"

I flew out of the bookshop and ran faster than I thought was possible to Caleb's office. I had to get there before my courage had any chance to falter.

I was in love with an angel, and I was going to make him mine.

SIXTEEN
Caleb

I'D ALWAYS BEEN A MORNING PERSON—ANGELS didn't have to sleep, so nighttime was boring now that I couldn't flit off to a part of the world that was awake. I already knew every language in the world—perks of being an angel, we got all the good downloads—and there was only so much to watch on TV. So the sun's first rays peeking through the gloom were a gift, each and every day I spent on Earth.

Except today.

Today, the cold light of reality shone like a beacon on all my regrets, all my failings. I'd lain in bed tossing and turning all night, and there I stayed. The way I'd lost my wings seven years ago echoed into the present, a burn of longing that I couldn't ignore. The longer they were gone, the more I felt the loss was permanent. My relationship with Josie back then mirrored the one that was growing now... starting with that earth-shattering kiss last night.

Even thinking about it hurt because it didn't make *sense*. How could something so perfect, that seemed so clearly ordained, be at the same time everything I'd ever wanted and everything I couldn't possibly have?

I was starting to understand why some angels fell permanently from grace. Being on the outside of love had never been a problem before Josie. It was my purpose, my *calling*, and I found great joy in it. But now? Now it felt hollow. Painfully empty, like opening the most beautifully wrapped gift in the world only to find there was nothing inside all the pretty paper.

I had to distance myself, stay apart from her, and that thought cut me to the quick. There was no other way to earn back my wings, and if I fell permanently... well, I'd never be worthy of her. Then, I wouldn't even have my duty to keep me busy. I'd be forced to wander the Earth alone, cut off from the Host permanently as darkness slowly ate away at the edges of my soul, and I descended into demonic ruin.

It simply wasn't an option.

The cruel irony that to be worthy of her I had to put her aside was like a knife twisting in my gut, and I couldn't see any way around it.

Fifteen more minutes of wallowing wouldn't fix it, though, so I dragged my sorry hide out of bed and into a lukewarm shower. I needed the discomfort to get myself moving.

By the time the sun was fully up, I was clean, dressed, and had found the day's couple. Jonathan and Kim had seemed like a simple match on the surface, but they'd proven otherwise over the years.

They had similar socioeconomic, political, and religious backgrounds. They were both only children who wanted to have a large family. They even had similar taste in movies.

And yet, I could not get the two of them together to save myself. I was mentally watching Jonathan grocery shop and

Kim teach a toddler gymnastics class when a rapid-fire knock sounded at my door.

Josie.

Her aura was amplified, the energy so loud it was leaking around the tiny cracks between my front door and the frame. Dread filled me as I crossed the space, but I tried to force a lid on the emotion.

It had been her idea to have a fake relationship; all I had to do now was honor that request. She didn't know much about an angel's Chosen; so she wouldn't understand how significant she was to me. That was one small pain I could keep from her, at least.

I pulled the door open and found her beaming on the other side, her voice intent as though she'd been up for hours. "Good morning!"

The wave of arousal that hit me when I opened the door was nearly enough to take me to my knees. I resisted the urge to shake myself as panic swamped me. I couldn't let this go any further than the kiss; I had to put the brakes on this relationship, once and for all.

I didn't want to consider the horrors that a fallen, twisted cupid could wreak on humanity over a millennium.

"I thought you'd already be at the shop."

She tucked a bouncy curl behind her ear, a flush staining her cheeks. "I was, yes, but I had to see you because... because today feels special."

"Special? Oh! Because the party went well?" I smiled, her enthusiasm contagious, but I didn't let her in. I needed the space to keep myself from getting too caught up.

"Exactly," she gushed. "It was... more than I ever dared hope."

Shit on a stick. I sucked in a deep breath through my nose, and instantly regretted it. Her arousal was heady, thick and sweet on the air. I wanted to drag her into my apartment, spread her out on my bed, and impale her with my cock. The way she smelled, the way her aura *glowed*, she'd not only let me, she'd beg me.

Fuck me sideways. I knew in that instant that there was only one honorable thing to do, even if it killed me. I had to use my powers to dampen that arousal, before things got out of control.

Regret burned inside me as I let the power out in a slow, miniscule trickle. Even it was reluctant, that power that usually leapt at my every command to create love and lust.

I had to keep her talking until it could take effect. "I'm so glad. I know you were uncomfortable with the idea of a fake date, but it all seemed to work out well. And thank goodness that's over now, right? I hope you weren't too embarrassed by the kiss, but that was the only way I could think of to sell it." I forced a very fake smile, knowing she'd see right through it.

She bit her bottom lip, searching my face intently. "No, I wasn't embarrassed, not at all."

My power still wasn't cooperating, but the rosy flush of her need was starting to dim, turning hazy black around the edges. Why was it turning *black*? I'd never seen that color before, and panic started to well in my chest. Was I hurting her?

She *seemed* fine. Confused, but fine. Was it because I was acting against my primary directive as a cupid, to *encourage* love?

I didn't know, but I couldn't risk hurting her by using my powers in a way they weren't meant to be used. I eased off, letting the flow of power stop. I'd have to put her off the old-fashioned way, and the thought wasn't any more appealing.

"Good, I'm glad. We hadn't had a chance to talk about it

before, but I was a little worried that you might have thought it was too far. Especially given our history. I promise you, though, it was *all* to put on a show for your parents. But your Nana was thrilled, and even Fred wants to come to the Bookish Cat. So, all's well that ends well, I suppose. Luckily, we won't have to do that again, right, old pal?" I pretend-punched her on the shoulder like we were old drinking buddies, barely making contact. Yet still, she stumbled back as if I'd put my weight into it and slugged her.

Or just hurt her feelings like a prick.

I hated myself for every word, but the longer she spent with me, the more off track her life was getting. I had to protect her, even from me. Especially from me.

I helped patch up a dozen other old family wounds, but she probably won't notice those for some time. That's all I can do; try to leave her better off than I found her.

"I—Yes. Exactly. That was always the goal." She smiled again, but this time it was her smile that didn't reach the eyes. A knife to my ribs would have been more pleasant. "You fulfilled your role excellently. I just wanted to come by and say thank you for all your help. That's it."

"Of course. You know that's my life's work, helping others."

So, why does it feel so empty standing next to her? The scent and glow of her need was all but gone, turned bitter black, like dead rose petals.

I would be mourning that loss for the rest of my existence.

"Of course, right. And that's the other reason I stopped by." She stood a little straighter, setting her jaw in determination. "We need to work on your couples now. Can you come by after the shop closes tomorrow?"

"Absolutely. I've got two couples left, and, fair warning, they're both doozies."

"Well, call me *The Little Engine That Could*, because we're going to get them taken care of in no time." She punched me lightly on the shoulder just like I had her, and then spun on her heel. "Got to get back to the shop now—so many things to do —but I'll see you tomorrow."

"See you tomorrow," I called after her retreating back. She didn't turn around.

I still want her to turn around.

"You've barely touched your lemonade. Are you sick? Do I need to call a doctor?"

Victory's joking question startled me out of my malaise as I stared at the passing traffic. I wasn't even using my senses. I was truly just staring out into the void.

Heavens help me, I had it bad. Seeing Josie that morning, keeping her at arm's length... It had taken a toll.

"I'm fine, just distracted." I forced a smile, but I knew she didn't buy it.

"Okay, well, you'd better drink up or else I won't be able to earn my tips today." She rapped twice on the table before leaving me to my gloom, heading off to a table of orc warriors. They could be mistaken for humans—most likely pro wrestlers, given their bulk, but humans nonetheless—if people didn't notice the small tusks protruding up from their bottom lips. An odd supernatural race because they looked terrifying but were actually quite family-centric. These were unmated males, though, perhaps looking for a female.

I might have used my senses any other day to see if there were any likely prospects I could nudge that way, but my heart wasn't in it.

Instead, I picked up my lemonade and took a swig to give myself something to do. It didn't taste the same, and I set it back on the table listlessly.

"Boy, for a man who just spent the evening fixing familial bonds so successfully, you look like somebody just kicked your dog. Or... do you prefer cats these days?"

I nearly spit out my lemonade at Gabriel's sudden appearance.

"Gabe, we're on a public street. You can't just *poof* into existence—"

"Relax, Caleb. Everyone passing by will think I've always been here. Nobody on this patio is even a little bit surprised by a sudden appearance." He shot me a cocky grin and propped one heel up onto his other knee, the epitome of relaxed indifference.

"The waitress is nearly human."

"The waitress is fending off five rowdy orcs who can smell that she's fertile. She didn't notice. What's gotten into you today?"

"Nothing," I snapped, and then immediately regretted it. Gabriel was one of the few members of the heavenly Host who'd stood by me, even when I screwed up. He had always been a friend, close as a brother. And here I was biting his head off.

"I'm sorry, Gabriel. Truly. I just... last night was complicated. And those complications overflowed into this morning."

"How so?" His pose didn't change a millimeter, but the energy in the air between us did, imperceptible to anyone without our talents.

I had to tread lightly, or even Gabriel wouldn't deign to visit anymore. And without him to recommend my reinstatement to the Host, I'd surely be struck down permanently. But what did I tell him?

"I had to kiss her. To sell the ruse. Her parents didn't believe I was really her boyfriend."

His eyebrows shot up, and his foot clunked unceremoniously to the pavers beneath our feet.

"You kissed the human girl?"

I nodded, unable to hide my grimace. That was all she was to him, some human girl. But to me, she was so, so much more. And all of her was out of my reach.

"Ah, I'm sure it will work itself out. Humans have short memories; even if you stunned her a bit last night, she'll move on." He raised a finger to flag Victory down, already over the news of the kiss.

Me, though? I would never get over it, over her.

I was an immortal being, and she wasn't. The enormity of it all was finally sinking in. I would be alone forever, after I watched my only shot at true love grow old and die. She would be married to someone else and have beautiful children. The best I could hope for after she was gone would be playing some twisted version of guardian angel over her descendants in between matching my assigned couples.

And all that time, for the rest of eternity, I would be unchanged—a stone unmoving in the river of humanity.

Never loved.

Always on the outside.

And for the first time in my long, *long* life, it felt like my heart was breaking. Turning black and decrepit, just like Josie's aura this morning.

"So, what are you working on today?" Gabriel asked after

ordering a cappuccino and biscotti. "You've only got two couples left on the list and the book of angelic seals to find, right?"

"Right. I'm still shadowing the couples, and Josie is going to help me with some ideas tomorrow evening, now that her party has been taken care of. Today, though, I have another man I need to ask you about."

I definitely wasn't changing the subject to keep him from prying into my disastrously misguided infatuation with a human.

He leaned forward, interested. "Who is he?"

"Josie's landlord. He's allergic to her cats and trying to make her get rid of them. I was thinking there might be a way to help him, and in doing so, help her." I pushed an impression of the man's face and energy signature to him, and he frowned, searching the angelic registers for him.

"Ah, yes. Herb Anderson. Looks like we have him down as a switch."

Interesting. So, he didn't have a pre-ordained mate, and his fate was up in the air. "So, if I can find him a match who's also available..."

"You would have the Host's blessing." Gabriel shrugged and stole a fry off my plate, not concerned about the fate of a switch in the least.

"Fantastic."

I had some research to do, but I already had someone in mind for him. I might not be able to make Josie mine, but I could still give her the best life possible, one that would allow her to keep her cats.

If that was all I could ever give her, then it would have to be enough.

SEVENTEEN

Josie

I STORMED INTO MY APARTMENT, SLAMMING THE door behind me with a satisfying bang. I kicked off my shoes and threw my head back in humiliated frustration.

"What the hell was I thinking?"

I chastised myself with every name in the book, shaking my head as if the motion could dislodge the memory. *Of course* the kiss had meant nothing. Caleb was my *fake* boyfriend, and it was all a performance, nothing more. Just an act for the crowd, no strings attached.

"That's what I asked for, isn't it?"

A cold feeling of denial washed over me as I muttered the words to myself, the echo of my voice in the empty apartment doing nothing to make me feel one stitch better. There I'd been, halfway to tearing my lace underwear off with my own nails, when it suddenly became clear that whatever hot mess I'd become, it had all been my imagination. He didn't reciprocate my feelings *at all*.

"Such an idiot. An overworked, sex-deprived desperate idiot."

My musing received a reply in the form of a familiar mewling sound. The trio of mysterious cats wound their way around my legs. I flopped onto the sofa and bent to scratch behind Matilda's ears.

"Look who decided to grace me with their presence," I cooed at them, my voice turning softer as I resigned myself to reality. "What are you, magician cats or something? How do you get in and out of places without the key?"

Maybe Caleb would know how they did it. *Screw that,* I shoved the thought away. This had to be a Caleb-free head-space for a while. Like forever.

I stood up and the cats trailed after me, their curious eyes following my every movement. The incongruity of their appearances and disappearances was almost comical. One minute, they were here, the next, they were gone, and then they would reappear at the shop when I least expected them, like feline Houdinis.

I scooped up Gatsby, his golden eyes reminding me a bit of Caleb. The thought made my stomach sink, and I found myself hugging the cat closer, his warm purr a comfort to my disquieted heart. The magician cats were a distraction, a comforting, furry distraction, which was exactly what I needed.

But as soon as I put Gatsby down, he and Matilda trotted off. Heathcliff waited behind, staring at the wall a moment longer, and then sprinted to follow.

"They're in a world of their own."

That's what I wanted. To rebuild my own world. I had been on that path before Caleb showed up, having the Bookish Cat to keep me busy. But now I just felt... less than.

Without thinking, I grabbed my laptop and opened FindYourGuy.com.

My inbox was flashing with a new message.

> RockCollector89: Hey Josie, how did the family event turn out? Hope it wasn't as rocky as one of my collections...

He remembered. That was sweet.

> Josie: It was good. Lots of fun, maybe a little too much.

> RockCollector89: Ah, sounds like a landslide of a party! Anything you want to talk about? I'm all ears, unless you count my rock-hard abs...

I laughed and shook my head. This guy, his humor, was a lot to take in. Was I ready to dive deeper into this? I had a lot on my plate already. Caleb's matches, the bookstore, Nana's bombshell of a revelation. But maybe that was all the more reason to just go for it. A distraction could be good. A non-celestial, pun-loving distraction. Though it wasn't easy to tell from his profile picture if the rock-hard abs thing was true or a convenient analogy.

> Josie: You're quite the comedian, aren't you?

> RockCollector89: I try. Keeps things light, you know? Otherwise, life would be as dull as dirt.

> Josie: It's refreshing.

I sighed. Anything that would make me forget about that asshole of an angel would hit the spot. Something light. Something... normal. And at least he didn't make a pun that time. I made a split-second decision and typed before I could second-guess myself.

> Josie: Want to take this to the phone?

> RockCollector89: Oh, I'd be delighted! But I have to warn you, my phone voice is a little, um, gravelly.

> Josie: I'll risk it.

I sent him my number before I could stop myself.

Here goes nothing.

The phone rang almost immediately, the sudden jingle startling me out of my thoughts.

"Hello?" I answered, my voice shaky.

"Hi, Josie," a warm voice greeted me from the other end, his tone soft and rich, reminding me of smooth, polished stones.

Oh look, he got me into the puns now.

"Hi... RockCollector89?" I replied, realizing I didn't even know his real name.

He chuckled, a sound like boulders clashing together in the most harmonious way. "Actually, it's Ethan. But I'll take Rock-Collector89 if you prefer."

"Ethan it is," I said, smiling despite myself. His light humor and the ease with which he approached the entire situation made it hard not to. And I had to admit that his voice was kind of hot. That was unexpected.

There was a small pause before he said, "Josie, I know it's sudden, but I've always been an in-person kind of guy. Would you like to go out tomorrow night?"

The suddenness of the proposition almost made me drop

the phone. But what the hell was I waiting for? Did I want to have phone sex with a geologist? No, sir. Worst case scenario, we talked about the controversy around quartz countertops for an evening. "Sure, Ethan. That sounds nice."

"Fantastic!" he replied, his excitement palpable through the line. "I promise I won't take you for *granite*."

"Ouch, that was a rough landing. Some might even call it... rocky."

He laughed, deep and sincere. "I'll text you details. See you tomorrow, Josie."

I hung up, and good sense immediately made me wonder what the actual fuck I was doing.

Hours ago, I was ready to throw my body and soul at Caleb. Now, I was going on a mystery date with an unknown quasi-obsessive rock enthusiast. What if he turned out to be a serial killer? The more I thought about it, the more I realized I had to be careful. Safety first. As long as he picked a public place and not a random abandoned parking lot to meet up.

That seemed unlikely. For all his strangeness, he seemed like a mostly normal guy. With a sexy voice. And maybe even rock-hard abs.

A sense of excitement bubbled up inside me as I tried to fall asleep. I was taking life by the horns. And for the first time in a while, it felt like the right direction.

THE NEXT MORNING, I arrived at the Bookish Cat to find Heathcliff, Gatsby, and Matilda already there. "Good morning, magic furballs."

They sat in the middle of the shop as if holding some secretive cat conference, their eyes glinting with hidden knowledge. Their inexplicable presence before me only added fuel to my magician cat theory.

Many new customers, including a class of second-graders studying mythology, kept me busy until late afternoon.

I turned to the shipment that had come in from England. Crates of books, their spines vibrant and uncreased, fresh off the press of an independent publisher. And I was their first stateside customer! I was going to put the Bookish Cat on the map, I could feel it in my bones.

As I began to arrange them, their familiar smell wafted toward me, a comforting mix of paper, ink, and something indefinably bookish.

I was in the middle of categorizing a set of dark police procedurals when my phone buzzed with a new text.

> Ethan: Hey, are you excited for our date or am I rocking the boat with my eagerness? Here's what I'm thinking...

I rolled my eyes at the pun but was relieved to see he'd selected a gorgeous little spot in the Central District. Very public, and not setting off my sketch-o-meter. *Perfect*.

I was just about to reply when the bell over the shop door jingled, and there he was. Caleb. His eyes met mine as I shoved my phone behind a stack of books. If Caleb saw that I was texting with another man...

So what if he did? I had nothing to hide. I was a grown-ass woman who owned her own business and was taking life by the horns, wasn't I?

Sure, Caleb's eyes sought out the deepest part of me as he

stepped tentatively closer, and the affection he felt was so obvious on his face that I couldn't help feeling a tiny bit guilty for trying to run off with someone just to forget him.

Stop it, Josie. He's not yours. You ought to forget him, and fast.

"Caleb! Is it time already?"

He looked at his watch. "Closing time has come, and here I am." His smile was nervous. "Just like we said."

He let out a long exhale, and the air of it washed over me like a sea breeze. Calming my anxious bones. It took every ounce of willpower I had not to wrap my arms around him and forget everything he'd said. Let our lips meet the way they were supposed to, searching hungrily for the other as I'd imagined all these years.

And like he'd done last night.

With a deep inhale, I veered the conversation into safer territory. "So, Caleb," I began, leaning against the counter. "Tell me more about this matchmaking mission of yours."

He blinked, as if surprised by my formal tone of voice, and then nodded, leaning back against a bookshelf. His eyes were serious as he spoke to me like a colleague, but his muscles flexed, and I remembered how strong he was when he pulled me into him. "Well, first I've got Jonathan and Kim, who are absolutely destined to be together and won't let me make it happen."

I pursed my lips to think. "Okay, sure. But if they don't want it, maybe it isn't meant to be."

"That's not how this works."

"Maybe you should explain it to me."

He scratched the back of his head, squeezing those fine lips to the side. "These are couples who should have been together already, but I made errors early on that got in the way. I'm lucky to have been given a second chance to correct my mistakes and help them find love now."

"Errors, huh?"

"Yeah. Lots of them." The sheepish look on his face was more boyish than man, and I got a glimpse of how he might have been if he hadn't been a powerful other-worldly being. "The list I was given, to prove my worth, was many couples long. Only two are left now, and I'm getting desperate to finish. Anything to be back in good standing. The alternative is... unbearable. I need this, Josie."

That vulnerability, the *honesty* of it, wasn't only utterly endearing, it was sexy beyond my ability to manage. A lock of hair fell into his eyes, and without thinking I reached up to move it aside. He looked surprised at first, and then the corners of his eyes filled with understanding. And then they filled with *something else*. From my fingertips straight to my core came that shot, the electrical wave that made my body react. I was sure he could hear my heart beating, it was so loud, so intense.

What am I doing? I reprimanded myself. *Why is everything in me rebelling against my better judgment, demanding that I touch him?*

His eyes were a study in emotions, flickering between earnest determination, frustration, and a gentleness that tugged at my heart. A heart that needed to remember boundaries. He had set those boundaries, clear as day.

But no matter how much I tried to convince myself, even the air around us seemed to change. Like being here now wasn't real life—it was the life we'd always wanted. The one we'd talked about seven years ago. It was a dream, sure, but I wasn't about to pinch myself.

"I need you, Josie." He meant with the couples. Probably.

Or did he? He stepped even closer, my breasts brushing his chest. "I need you."

Fire. That was the only way to describe what happened when his fingertips touched my cheek. As if all of the Bookish Cat had gone alight and I was burning from the inside out. Everything around us was fine, but I wasn't. I was anything but fine. I needed him, needed him that second, and I couldn't bear it anymore. Everything in me screamed that this was right, that it had to happen, that we needed each other, and I was incapable of thinking anything else.

I pressed my body against his and he knew. He felt it, too. He had to. The question didn't linger long in my mind because I was overcome by the warmth emanating off him as he leaned in, leaned closer, and took my lips with his.

Perfection.

My body knew it. My soul knew it. Even if my brain was calling me crazy, there was no other choice at that moment. I didn't even care that the door to the shop was unlocked.

"I want you, Caleb," the words were a husky admission. "Don't stop."

His mouth crashed against mine again, harder this time. He pressed me against the row of high fantasy novels, his hands gripping my waist, pulling me closer to him as his tongue swept my lips, eager to taste. The heat from his body burned through my thin shirt as the ridges of book spines pressed into my back.

Our kisses deepened with each one, tongues tangled as our hands explored, desperate, as if this couldn't last. His fingers traced the line of my jaw before caressing my side and lifting the edge of my shirt. He reverently palmed my cleavage, grazing the lace of my bra. He pulled back to look at me, eyes filled with desire. His breath, still like the sea breeze, sent shivers down my spine. I let every fear of him leaving again melt away as his cock grew harder against my hip.

"I need you," he replied and his lips crashed against mine with more urgency, his hand gripping my jaw as he pulled me closer. His tongue demanded entrance to my mouth, and I eagerly obliged, letting him plunder every word I couldn't say. My heart raced as his body heat sank into mine, our chests pressing together tightly. The soft rustling sounds of the street faded away, and I felt free even though the walls held us close.

I lifted my shirt off, wanting to drink in the sight of him watching me.

He slipped my bra strap off my shoulder with a gentle tug, exposing a bare inch of skin. My nipples hardened immediately at his touch. "So beautiful," he said. His smile was hungry as he softly bit my shoulder before trailing more kisses down my collarbone.

He kissed my lips, his fingers entwined in my hair, pulling me closer to deepen the kiss while his free hand roamed up to cup my breast through my bra. He gently squeezed it before reaching around to open the clasp, freeing me in multiple ways.

"Like no time has passed," I whispered with my eyes closed, reliving the moments from before but with a body that now knew exactly what it wanted.

He slowly tugged on the elastic band of my skirt and panties before slipping his hand inside and skimming one finger lightly over my wetness. It felt so good, so divinely right, having him touch me this way. "Like no time has passed," he repeated, tenderly pressing against me, his strong fingers restraining themselves. Firm but gentle.

He froze there for a moment, his touch sending shock-waves through me as I instinctually arched into him.

And I couldn't hold myself back any longer.

"More, Caleb," I whispered against his shoulder urging him onward with every fiber of my being.

With a growl, he roughly yanked off my skirt and panties in one swift movement, leaving me completely bare to him. He lifted me as if I weighed nothing and carried me down the row, setting my ass on top of a box of dictionaries that reached waist height. His eyes darkened further at the sight of my pussy as he leaned in to taste me, his tongue swirling around my sensitive core before plunging inside, causing a wave of pleasure to wash over me.

The smell of books mixed with our sweat and lust, creating an intoxicating aroma that blinded me to every other thought except him. He held me against his face while his free hand roamed up to cup one breast, pinching one nipple, and then the other. "So beautiful," he murmured again before rising up to take one hardened nipple into his mouth, sucking enough to make me squirm, my pussy clenching with need to be filled.

I could feel his cock pressing against my thigh, straining against his jeans. With trembling fingers, I reached down to undo his belt and zipper. He groaned against my breast as I wrapped my hand around his length, stroking him slowly.

I whispered in his ear. "I want you."

"I know you do." He pressed my clit with his finger.

"No," I took his head in my hands, tugging on his hair so he had to pull back, see the intent in my eyes. "I want *all of you*. Now."

He moaned, closing his eyes. "Josie, if you only knew..."

"Caleb, shut up and *fuck me*."

Caleb pulled away slightly, his eyes darkening with desire at my dirty words that sent a fresh thrill thrumming through my core. "You don't know what you're asking for," he said, his words a raspy whisper that only drove me higher.

But as I stared up at him with challenge and invitation, he groaned softly. He reached behind his head and yanked his shirt off in one fluid movement, kicking his pants off a second later. Then he pulled me closer, notching the head of his cock against me as he lifted me effortlessly. "I have to," he murmured, whether to me or himself, I couldn't tell.

My heart raced in my chest as we made eye contact for one last moment before his lips crashed down on mine once more —hungrily devouring me.

His muscles rippled down his body, and I feared I'd fall off the dictionaries right there and then, nearly fainting at the realization that I finally had him. After so long, I worried this was just a hallucination. But the heat of his skin on mine was too real to deny.

He wrapped his arms around me, keeping me steady as he lowered me to the reading bench in the corner.

His cock teased my entrance for way too long, need and pleasure making me impatient. He teased me mercilessly, running the head along my folds without quite giving me the pressure I craved. I bucked my hips, silently begging for more as I kept my fingers tangled in his golden curls.

I moaned and arched my back as he carried on, circling and dipping inside of me slowly. It was electric, sending shockwaves through every inch of my body. I held my breath as he continued to explore, building a rhythm that had me squirming in his grip.

"Mine," he whispered hoarsely as he pushed into me at last, and I was sure I had just shot into the stars. He continued, going deeper with every thrust, and I let out a moan at the fullness. He was stretching me in the best possible way. The sounds of our heavy breathing filled the air, punctuated by the occasional whirr of a car going by.

He held me close as he thrust faster into me, tangling his tongue with mine as I let my nails dig into his back. Each push took me somewhere new until our bodies were one, chaotic and perfect and somehow *more* at once. My core clenched, and I screamed my release.

"Yes," he moaned as my screams turned hoarse and he pulled out slowly, leaving me feeling too bereft, too empty. "That's what you needed."

"Me?" I wasn't letting him get away with it. I wrapped my hands around him, the thickness of his cock throbbing as I stroked it, watching his eyes. "What about what *you* need?"

I could tell he was seconds from exploding. His shoulders pulled forward as his breathing quickened, and he moaned my name as he came, staring deep into my eyes as his cum spurted over my belly, painting me with his release.

He rested his head against my chest and breathed heavily. As I stroked his hair, I had exactly zero thoughts running through my head, for the first time in—well, possibly ever. I didn't want to think. Thinking would only bring me back to reality, and I still wasn't sure what was happening here.

Caleb lifted his head and then gazed down my body. Sticky warmth that felt cool as he pulled off me.

"Let me help." He inhaled and then blew along my skin, chest to stomach, and I braced for the cold. It didn't come. Instead, all traces of his orgasm disappeared, leaving nothing but pleasant warmth and the tingle of goosebumps in his wake. He ran his finger along the place it had been. "Like new."

Like it never happened, I couldn't help thinking and gulped as anxiety started to creep in. I didn't have the will to move, too afraid of the passing time, of what would come next. Was he going to tell me this meant to him as much as it meant to me, followed by a big "but"?

"Sweet Josie." He kissed my cheek and then reached into empty air, where my clothes suddenly appeared in his hand. He lifted my foot, gently passing my panties over one, then the other.

He was taking care of me, which was sweet. So why did I feel like he was also saying goodbye?

He half-smiled, a huff of air escaping his lips. "That was... something else. If only the world were different, my perfect girl."

There's my answer.

The weight of responsibility in his tone told me everything, and he wouldn't meet my eyes. That stung.

"Right, right. This was for old time's sake. For getting it out of our system!" I said with a little too much enthusiasm. Anything to cover up how I really felt. Like he was oxygen, and I was suffocating. Like he was the sun, and I was the moon, trailing him for eternity but never catching him.

He had made as much clear to me even without a word—I was the one who had gotten carried away with... what exactly *was* that? I had never felt something so intense, a driving force that I knew came from deep within me. *Us.* Seven years of asking, "What if?"

The look on his face told me all I needed to know. What had just happened between us was nostalgic, a throwback to what we had been, and not what we might ever become. I swallowed a sob that threatened to escape me. I would *not* be the girl I was seven years ago, pining for a love I couldn't have. I had changed. My heart longed for Caleb, and I might never be the same. But I wouldn't let him see that now.

Caleb's jaw was set in that determined way I knew too well. There was sadness etched in the lines around his eyes, a heaviness in every slow, deliberate movement as he redressed me, as if each move was an effort against a tide of disappointment. He was trying to hide it, of course—he always did—but I saw the fragile cracks beneath his calm façade.

Whatever was holding him back from me, this chasm between us, couldn't even be addressed until he took care of the brokenness in him from losing his wings. The fear in his voice as he'd described what his future would be without them was enough for me to dampen any disillusionment I felt now.

I owed him. He did his part at Nana's birthday, and now it was my turn to come through. Even though watching him covering up his own cracks was fracturing me inside.

Which was easier now that we were fully clothed. We could pretend that whatever *that* was didn't really happen. Not in this plane of existence.

"So..." I sucked in a deep breath. "There are couples relying on you to set their future straight, and you"—I avoided saying *need me*—"want my help."

He let out a long breath, relief at my change of subject clearly setting him at ease. "Exactly. The biggest challenge right now is getting this next couple, Jonathan and Kim, to just be in the same place at the same time."

I frowned, knowing what I now did about his capabilities. "Why is that so hard? Can't you just, I don't know, manipulate their schedules or something?"

Caleb sniggered. "I wish it were that simple. They're like magnets facing the wrong direction. They just refuse to be in the same vicinity, and they're running out of time."

The image he painted was almost comical—two people unwittingly avoiding each other while an exasperated cupid tried to push them together. But behind the humor was a deeper struggle, one that Caleb was bearing the brunt of.

"Any ideas?" he asked, aiming those deep blues at me.

I thought for a moment before a spark ignited in my mind. "The first step is to test your theory. Let's see if we can twist the magnets around. You need to lure Jonathan and Kim to the same place, for different reasons. Once there, if they naturally gravitate toward each other, then we can work with that. If they repel..." I trailed off, frowning. "Then we're going to have to be extra creative."

Caleb nodded, his eyes bright with interest. "Yes, brilliant. There's a concert tonight at the Showbox that just might do the trick."

"Perfect." I smiled to show both that I was serious and that I was on his side. "You can tell me all about how it goes tomorrow."

He cocked his head, his expression earnest. "You're coming with me, right?"

A knot formed in my stomach. I was meeting Ethan, for a real date, not a fake one, and not one who was a dream from seven years ago. "I can't," I admitted, bracing for his reaction. "I have a date."

For a split second, his face fell, and a part of me wanted to cancel the date right there and then. What we'd shared was something I'd probably never experience again, and our history was far more complicated than any normal exes.

But I didn't owe Caleb anything, not with the way he'd shut down any idea of us just minutes after he'd spurted his cum across me.

He collected himself, nodding slowly. "Of course, I understand. I was just hoping... Well, never mind. Not important." He ran a hand through his hair, mussing the perfect golden strands. "You're a fantastic partner, Josie, and I can run with this. I want *you* to have a good time tonight. Maybe you can"— he cleared his throat—"tell me how it went when I report back on the couple." He tilted his head to the side, and I thought he might say something more. "I hope he's a great guy, Josie. Catch you later."

As I watched him leave, it felt like a door was closing. And I had no choice but to bolt it shut.

"Goodbye, Caleb."

EIGHTEEN
Caleb

I CAN'T. I HAVE A DATE.

The words echoed relentlessly against my skull. I had no right—not to be upset or to be angry. None. And yet I stormed away from the Bookish Cat with all the thunder of an avenging angel, not a cupid.

Watching the woman who felt like my Chosen choose another man over me shortly after she'd just squeezed my dick with her orgasm and screamed my name until she was hoarse struck so close to the quick, I couldn't breathe.

I could—not—breathe.

And yet, I had to move forward. I couldn't march back in there and demand she cancel with this inferior human man who couldn't possibly make her happy.

I can't. I have a date.

The words mocked me. Mocked everything I felt about what could have been between us. It was earth-shattering, heavens-shaking. I turned down an alley—one mostly free of humans—and punched the side of a brick building. It shuddered under the force, and I quickly snatched my hand back, horror washing over me.

I could have killed someone. Knocked down the whole damn building in a fit of temper over a first date. I had to get a grip.

This is why I can't have her. She goes on a date, and I accidentally almost murder a building full of people.

Shaking out my hand, I darted out of the alley and used a bit of supernatural speed to put more distance between us. I had to, or I'd do something truly stupid, like kidnap her so she couldn't go out with this... I let my senses unfurl and search the surrounding area for a male signature focused on Josie's.

Ethan.

It only took seconds, and it was a bad idea. He wasn't far away, and instead of kidnapping her, I could kidnap him, and then—

No.

Caleb, get your shit together!

I pointedly turned the opposite direction of Ethan's signature, away from this blissfully ignorant human. I had to focus on my match and getting Jonathan and Kim together as quickly as possible.

The sooner I got them matched, the sooner I could get the fuck out of Seattle. Because I knew something now, after tonight. I knew without a shadow of a doubt, I couldn't stay in Seattle and watch her move on.

It would kill me, even worse than the loss of my wings. Losing Josie? Watching her fall in love with someone else... the edges of my vision went black, and horror filled me as I froze to the spot.

I was falling. Falling from grace.

I sucked in a deep breath, then another, desperately trying

to let the anger and resentment and all those horrible things an angel wasn't supposed to ever feel *go*. I don't know how long it took, but eventually the black receded from my vision, the normal golden halo at the edges of my life returning.

Thank fuck.

But I wasn't out of the woods, not by a long shot. If sex with her could push me to the limits that quickly, there was no choice. I knew what I had to do.

Fix my matches and get as far away as possible from Josie—sooner rather than later. I knew she'd eventually find someone to marry and settle down with, but I couldn't bear to stay here and watch it. I would fall from grace permanently, that demonic influence taking hold forever.

If I asked, the Host would probably assign me to matches on the other side of the globe for a few years, or fifty, until she'd passed on. It was my only chance of not turning against everything I stood for. If I stayed where she was, the constant temptation that was Josie would be too much for me to resist.

I STOOD a few dozen yards from the famous gum wall, trying to ignore the tourists taking selfies, and focusing on my match. The Showbox was buzzing, but I happened to know that there were two tickets waiting at "will call," one under the name Jonathan Lyle and one under Kim Brezzo. The seats just happened to be next to each other. They'd been notified of the free tickets, and I was just waiting around for them to show up, so I could ensure the meeting went smoothly.

The problem was I couldn't concentrate. I'd be homed in on Kim then find myself glaring at a tourist while I mentally watched Ethan slick back his hair, wearing a... was that a tie covered in *rocks*?

Who was this bastard? Where had she found him?

And the question that had *really* been plaguing me since I'd left the Bookish Cat: if she'd had this guy in the wings, why make *me* her fake date to Nana Geraldine's birthday? Why reel me back in at all?

It didn't make sense, and I hated that it didn't make sense.

Maybe she was actually into you before you basically slammed the door in her face earlier. You screwed everything up when you turned your powers against her.

That's how the fall started. It seemed innocent enough—that's just a piece of fruit, over there. What's the harm in one taste? One glorious, poisoned taste.

The tiny voice in my head was officially dead to me. I couldn't go there. But what I wouldn't give for things to be different. If only.

Voices around me slipped into the edge of my hearing.

"What is up with that guy?"

"I don't know. He looks creepy. Let's just... go to the other side of the street. Maybe we should call the cops. He's been there a long time, and he looks suss."

"*Total* suss."

I cast a glance around to see who the tourists were planning to call the cops on—I could take care of any garden-variety criminal much more quickly than the police, after all—and realized with horror that it was *me*.

Apparently, standing on street corners immobile while brooding made one look *suss*, which I knew, thanks to a lovely little site called the Urban Dictionary, meant suspicious. Human language was always evolving, but it had gotten much easier to keep up with since the invention of technology.

157

Though I'd learned the hard way that it was best not to dig *too* deeply into the Urban Dictionary.

I started moving, since I wasn't anxious to coerce a few police officers into ignoring the *suss cupid*, and causing a scene was bad form for both my lines of work.

If it wasn't for bad form lately, would I have any form at all? That was a big fat no.

Keep it up and you'll have a demon form.

That depressing thought could go straight to hell. I wasn't going to let myself fall. If it came to that, I'd call Gabriel and ask him to take me out. Better to cease to exist than to turn into a demon.

I let my attention wander as I walked, not focusing on where my feet took me. The streets of Seattle were busy as always at this time of the evening, and it was easy to get lost in the mass of humanity. I let my senses go, ignoring the pull of so many people pressed so close. Twenty minutes of angelic-speed-walking later, I stopped on a quieter street, my head clearing as if from a fog.

When I looked up, I groaned. I was on the street next to a restaurant, and through the shiny glass entryway, I could see rock-tie guy nervously fiddling with his tie pin. I cast out my senses and sucked in a breath when I realized that Josie was nearby. If I didn't move and *fast*, she'd see me loitering like a stalker on the street at her date.

The date she hadn't told me the location of, nor invited me on.

Yeah, I was batting zero on the non-suspicious activities tonight.

She's coming!

Making a knee-jerk decision, I dove into the bushes, where I still had a good view of the windows.

Was it utterly ridiculous behavior? Yes. Was I going to leave and let her have a date in peace? Absolutely not. Would I ever admit this to a soul? Also no.

Josie walked around the nearest corner, and I felt her aura dance across mine like the best tart lemonade. As she cleared the front steps of the restaurant, I caught a glimpse of her and time stood still.

She was a vision in red, the bold color of the wrap dress setting off her creamy skin and dark curls. She'd gone all out for the evening, with tall black heels and a shiny clutch purse. Jealousy, hot and acrid, ate the back of my throat.

I hadn't even gotten to see this new, vivacious side of her before, and here she was, going all out for a stranger.

Well, I assumed he was a stranger. They both had auras tinged with nerves, typical of a first-date meetup. I watched as she pulled the restaurant door open, scanning carefully for her date. When she spotted him, her lips turned up in a warm smile.

What had I done? *Why did I come here?* Black tickled the edges of my vision once more, but I was powerless to stop it.

I should have left, but I was stuck like glue. I would only watch for a minute or two, make sure the guy seemed safe and on the up-and-up, and then I would go, darker side of me be damned. This wasn't healthy or fair. I couldn't be with her, and the fact was, she needed to find herself a nice man to be her companion, to lean on in the hard times.

It couldn't be me, no matter how much I longed to be the one to unwrap her from that delicious dress at the end of the night.

It isn't my right. The darkness flared at the thought, and I didn't even try to tamp it down. I was on the fast track to hell, but I couldn't find it in myself to care.

They were seated quickly, and I watched sadly as the man pulled out her chair with a smile. They chatted in fits and starts until the waiter came and dropped off waters. After he left, rock-tie guy reached across the table and brushed something off her shoulder. She leaned in to let him. My stomach turned, and I knew it was time to go, before the tremulous hold I had on my powers snapped.

I glanced around, trying to stay low so no one inside the restaurant caught sight of me, and looked for the nearest break in the bush where I could let myself out. Instead of an opening, I found an impenetrable wall of foliage.

Just my shitty luck.

I shoved my hand into the bush to create a place to step through when I heard an angry buzzing. I didn't stop pushing forward because bugs didn't bother angels.

Apparently, nobody told those wasps that.

As soon as I stuck my leg through the opening, I felt three stings on the back of my knee in rapid succession.

I howled as I jerked it back, the reaction involuntary. Thankfully, the wasps didn't pursue, because I didn't have anywhere else to go to get away from them.

I'd straightened when they stung me and was now back in an awkward half-crouch, rubbing the back of my leg when I heard someone say, "Is that a man in the bushes?"

I spun and saw a waiter pointing directly at me from inside the restaurant. People all over the restaurant were standing up and peering in my direction, but I wasn't worried about them. It was Josie's eyes, shocked and dismayed, that would be branded in my memory for the rest of my eternal life.

NINETEEN

Josie

It had thus far been a picture-perfect Seattle evening, the city's lights reflecting off the leaves of massive trees, casting a magical ambiance over the small restaurant. Ethan had been sharing a sweet tale about the time he found an age-old fossil in his back yard with infectious excitement, his hands gesturing wildly, when the commotion caught our attention.

"Weirdo in the bushes!" someone cried.

That was when I saw him. A familiar figure, hunched and oddly out of place, head peeking out from the bushes right outside the restaurant's large windows.

Caleb.

The sight of him should've been comical—a grown-ass man attempting to half-hide in a highly visible bush—but it wasn't. The tension that knotted in my stomach made sure of that. Yet what I felt wasn't just the expected awkwardness of, *Oh look, there's my former lover of this afternoon spying on me,* though that would have been entirely reasonable.

No, I sensed something else. A shadow, as if the light was

angling off him in an unnatural way. But it must have just been the streetlight, or the fact that he was caught in shrubbery.

Whispers started around the restaurant as others noticed him, too, speculating about his strange behavior.

"We ought to call the police," one woman said, a silver-haired lady in the next booth.

But I quickly reassured her, "Oh, he's harmless. Just a friend trying to play a prank."

Ethan, not missing a beat, responded with, "You can never be too careful these days. There are a lot of strange people out there."

I swallowed back an ironic laugh. If only he knew the extent of the strangeness I was dealing with.

Caleb ducked out of sight like a secret agent caught in the spotlight, blending into the darkness in a swift movement that would've been impressive if it wasn't so exasperating.

My heart pounded in my chest, not in a fluttery, romantic kind of way, but like the rhythm of a war drum. Caleb was gone from sight, yet his presence lingered, prickling at the back of my neck. The sensation of being watched persisted, just like that shadow hovering where it didn't belong.

Is he still out there somewhere?

For fuck's sake. A flicker of defiance ignited within me. Couldn't I just get one normal date with a normal guy? This was *my* life, *my* date. Caleb had no say in it. He had made it crystal clear that he didn't want me. But did that mean I was supposed to sit alone, awaiting his approval on who I could or couldn't see? I was Josie Ray, proud bookstore owner and cat herder, not some damsel in distress waiting for a prince who clearly had no intentions of sticking around.

A new determination rolled through my veins. I would not

let Caleb's ghostly watch influence my actions nor my emotions.

If he wanted a show, I'd give him one.

With renewed spirit, I turned to Ethan, his dark hair catching the soft glow of the restaurant lighting, his hazel eyes waiting patiently. He seemed like a good man, a bit socially awkward, perhaps, but kind and endearing, not to mention devilishly handsome. He was the dark antidote to Caleb's golden light, and I appreciated that difference on a cellular level. A part of me felt a pang of guilt, but it was dwarfed by the empowering surge of control.

"Ethan," I started, offering my most charming smile. I could feel my cheeks heating up, but I held his gaze.

Gathering all the confidence I had mustered, I leaned across the table, willing my eyes to twinkle with mischief under the warm glow of the fairy lights dangling from the restaurant's ceiling. My hand reached across, gently touching Ethan's, whose eyes widened slightly at the sudden contact.

"Oh, Ethan," I cooed, my voice a soft purr, giving his hand a squeeze. "You know, you're quite a gem yourself. You're like —" I desperately tried to remember the name of that rock I studied in seventh grade science. "A *geode*. Ordinary at first glance but extraordinary once you look closer."

Ethan blinked at me, his lips parting as if he were saying "oh," but nothing came out. His reaction was funny, poor guy, like a deer in the headlights. I bit back a laugh, pressing on, my heart pounding in my chest with a mix of thrill and amusement.

I added, "And who wouldn't want to crack open a geode as handsome as you?"

Ethan blinked, a look of utter bemusement crossing his

features. I could almost see the wheels turning in his head as he tried to make sense of my forwardness.

Leaning back, and taking my hand with me, I said, "I mean, I can see layers and layers in you, just waiting to be explored," I continued, giving him my best come-hither look.

He swallowed hard and tilted his head.

I felt emboldened, drunk on the power of my own charm, fueled by a defiant need to show Caleb, wherever he was, that I could play this game, too.

I don't need him.

Ethan bit his lip. "I have always been very intrigued by the complexities of modern social engagements." He grimaced, perhaps noticing the odd turn of phrase in his own words.

"Sure," I offered. "Complex social engagements are very hard to untangle." I reached out and put my hand on his once again, as much to comfort him as to carry on the flirt.

Ethan's eyes flicked from my own down to where my hand rested over his and then back again. His gaze was similar to that of a child faced with a difficult math problem, completely clueless, yet undeniably eager to understand. I suppressed a chuckle with a coy smile instead.

A young waiter sauntered over, and I took a big gulp of water to help me keep my course. His nametag announced "Stephen," and he folded his hands in front of him. "Good evening. Can I bring you any appetizers?"

Ethan continued to stare at me, blinking like an owl caught in daylight. Then, as if a lightbulb had flickered on, his face broke into a broad grin. "Oh," he said, his voice rich with sudden understanding. "You're flirting!"

I nearly choked on my water.

"I can come back." Stephen backed away with a bemused

smile. As he scampered off to attend to other customers, Ethan leaned in closer, his smile cheeky.

"I must admit," he confessed, his gaze locking with mine. "Innocent rock puns roll off my tongue more easily than flirtations. But I think I can get the hang of it."

True to his word, the rest of the evening unfolded with a natural ebb and flow of lighthearted teasing and laughter. Ethan, once he was over his initial surprise, played along with my flirtatious antics, even throwing in some quips of his own that had me giggling.

It felt easy, uncomplicated, and completely under my control.

The sense of being watched remained, but I used it to fuel my playful defiance, maintaining the pretense of a budding romance with Ethan.

Assuming Caleb was out there, I hoped he was taking notes.

We strolled back to my apartment, Ethan ever the gentleman offering to walk me home. We made the last turn when he was still passionately explaining that the Bookish Cat might be the most important thing to a young boy someday.

"It was a book I found in a shop just like yours that changed everything for me, opened up a whole world below the surface and in towering mountains. Don't underestimate how important your work is."

"That's very sweet of you to say, Ethan."

Standing at the doorstep of my building, bathed in the soft glow of the light, there was a nagging pull at the back of my mind, the lurking presence that I'd felt all night. Caleb had to be out there somewhere, watching us.

"Well, this has been fun." Ethan turned toward me, his eyes soft and kind. He extended his arms for what seemed like a friendly hug—and then I felt those watching eyes even stronger, waves of him reaching me, and it felt utterly unfair.

You can't have it all, Caleb!

Before Ethan could reach me, I stepped forward and threw my arms around his neck, pulling him down for a kiss. It was a desperate move, fueled by the irrational need to make a point.

The instant our lips met, I felt the sensation of being watched dissipate, like smoke being swept away by a gust of wind.

Caleb was gone.

But the kiss—um—could it even be called a kiss? It was more of an accident of two faces pushing together. There was no spark, no magic, just the touch of lips and the awkward fumbling of a man caught off guard.

It left me hollow inside instead of triumphant.

We pulled apart, and I could see the surprise mirrored in Ethan's wide eyes.

"Well," Ethan stammered, his cheeks flushing a shade of red. "I sure appreciate your enthusiasm, but..."

I forced a smile, trying to keep the mood light. "But we're probably better off being just friends, right?"

"I'd love that." He extended his hand, and I shook it, a formal end to an evening that had not gone as expected.

As he waved goodbye and walked away, I sighed. Anything I ever could have felt for Ethan had fizzled right out in the anticlimax of that kiss.

It was nothing like the kiss at Nana's party. Nothing like Caleb *at all*. God, everyone was measured against Caleb, and nobody ever compared.

I closed my apartment door behind me, stepping into the quiet emptiness of my apartment. Not a single cat in sight. *Big surprise.*

But with no distractions, no comforting purrs, it was just me and my swirling thoughts.

And I couldn't handle it. If Caleb was going to be on my mind, then he might as well be in front of me. I resigned myself to the fact that as long as he was on this plane of existence, he was going to be a great big distraction. Maybe we couldn't be together *that way*, but my soul wouldn't let me drop him like a hot potato either. He was watching me on the date because he cared. And I knew a part of him wished it could be different, too.

That's what I felt when we made love, whether he wants to admit it or not.

Almost instinctively, I was out and walking toward the Showbox. There was still plenty of time before the late-night concert would begin.

And there he was, as if he'd been there all the time, staring at his phone with hunched shoulders, and for once, I was sure he didn't know I was coming.

"So," I said like it was the most normal thing in the world. "What's the update on this couple we're matching?"

TWENTY

Caleb

MY BRAIN HAD TO BE SHORT-CIRCUITING; I'D FINALLY lost it, seven years into my life as an earth-bound angel. Because there was no way I was *actually* seeing Josie, here and now, after I humiliated her on her date. I'd followed their auras from afar, all the way back to her apartment, until it got too painful.

Even with my senses, I had to break it off when she pulled him in for a kiss.

And yet, instead of at home, having a post-date coffee with Ethan, she was... here?

"Josie? What do you mean? You had a date, and I already—"

"Shh. It's okay."

"It's not, and I'm sorry. I didn't mean to embarrass you or ruin anything—I didn't even mean to be there. My feet just... took me there. And then I thought I'd make sure he seemed like a safe guy. I was trying to leave when the stupid wasps got me."

She bit her lip, trying to hold back a laugh.

"Yeah, yeah, really funny! I know how ridiculous it

sounds, okay?" I threw my hands up in frustration, nearly losing my cell phone in the process. That dark pulse around my vision was tearing me up, but damned if I knew what to do about it.

She placed both hands on my chest and looked up into my eyes, and like silk sliding over stone, that demonic influence slid away to nothing. I was breathless at her complete sincerity when she said, "I forgive you."

How did she do it? *We weren't meant to be*, so how did she wipe away the stain on my soul with a single touch? It flew in the face of everything I knew, but I couldn't push her away. I slid my hands up over hers to hold them in place. Her touch felt right.

Everything with her was right, easy.

But I didn't deserve her forgiveness, not this time or the last time. Yet here I was, receiving it anyway. She patted me lightly and stepped back, squaring her shoulders as she turned to face the Showbox, where the streets had emptied as the show got started.

"Now, tell me about this couple," she said again, prodding me lightly with her elbow when I didn't answer right away.

"They're inside, watching the show. Happy, based on their energy signatures. They both love this band. I can sense them talking to each other, and that's already a step in the right direction after so many failed attempts."

"So, what do we do now?"

"Nothing. We let them have a good night, and we check on them tomorrow."

"Oh, okay." She tucked a strand of hair behind her ear. "So, I walked all the way over here for nothing, huh?"

I looped an arm around her shoulders and pulled her a little bit closer to my side, against all my better judgment. "Can

I buy you a slice of cake for your troubles? Giordano's is only a block over, and they have your favorite."

"Italian cream? Really?"

"Really."

She nearly broke into a jog, tugging me along.

"It's the other way," I said with a laugh.

She changed directions without missing a beat, still tugging my hand. "What are you waiting for, Caleb? Let's go, let's go!"

THE NEXT MORNING, I was up before the sun, dressed in my nicest casual private-investigator clothes and standing outside Josie's favorite coffee shop precisely fifteen minutes before the Bookish Cat opened. Which was how I was waiting for her with a smile on my face and her favorite latte precisely five minutes before opening, when she walked up. Her skin shone in the morning sun like a beacon. So much beauty afforded to the woman I couldn't have; she truly put many of the female angels to shame. But the fact that I wasn't allowed to love her didn't mean I couldn't love the sight of her. And damn, she took my breath away.

"Caleb! What are you doing here? Also, why are you so perky? I'm beat. We stayed out way too late last night." She stopped, sniffing before pointing to the coffee. "Is that for me?"

"It is. And I didn't hear any complaints last night when they brought you the second slice of cake."

"Okay, one, it's rude to complain when someone brings you cake. And two, shut up." She took a sip and groaned, the sound sending all sorts of inappropriate thoughts racing through my head. Damn, I was jealous of the coffee sliding down her throat. "This is heaven. Thank you." She smiled and opened the door, letting me in with her.

"I should be thanking *you*. Jonathan and Kim are both glowing with happiness this morning, which I think means their unplanned date went very, very well."

"Excellent. So, do you have to meddle some more today, or—"

"Josephine Ray! You have well and truly done it this time!"

The front door of the shop flew open with a bang, startling Josie so much she spilled her piping-hot coffee. Anger tore through me at the minor wound, and I didn't even think before sending out a thread of power to snap the offending liquid from her skin, following it with a cooling rush of healing.

"Mr. Anderson! What's the matter? You startled me!"

Her aura was turning prickly, but the overwhelming fear had me stepping between her and the angry landlord. Thankfully, he hadn't noticed the coffee evaporating.

"*This* is the matter. It's not enough that you've filled my property with scurrilous, allergenic felines, no! You've got to go and bring the tax man down on me? No! This will *not* stand!" He was angrily waving a sheaf of papers in the air, too quickly for me to read them.

I reached out and plucked the papers from his hands, and Josie snatched them from me just as quickly.

"I don't understand, Mr. Anderson. How could I have brought you trouble with the tax man—my business only just started, and I always file on time. This doesn't make any sense." Her hands shook as she read, and I found myself glaring at Anderson, running through all the ways I could kick him to the curb without breaking any of my angelic vows.

Taxes weren't something I was familiar with, given I didn't technically *exist* according to the US government, and had never filed any. They weren't equipped to deal with angelic immigrants, so it was just best for everyone that way.

"Oh, it's not your *sales taxes*," he spat. "Apparently, you've been importing foreign goods to sell on my property without filing any of the proper paperwork or paying the business and occupational taxes for an importer!"

His entire face was red, his aura boiling with rage, and was that... desolation? I sent the suggestion that he calm down, and the man rocked back on his heels, eyes falling briefly to half-mast before springing back up. Apparently, it was stronger than my usual subtle intentions.

Tone it down, Caleb. This is not life or death.

I sucked a breath in through my nose, not letting myself do anything else but be a staunch presence by Josie's side. But the color was steadily draining out of her cheeks as she read further down the paper, so whatever the issue, it had to be legitimate. That was a hard blow for my rule-following girl, but everything was fixable. I'd help her sort it out and make things right.

Something about the man's aura was niggling at me. This was more than just a tax problem. It had to be.

"You don't even deny it. Well, know this—you'll be hearing from me again, and soon. I'm not going to allow this kind of reckless flaunting of the law on my property, I can promise you that!" He sneezed, turning for the door.

"Mr. Anderson, please! Give me a few days to sort this out. I didn't know these taxes *existed*, let alone that I could get you into trouble as the property owner. But now that I do, I'll have everything filed and paid up immediately. Please!"

He sneezed again as he snatched the door open, not giving

her a backward glance. "I've had about enough of you and your lawlessness for one day, Ms. Ray. This is not over."

The door slammed behind him so hard it sent several bookshelves rattling. Josie sank heavily against the counter, shaking like a leaf.

"I've really fucked up this time, Caleb. What am I going to do? I don't know how to file all this stuff! He already hates the cats. What if he uses this as a way to evict me? I can't afford to lose my deposit and re-open in a new location, not without the shop's income. I used every penny I had to get this place up and running as it is."

Tears lined her lower lids, and I leapt into action, rubbing her arms lightly with my hands to distract her as I spoke. "No. That's not going to happen, okay? There are rules, laws, about tenancy rights, aren't there? You just have to figure this tax situation out. I've got a plan for him and the cats, and I'm already working on it. Don't worry about them."

As if talking about them made them magically appear, all three cats were suddenly purring and rubbing against Josie. Gatsby and Matilda were on the floor, keeping her ankles warm, and Heathcliff on top of the counter, rubbing his cheeks against her shoulder.

Good cats. I thought the praise, but the black one turned and made eye contact with me as if he'd heard it, a flash of magic in his eyes giving me a second of pause. But I quickly snapped out of it; Josie needed me, and I was not going to let her down.

"I'm going to follow him, see if I can move my plan ahead sooner. You stay here and read up on the taxes. We're going to fix this; I promise." I squeezed her shoulders and planted a reassuring kiss on her forehead, but she barely responded. Shock was rolling over her, tangling with the fear in a toxic combo.

I pushed a—very, *very* gentle—wave of calm at her, hoping it helped her settle enough to focus on the problem. After my last time using my angelic powers to calm her, I was terrified it wouldn't work, but the power leapt at my command, clearly fine with soothing her, just not dampening her libido. Relief surged through me as her aura filled with a lighter blue, a sense of peace taking hold of her.

"Okay, you're right. Yes. I need to look up these... B & O taxes and see how to file the paperwork."

She was still wobbly, but she was moving forward, and I could see the determination in her eyes, trying to win out over the trepidation as she stepped around the counter to start up her tablet.

"We'll work this out. I can sense Barb down the street. She's on her way here, so you'll have company. I'll be back as soon as I can, okay?"

"Okay," she said, her voice small as I raced out the door to catch up to the landlord. I hated to leave her when she was upset, but I needed as much time as possible to figure out what was going on with him, to see if I could fix this.

Josie losing the Bookish Cat was not going to happen, not as long as I was around.

TWENTY-ONE

Josie

I STARED BLANKLY AT THE TABLET'S SCREEN, THE harsh blue light illuminating the darkened space of the Bookish Cat, where I'd come back before sunrise in the hopes of having a little bit of divine inspiration.

But even running my fingers over the cover of the journal had no effect. I'd been shaking since Mr. Anderson showed up at my door yesterday and couldn't sleep a wink. Every moment was dedicated to deciphering the complex labyrinth of US tax laws, reminding me just how much *I didn't know* before I made those orders from England.

How could I have made such an awful mistake?

Spread across my screen were the intricate details of import taxes, paragraphs filled with dense legalese that threatened to drown me in a sea of confusion. Each sentence, each word seemed to be a carefully coded riddle, a cipher I couldn't crack. No wonder no other bookstores around were working with these foreign booksellers, because the sheer wall of confusing text was enough to make me cry.

I specifically went into the world of books and not accounting to avoid moments like this.

My temples throbbed, the incessant headache a result of too much caffeine and too little sleep. I was no closer to a solution than I was when I began.

"Come on!" I slammed my hands down on the counter in an uncharacteristic temper tantrum. The cats jumped at the sudden noise, scattering in different directions, though Heathcliff shot me an accusing glare before making himself scarce. I watched them flee with a twinge of envy. Their lives were simple, despite their ability to seemingly move through walls.

The more I wrestled with the intricate language of US tax laws, the more I was entangled in an administrative spider's web that threatened to eat the Bookish Cat whole.

I heaved a sigh, massaging my temples as I tried to make sense of the dense paragraphs on my screen.

"'The Harmonized System...' Ugh," I read out loud, my voice a frustrated grumble. "'The Harmonized System, also known as the HS Code, is a multipurpose, international product-naming system used around the globe. Import duties and taxes are calculated based on the HS which is uniform across all countries in the WCO'—ugh, another acronym to look up—'determining the basic category of the product.'"

As I recited the next line, "'Different countries can assign specific numbers to classify goods in more detail for their own use,'" a sudden warmth spread across my shoulders. Startled, I jumped, my words trailing off into silence as I turned to see Barb's concerned face right behind me.

"Josie, you look terrible," she said, her voice carrying a worried lilt as she looked over my shoulder at the screen.

"I didn't hear you come in."

"I don't think you're hearing much of anything—you look

halfway to zombie, and I'd like to keep my brains intact, thanks. Have you been working on this tax issue all night? How long have you *been* here?"

The glow of the tablet illuminated her worried face. "I have to figure this out, Barb," I responded, my voice resolute, if exhausted. "I have to save the Bookish Cat."

Barb shook her head, her stern gaze softening as she crossed her arms. "You're working yourself to the bone. You'll make yourself sick."

I blinked up at her, my throat tight. "Then let me be sick," I declared, my tone leaving no room for argument. "Because I have no choice. This is my life's work. Everything I ever wanted is between these four walls."

Except Caleb. Even that depressing thought couldn't make this shitstorm any worse.

"Poor thing." Barb wrapped her arms around me, but I couldn't tell if it was because of the tax situation or because she thought it was sad that the Bookish Cat was the only thing with meaning in my life.

After releasing me, and with a sigh, Barb crossed her arms over her chest. "Josie," she started, her tone surprisingly firm. "Why haven't you done the most logical thing yet?"

I bristled at her words, my anxiety morphing into irritation. "And what would that be?" I snapped, my tone sharper than I intended.

Barb raised an eyebrow at me, peering over the rim of her glasses. "Do I need to remind you that your family runs one of the most prestigious accounting firms in the state?"

A bitter laugh escaped my lips before I could stop it. "No, Barb, not possible," I retorted, my tone laced with acerbic humor.

"Josie..." Her tone lowered, giving me her best motherly voice. "You've got to consider—"

"I said *no*."

She let out a tense sigh, but after a moment, her expression softened, and she patted me resolutely on the shoulder. "You keep at it then. I'll take care of the shop today."

"But I can only pay you for the half shift."

She waved her hand dismissively. "I'm volunteering. Let's save this Cat."

As she said it, Matilda, Gatsby, and Heathcliff sauntered back in, taking up napping places around me.

"Thank you. Thank you, all," I added for the cats in a whisper.

Regret filled my chest as I thought of my parents. But there was no way I could go to them now, not after everything. I couldn't bear the thought of looking like a dog with its tail between its legs, begging for help. I had to figure this out on my own. The very idea of them knowing about my struggle, of them holding this over my head for the rest of my life, was unthinkable.

Their staunch disapproval of the Bookish Cat, their dismissal of my passion, had inflicted wounds on my spirit that were as deep as they were jagged. Their failure to see the merit in the path I had chosen for myself, the life I had so lovingly crafted, had formed rifts too vast to cross. Even though a touch of a bridge had been built at Nana's birthday, we were far from anything that resembled a relationship.

Asking them for help now would only reopen those wounds, and there was no guarantee they'd even help.

I'd rather read tax law by myself. Even if it was convoluted, soul-sucking gibberish.

After hours and hours of it, I leaned back in my chair, a

heavy sigh escaping my lips as I pinched the bridge of my nose. My eyes were heavy, my body was aching, and my mind was a blur of taxation and legal terms.

That's when I saw the slip of paper tucked in the mail slot.

Hang in there, it said in a scrawl that rivaled a Shakespearean missive. *I don't want to interrupt your concentration, so just know we'll figure this out.*

I opened the door, looked left and right, but who knows how long ago Caleb dropped off this note. I settled back behind the counter, the note under my fingers, and somehow felt lighter for having it. I traced the letters with my fingertips, the curves soothing, and I fell into a meditative state. Just a short break. The cold, hard surface of the counter was so inviting...

I must have fallen asleep because when I opened my eyes again, it was pitch black outside. The lights of the Bookish Cat were dimmed, the familiar rustling of books and purring of cats silenced. I sat up, rubbing at my sore neck as I glanced around, noticing for the first time that Barb and the cats were gone, the shop locked up for the night.

My heart ached as I slipped out of the store, the reality of my situation pressing down on me like a ton of bricks. Another day passed, and still no answers.

I couldn't give up, not yet. I would find a way to solve this mess. I made a promise to myself as I locked the door behind me, vowing to figure it out in the morning.

As THE HUMID and crisp air filled the streets of early morning Seattle, the city was buzzing to life with coffee shops, fast-walking folks in suits, and the rhythmic patter of joggers. It was a picture of serenity and promise, which I hoped would set up my day for a breakthrough.

I made my way back to the Bookish Cat, my mind heavy with exhaustion and the unresolved weight of the previous night's efforts, but with a bit of hope peeking in with the sun.

As I turned the last corner, I yearned to see Caleb's warm smile, the reassuring sight of him with two coffees in hand.

But as my gaze fell on the bookstore, instead of the familiar figure, my eyes locked on to a stark, yellow notice plastered to the door.

A cold shiver of dread ran down my spine. The door, which I firmly locked last night, was ajar. The ominous yellow notice fluttered in the breeze. A sinking sensation hit my gut, the bitter taste of dread filling my mouth. What fresh hell was this?

With a deep breath, I pushed open the door, steeling myself for the worst. Inside, I found Mr. Anderson standing amidst the stacks of books, his thin lips curled into a sneer.

"You don't have the right to be in here, Mr. Anderson."

"Ah, but I do. I suggest you read that notice very carefully, Miss Ray," he said, his voice echoing unpleasantly through the shop. His eyes flicked to the yellow paper tacked to the door. "You have exactly seven days to fix your tax issues, or I'll have no choice but to take legal action, closing up your shop in the meantime."

"But... Mr. Anderson..." A harsh tremor rattled through me, my nerves suddenly feeling as fragile as glass. A clammy chill spread across my skin, a sheen of cold sweat prickling at my temples.

Just then, the door swung open behind me. Caleb and Barb arrived at the same time, stepping into the store. Their expressions fell as they took in the scene: Mr. Anderson's triumphant smirk, my white-knuckled grip on the counter, the ominous notice on the door.

A sudden realization struck me like a lightning bolt as Mr. Anderson brushed past me to walk out.

"Wait!" My voice echoed in the nearly empty store, an agonizing plea. "Where are the cats?"

He paused, turning to face me with a grimace. "Far away from my sneezing face!" The door jingled as he marched out.

His words hit me like a sledgehammer. My knees buckled, and I found myself collapsing onto the checkout counter, my body shaking with the onslaught of my emotions. The cats, my precious companions, were gone. The Bookish Cat felt hollow without them, as hollow as I felt inside at all this horrible news.

Barb and Caleb were at my side in an instant, their hands on my shoulders, their voices a soothing murmur in my ears. But their words were lost to me. I was drowning in a sea of despair, the tide of my problems pulling me under.

"Please, Josie," Barb pleaded. "Consider contacting your family."

I shook my head, fighting back the tears that threatened to spill over. "You don't get it, Barb," I managed to choke out, my voice raw with emotion. "They won't help. They won't come. I dug my own grave with them a long time ago."

Even as Caleb and Barb wrapped me in a comforting embrace, I was lost in the storm, adrift in a sea of my own making. All because of a silly dream of sharing books from faraway lands.

The Bookish Cat, my dream, my life's work, was sinking, and I felt like I was going down with it.

TWENTY-TWO
Caleb

TWENTY-TWO FORTY-SEVEN... FORTY-NINE... FIFTY-
one. I came to a stop outside the unassuming office, letting my
senses reach out and inspect the interior. The small waiting
room held two normal human women and one quarter-elf
man, plus a receptionist who was part... goblin? Interesting.
They weren't held in terribly good standing in the magical
community, though I'd always thought they got an unneces-
sarily bad rap.

Finding one working here was a good sign. My hand was
on the door handle when my phone rang.

"Hey, Josie." I waited to see her state of mind. She hadn't
been the same since the shock of the landlord removing her cats
yesterday morning , and I'd been working around the clock
ever since to fix it.

"Hey, Caleb. Are you coming by today?" Her voice was
quiet. I could tell she needed company.

"Yep. I'm almost done with my plan for the cats. How is
operation fix-up-the-taxes going?"

Her voice broke as she said, "It's not."

I let the door handle go and leaned my back against the glass window instead. "Tell me what's wrong."

"I don't understand any of this. The filing is complicated, the forms are ninety million miles long, and I don't even know how much I need to pay! How can I fix what I don't understand?"

"There has to be someone who can help you with it."

"I called the small-business support line, but they are all booked up and can't help until next week. By next week, Caleb, the Bookish Cat will only be an empty shell!"

I sucked in a breath, knowing that I had to be careful with my next words. "Desperate times call for desperate measures. And things are desperate, Josie."

"Are you going to suggest again that I contact my family? Because I thought I made it very clear that—"

"I can feel your frustration from here." Literally. I was so attuned to her aura that I could pick it up from anywhere on this continent. Her frustration and despair were a thick, dark cloud. "Only your family gets you *that* level of twisted up, but this has to be about the bigger picture. I hope you'll at least consider calling one of them."

"They told me I'd never make the Bookish Cat work. I'm not about to prove them right."

I rubbed the spot between my eyebrows, unsure how much to meddle and how much to listen. Being a good angelic friend was hard sometimes. "What about Fred?"

"What *about* Fred?"

"Remember what he said at Nana Geraldine's party? He was warming up to the idea of the shop and even said he might want to stop by. He's *also* a CPA. Maybe you call him and just ask if he's familiar with the form and can give you some tips. You don't actually have to tell him the problem, if you don't feel like he'll be understanding. But there was improvement, an olive branch between you two at the party. Maybe calling and asking for his help could be another one."

"I hadn't thought of it like that." I could hear the uncertainty, and it broke my heart. No matter how much encouragement I gave her, though, she had to be the one to make the choice. The choice to reach out, to open up.

"You don't have to. It's just an option. If that one doesn't work for you, you'll find one that will."

"Right, of course. I should probably let you get to your appointment. I'm making you late."

"I've always got time for you, Josie. Late or no."

"You're sweet. Go. I'll figure this out."

I smiled at the determination in her voice. That was my girl. She never gave up, no matter the odds. It was part of what had drawn me to Josie in the first place. She had *spunk*.

"Yes, you will. Talk soon."

"Bye."

I hustled into the office and gave the receptionist my name. She was petite, the tips of her ears barely pointed—a fact that was hidden in plain sight by a cleverly placed piercing—and her eyes were a deep purple, but there was no hint of the green skin that most goblins had.

"Dr. Elwyn will be with you shortly. If you'll just take a seat." She smiled and pointed me to the waiting area.

Dr. Elwyn didn't keep me waiting long. She called me back herself, wearing a white coat and purple patterned scrubs. I followed her to the end of a long hallway, to the very last patient-treatment room.

"So, Mr. Starr, what can I help you with?" She tilted her head to the side. "I get the feeling you're not here for my Western medicinal services. Though, frankly, I'm not sure what

I can offer that you couldn't do for yourself." She propped one hip on the small counter and cocked an eyebrow at me in question.

"You're correct. I'm not personally in need of your services. I'm wondering if you can help someone else for me, though. And I'm open to your preferred method of help, Western or *otherwise*." She smiled at that, a sparkle of her inherent magic playing over her skin before she quickly reined it back in. "He's proven a tough nut to crack, and I think you're the one for the job."

"Why can't you help him?"

"Well, for starters, I'm not an allergist. He's got a pretty severe cat allergy, but..."

"But what? Don't think I don't know what you are, *cupid*."

I held up both hands in a placating gesture. "I wouldn't dream of underestimating you, or your magic, which is why I'm here. If you're willing to see him, he's just walked in the front door. The 'but' was about you and what I might be able to do for you in exchange for helping Mr. Anderson."

She scoffed, turning to straighten the long cotton-tipped swabs in a glass jar on the counter, her aura turning scarlet. I still had to convince her.

"Dr. Elwyn... Angie, I know you're aware that certain angels have extra powers. But are you aware that cupids can do more than just make people fall in love?"

She froze, hand on top of the swabs, the little sterile pouches crinkling under the weight of her hand.

I could tell exactly what she wanted. "Your case is advanced, but I'm able to regenerate nearly any reproductive tract organ and restore fertility. If you would want that, of course. I would never overstep in that way if you didn't—"

She spun, both hope and terror in her eyes. "I do. I want you to do whatever it is you do and fix me. Please. I'll take care of your friend's allergies if you can help me."

I nodded. "I would do this for you, even if you couldn't help him. Just so you're aware, this isn't a quid-pro-quo situation." She nodded rapidly, not at all concerned with what I was offering her, or asking for her help with. "You may feel some discomfort, and you should probably lie down. I'll do my best to make it quick, but as I said, your case is severe, and regrowth—"

She grabbed my hand, shocking me into silence, the feel of her witch's magic brushing against my power was unusual. It had an earthy quality, almost like brushing my hand through tall, downy grass.

"It's worth the pain. Do what you need to," she said resolutely as she lay down on the procedure table.

I nodded and closed my eyes. My hands hovered over her abdomen, and she didn't make a single noise as I worked. Sweat beaded on my forehead, nothing moving but the hands on the wall clock. Once I was finished, I sagged back against the wall.

"Is it done? Did it work?" Her voice was hoarse, and she didn't move from the table.

"It's done."

"How long until...?"

"You'll be experiencing a greater than average surge of fertility for the next twelve or so days as a result of the lingering divinity in your body. After that, your normal cycles will resume, and your chances of conception will be the same as any other healthy female your age."

It wasn't hope that lit her features now, but determination. "Twelve days. I can work with that."

She strode to the door, giving no sign that she was fatigued or in lingering pain from the intensive work I'd just done on her. She propped it open and called down the hall to her receptionist. "Bring back Mr. Anderson, please, Tiffy!" She turned back to me, where I was still sagging against her wallpaper, drained after the effort it took to help her. "You'd better skedaddle. I've got a lot to do with this man and not much time to do it in."

I stepped into the hallway, trying not to grin as I walked toward the exit. I pulled my hat down low over my face as I walked past Josie's landlord, not wanting to color his impression of the place by seeing me and connecting it with his troubles.

I slowed down, shamelessly eavesdropping as Dr. Elwyn greeted him.

"Mr. Anderson," she purred. "It's lovely to meet you. I see here that you've got a severe cat allergy. You're in luck. I've got a new allergy medicine which alleviates symptoms in as little as seven days."

And then began the fireworks.

Knew it.

As I suspected, attraction flared between the two of them, kindled by mutual hope as well as compatibility.

It wasn't easy finding an allergist in Seattle who augmented her Western medicine with magic. But it was even harder finding a single one who was compatible with the very persnickety Mr. Anderson.

But what was the point of being a cupid—even a fallen one —if I couldn't bring together two lonely people, each of them needing something from the other? It was some of my best work, and if I wasn't mistaken, within a matter of days, those two lonely hearts would be singing a whole different tune.

Now, I just had to tell Josie that I'd solved her cat problem and try to help her deal with the tax situation. But I was holding out hope that she'd reconnect with Fred. I could already tell it would be good for both of them, as long as they were ready to set their egos aside. He could help her far more than I ever could.

Unfortunately, cupids didn't hold any sway with the IRS.

TWENTY-THREE

Josie

To call Fred or not to call Fred, that was the question.

What I would have done to pet Heathcliff right then. The purr he gave as I scratched his belly was like my own personal catnip, a calming elixir.

For now, I had to trust that Caleb was working on a solution for those fur-babies. I still had to save my book-babies, or else I would be jobless and homeless, and not have anywhere for the fur-babies to come home to.

What to do about Fred, though. The debate had been raging within me since I hung up with Caleb. On one hand, he was my brother, a Certified Public Accountant, and possibly the only lifeline I had in this tax mess.

On the other hand, reaching out would mean swallowing my pride and admitting my failures not only as a business-woman but also as a sister who had insisted on going it alone.

And also risking that he might flat out say no.

It felt like being in the middle of a shit sandwich, a tug-of-war between my pride and the potential salvation of the

Bookish Cat as I scribbled down pros and cons on a discarded invoice.

The pros list started with the most obvious point: "Fred can solve the tax problem." This was followed by a hesitant, "He might do it for free" and a very desperate, "He could stop the Bookish Cat from becoming the Bookish Tax Evasion Case."

But as my pen moved to the cons side of the paper, it hovered for longer than I expected. "Fred will lord it over me for the rest of my life," was the only real con I could find.

There has to be worse than that...

As I began to let my mind wander, the list started to resemble a collection of exaggerated doomsday scenarios.

"Fred might demand that part of the Bookish Cat be turned into a CPA study center, swapping out *To Kill a Mockingbird* for *Tax for Dummies*," I wrote down, envisioning the horrified faces of my regulars as they found their beloved classics replaced by dreary tax literature.

Then I jotted, "Fred might become a Scrooge, counting coins and terrifying the cats with his abacus."

Then the ideas started flowing.

"Fred could recreate the *Cask of Amontillado*, trapping me in the basement with nothing but a tax manual for company."

As the list grew longer, each scenario more absurd than the last, I found myself chuckling, which was a relief after all the stress. But behind the humor, the fact remained that Caleb and Barb were right. Calling Fred was the only possible next step, if I wanted to get help before Mr. Anderson closed the doors on the Bookish Cat forever.

With a sigh, I laid down the pen, picked up my phone, and dialed Fred.

Here goes fuck-all.

"Josie?"

I hung up.

Why did I do that? It was such an instinctual reaction at hearing his voice, like my autopilot took over, screeching, "Danger! Abort!"

"Get it together," I told myself out loud and dialed again.

"Josie? Can you hear me now?"

"Hi, Fred, yes, sorry. I dropped the phone." *Terrible excuse.* I cringed at the blatant lie. "I hope I'm not bothering you."

"Not at all."

"And I'm guessing you have a lot of things planned for the day—"

"Some, but nothing critical."

"It's just, I was thinking, you know... You're a CPA."

"Sure am."

I winced. Was he getting sarcastic already? Best to just tear off the band-aid.

"I'm in some trouble."

There was a pause on the line as I tried to think of my next words, but I couldn't figure out what they should be.

Fred answered before I had to. "I'll be right there."

In that instant, a weight lifted and I had to keep my knees from buckling. Thank you wasn't enough, but it was all I had. My voice broke as I said, "Thank you, big bro."

There was a pause, and I waited on tenterhooks for whatever chastising might come next. But it didn't. Instead, he chuckled.

"You make the coffee. Lots of it, little sis."

I watched as Fred rifled through my disastrous accounting records with a furrowed brow. He sat at the small desk in the back room of the Bookish Cat, surrounded by stacks of paper and an empty coffee cup that had seen at least three refills in the last hour. I hovered anxiously nearby, wringing my hands and biting the inside of my cheek.

Fred picked up a document and squinted at it through his glasses. "Josie, this is your 1120-S tax return. It says here you elected S-corp status?"

I swallowed, my throat suddenly parched. "It looks that way."

He looked at me with a puzzled expression. "And you know this means you're a pass-through entity, right?"

A pass-through entity? I thought, my anxiety spiking.

Fred, noticing my blank expression, sighed and massaged his temples. "That means the corporation's income, deductions... everything has to pass through to shareholders for federal tax purposes. Have you identified yourself as a shareholder in the business?"

My mouth opened and closed. No words came out. This was as good as Greek to me.

"I... I don't know, Fred. I thought I was doing it right. I filed with the state. That should be in the pile somewhere."

Fred ran a hand through his hair, clearly exasperated. "You still have to file the necessary tax forms for your personal return. Where's your Schedule K-1?"

I shrugged, blinking back the tears. "I don't know," I whispered, "I thought I could do this on my own."

"Everyone uses a CPA, Josie. Coffee shops, hair salons, even CPAs use CPAs!"

I looked down at my shoes, fighting the burning tears threatening to spill over.

When I looked up again, Fred's stern expression softened. My hands were trembling. He took off his glasses and studied me for a moment. "Josie," he said in a softer tone. "Strong-headed, emotionless Josie. What's happening to you?"

I somehow managed to meet his eyes. "Strong-headed? Emotionless?"

"That's how you always made us see you. There was no convincing you of anything, ever. You remained aloof unless you were biting our heads off."

"That is not true..."

Except it kind of *was*.

Fred and I stood staring at one another, perhaps for the first time realizing how out of control things had become. He'd said things he shouldn't have, but so had I.

"Hey, sis," he said in the big brotherly tone he hadn't used in years. "We've got time to figure out the past. Right now, we've got a bookstore to save. And I'm going to help you do it."

Thank God. I resisted the urge to bawl in my big brother's arms by nodding quickly and tightening my fists at my side.

He let out a quick exhale. "Come here, you crazy kid." He pulled me into a bear hug that I'd needed all day. All week.

Actually, I'd needed it for years.

"Now," he said, fitting his reading glasses back in place. "We've got some serious paperwork to do."

"Right. I'll get more coffee!"

He looked at me over the rim of his reading glasses, and I swore I saw a smile sneak onto that stern big-brother face.

THE BELL JINGLED over the door, and I saw Caleb's wide smile heading in our direction. Not wanting to disturb Fred's concentration, I quickly raised a finger to my lips, signaling Caleb to stay quiet. He froze, mid-step, then nodded.

A wave hit me as he tiptoed to the counter, that it might be the sexiest thing on the planet to see a divine being try not to break a CPA's concentration. Or maybe it was just that he was walking in front of the dictionaries we defiled during our evening of reckless debauchery.

They'd still been in the box—they were fine. But they would always be *those dictionaries* to me. Just walking past them sent a tingle through me, as if my clit wanted to remind me of exactly how well we'd been treated.

Fred was hunched over my tablet, his fingers clicking away on the Bluetooth keyboard in a steady rhythm. Finally, with an exaggerated flourish, he struck the enter key, and his face broke into a triumphant grin.

"Done!" he declared.

Caleb and I exchanged a glance, a spark of hope kindling between us. Fred turned, finally noticing Caleb in front of him.

"Caleb! Good to see you again, man." Fred extended his hand, his professional demeanor on full display. Caleb took it, shaking it firmly.

"Likewise. And it sounds like you've had a breakthrough."

Beaming, Fred launched right into it. "I had to rework the existing status registered at inception but considering that we were within the guidelines as published in the most recent bulletin for non-dangerous goods, I couldn't see any reason for a notwithstanding clause—"

He paused and seemed to notice the blank expressions on our faces.

"Let's just say I've tackled the immediate issue. Josie, you won't be losing the Bookish Cat anytime soon."

A whoop of joy escaped from Caleb, so loud that even Fred and I jolted. "I knew it! I knew things would turn around," Caleb said, his smile infectious. "We are on a roll today!"

Hope fluttered in my chest. "The cats?"

"Cats?" Fred stood taller. "You've got some furry-shmurry-cuddly-fluffballs?"

Caleb and I stared at Fred, mouths open.

"What?" He shrugged. "I friggin' love cats."

I laughed. Today was becoming so much more than I could have expected. "You *do*?"

"Sis, you and I have a lot to catch up on. But first, what's the deal with the cats?"

I explained about how Matilda, Gatsby, and Heathcliff had taken up residence here, leaving out the parts where I was pretty sure they had some magic up their paws. Fred and I were only just reconnecting, and I couldn't see him being at one with the supernatural. Though I clearly had much to learn about him.

Fred's eyes widened when I told him about how Mr. Anderson had them taken away, and that I'd had to focus on the tax issues before going on a quest to find where they'd ended up.

"And that's where I came in," Caleb said with a smile. I threw him a look that I hoped said *please don't let on that you're an angel*, but fortunately Caleb kept it all human-friendly. "But a private investigator needs to keep some secrets."

"So, you have news about the cats?" I bit my lip, and Caleb's eyes flashed at the movement. He wet his own lips before continuing.

"Not yet, but I think we will soon." With a smug look, Caleb added, "Let's just say that love is in the air."

TWENTY-FOUR
Caleb

I was flying high on a wave of excitement that we had nearly resolved Josie's problems. We only had the hurdles of physically getting the cats back and Mr. Anderson giving the thumbs-up to our fixes. That excitement was pushed even higher as I watched her exchange an emotional goodbye hug with Fred after he gathered up his things.

"I really can't thank you enough, Fred. You've saved my bacon, truly." Josie's hands were clasped in front of her, her aura soft with love and hope that I hadn't sensed in her before when dealing with her brother. My heart was singing at the reconciliation, so sweet after so many years of strife.

This is what cupids live for.

"Your bacon is worth saving, sis." He hugged her again, patting her head lightly before letting her go one last time. "From now on, just send me your receipts every month, and we'll keep things straight."

"Thank you. Seriously."

"I had to do it; your books deserve better. Your *financial* books, not just the ones on the shelves."

Josie blushed at the lightly teasing tone, and Fred gave me a final wave before letting himself out.

The door clicked shut, and the comforting silence of the bookshop enveloped us like a cozy sweater. Josie turned to me, a relief in her eyes that I hadn't seen since we'd reconnected. She stopped a pace or two away, running her hands through her hair.

"This is it, Caleb! Fred gave me a file to show to Mr. Anderson. He handled the B & O issue, and fixed like three more problems I didn't know I had yet. I'm filed, paid up, and good to go. I'm not going to lose the shop."

Her voice quavered at the end, and I crossed the scant distance between us, scooping her into a hug. She fit so perfectly there, tucked under my chin against my chest.

Josie was tentative at first, but within a few seconds, she melted against me, letting her hands loop around my waist, settling comfortably on the small of my back. Even the innocent touch over my shirt felt like a brand against my skin. Her soft curls falling over my hands were pure torture, urging me to twine my fingers in them and pull her lips to mine. I dropped my cheek to the top of her head, reveling in a bit more of the silky softness.

I suffered in silence, savoring the little bit of her sweetness I could still let myself have, when she shocked me by moving. Her hands followed along the hem of my shirt until she reached my forearms and traced them up to the back of my neck, fingertips barely brushing my bare skin.

"You're so warm," she murmured, pressing her palms flat to my skin.

I hadn't moved, but heat was pulsing through me, my powers amplified ten-fold by such close contact with her.

"You're intoxicating," I whispered to the crown of her head. "And far too tempting."

"Tempting?" She leaned back, arms crossed and eyebrow raised in a challenge. "You're an *angel*, Caleb. How could anything tempt you? Aren't you all perfect and untouchably holy?"

I laughed and let my hands do what they wanted, sinking knuckles-deep into her hair, scraping my nails lightly over her scalp in a gentle massage. Her eyes fluttered, but she forced them back open, as if she was unwilling to look away, like she didn't want to miss a single second.

"You've been tempting me since the second I laid eyes on you all those years ago. Tempting."

I dropped a kiss on her forehead.

"Distracting."

I dropped another on her cheek, next to her long lashes.

"Calling to me."

I whispered the last against her ear before gently pressing a firmer kiss to the tender skin below it.

She shuddered and gasped at the sudden heat, clinging to me more tightly as I pulled back, watching her eyes as much as her aura. They were dark and wide, full of the same longing I felt. Her aura was turning that rosy hue I now knew meant we were in the danger zone of desire.

After last time, with how dark my own aura had turned... I couldn't afford to let things between us go any further physically. *Temptation* was the least of my worries. I pulled back with regret.

"I should go, Josie. We shouldn't let things get too far. You have a boyfriend now, and—"

"Boyfriend? I certainly do *not*."

I was rooted to the spot, riveted by the words dripping from her lips.

"But the date, the man..." *Do I tell her I saw them kissing?* "What happened?"

She shrugged, noncommittal. "It didn't work out. He was a nice guy but not... the one." She said the last words succinctly, and I felt like I was missing something. I couldn't focus on that, though, because what she was telling me was oh-so-dangerous.

Josie, my Josie, was available. Completely free, unencumbered, and in my arms.

Where I wanted her to stay forever.

I was torn, so torn. The right thing to do would be to walk out that door and not look back. Let her be free to find someone who could love her, be with her, give her children, and build a life together. I couldn't offer her that; I could only offer her temporary. And frankly, that wasn't safe. If the fall took hold, if I couldn't get my wings back...

The heat between us, though, wouldn't be denied. She inched up on her toes, eyes fastened to my mouth. I might hate myself for it later, when I had to leave, but I could not deny her in that moment, any more than I could deny my angelic heritage. Something about her drew me in, no matter how much I tried to resist. Body and soul. It's why I'd believed she was my Chosen all those years ago, human or not.

She abandoned my back, grabbing onto my shoulders with one hand and pulling me down closer with the other. It would have been so easy to push it further, to take more than I should have.

When our lips met, we were bathed in a golden glow. She was everything, the sun in the sky, the breath in my lungs, the love in my heart. I dropped one hand to her hip and pulled her closer, pressing our hips flush together. Her lips parted on a sigh that I felt like a caress down my spine, and I tilted my head to deepen the kiss. I needed her to know I felt the same.

I feel it all.

With Josie, for the first time in my life, I wasn't on the outside.

I couldn't say how long we stayed wrapped together; time lost all meaning. All I knew was that when we finally broke apart, it felt like I'd been fundamentally changed. Something inside me shifted, different. But I was playing with fire every second I stayed in her arms. I had to go, put distance back between us.

There it was, as soon as I stepped away from her, that threatening tinge of darkness that made my vision warp and my hands shake. *Shit.*

I couldn't ignore it, but I couldn't ignore her, either. What was I supposed to do?

Josie was branded on my soul, and I knew the mark of our time together would never leave me. She looked into my eyes questioningly, as if afraid I was going to bolt again. But I wouldn't. I *couldn't.* To leave her now would be to leave a piece of myself behind, even if she didn't know it.

"Caleb, are you okay?" Her tone was worried.

I frowned down at her. "Of course. With you, how could I not be?" I blew off her concern, knowing I was out of sorts but not wanting to worry her. Could she tell I was falling? Could she see the damnation in my eyes?

"It's just you look... strange."

She grabbed my shaking hand, and her eyes went wide as she looked back up at me.

"A second ago, you turned all *dark* and shadowy. But

now... you're, um, *glowing*." I looked down at my hands, and sure enough, she was right.

A golden light gilded my skin, my angelic heritage shining through physically. The darkness was gone, again.

The second she touched me.

"Does the glowing thing usually happen when you—" She trailed off, eyes dropping as a blush heated her cheeks.

"No, it's never happened before. I'm not *quite* sure what's happening right now," I admitted, fear coursing through me and knocking back some of the heat which had taken over my brain with her pressed against me.

"It's faded a little. You might just need to, uh, stop kissing me."

Of course. Josie calls to my power, and with her instigating that kiss... my power is trying to form the seal, as if she were my Chosen.

But with my powers incomplete and my wings gone, what would happen? If the seal had already begun forming, she would be unable to be with another man. *Ever.*

Even though she was human and couldn't complete the Chosen bond. Right?

Was that why the darkness kept creeping in? I thought back, trying to remember precisely when it had hit last time. It had been after we'd had sex, but we'd separated for her to go on her date.

This time, we'd kissed—and as soon as I'd stopped it, demonic energy.

Nausea roiled in my gut at the idea. I let my eyes roll up to the ceiling, saying a silent prayer to the Host, beseeching.

Please don't say I ruined her life with a moment of passion, please. It's not fair to her. God, my power was on the fritz again, as if it were trying to claim her. It was getting *worse* than before when it didn't want to push her away.

A part of me was desperate to explain everything to her, to share the divine knowledge so that she could understand why I had to keep this space, the depth of the risk we faced. But she had so much going on, so much wrong right now. We had time; I didn't have to drop this in her lap as well. Especially not while it was just a horrible suspicion.

"It's working. You're almost back to normal now." She smiled up at me, completely unaware of my internal struggle.

I wouldn't tell her tonight. Tomorrow, she'd get her cats back and her business. After that... I would find a time to share the truth.

She deserved to know, especially if I'd somehow fused our souls without meaning to. I didn't know if it was possible, but I knew who I could ask.

With any luck, Gabriel would be down in the next few days to check on me, and he'd know. This issue with Josie would be unprecedented, but I trusted him.

And if it was true, if I'd started the seal that bound her permanently to my side, to my soul... he would be furious. But Josie was more important than his anger, and I would make this right somehow.

For her, I would risk anything, give anything, even if it would kill me. I knew that now. She'd become the most important person in my life, no matter how hard I tried to keep her at arm's length, to be the good angel. For Josie, I was willing to cross lines.

But how would *she* feel when she found out that she couldn't be my Chosen and that I might have unintentionally taken away her choice?

TWENTY-FIVE

Josie

I DIDN'T DARE TO TAKE MY EYES OFF MR. ANDERSON as he roamed around the Bookish Cat with his nose in the air like a hound on a scent. He moved through each aisle methodically, his eyes narrowed in focus. Sword and sorcery, mythology, high fantasy... then through the non-fiction aisles, self-help, psychology.

His gray suit contrasted with the warm tones of the surrounding books, his eyes reflecting the soft glow of the fairy lights we'd strung up along the shelves.

Every few steps, he paused, tilting his head slightly as he inhaled deeply, his bushy eyebrows furrowing in concentration. Then, he moved on, his polished loafers clicking softly against the wooden floor. From behind the counter, I watched him, biting my lower lip, while Caleb stood next to me, his arms folded across his chest. Dr. Elwyn, his allergist, stood beside us with a clipboard in hand, her gaze fixed on Mr. Anderson with an intensity that seemed to outstrip that of any allergist I'd ever met.

After what felt like an eternity, Mr. Anderson approached

Matilda, who was perched upon a table of award-winning classics. He eyed her warily, as though she were a live grenade ready to explode. Then, with a visible exhale, he reached out a hand and began to awkwardly stroke her soft fur.

I gulped. The moment of truth was nearly upon us.

His hand was stiff and unpracticed, moving in halting motions over her back. It was clear that Mr. Anderson was not a cat person, or rather, he was not an animal person at all. Yet, there was a strange sort of determination in his eyes, a willingness to face whatever reaction his body might have.

Matilda looked mildly annoyed but endured his clumsy petting with resigned grace.

Then, with the dramatic flourish of a Shakespearean actor, Mr. Anderson rubbed his eyes with that same hand. I gasped, anticipating a swift and severe allergic reaction. Caleb winced next to me, ready to jump into action if needed. Dr. Elwyn, however, simply watched calmly, pen poised above her clipboard, ready to note down any reaction.

"I'm starting the clock, one hundred and twenty seconds," Dr. Elwyn announced and tapped it into her phone.

And we waited.

When your whole future waits upon one hundred and twenty seconds, they last longer than the Superbowl.

I scratched behind my ear. I searched out Gatsby who was hiding behind the offending box of gorgeous books from England. I couldn't see Heathcliff. It must have been nearly time...

"Ninety seconds."

Come on!

Mr. Anderson didn't move. He stood like the sketch by Michealangelo of the Vitruvian Man, arms outstretched and legs wide, an eyebrow raised like he was as eager to know the result as we were. When he wasn't complaining or shouting, he was actually a pretty agreeable guy.

"Forty-five seconds."

You have got to be kidding me. Wait, no, what's happening to him...

Mr. Anderson's nose twitched. I know I saw it, and Caleb must have, too, because he sucked in a breath.

This had to work, it *had* to. It had been such a massive relief when Mr. Anderson nodded in agreement at the tax paperwork, but without the cats in the shop, the Bookish Cat couldn't and wouldn't be the same. On top of that, I had no way to ensure they wouldn't make their way back. I'd have to send them across the country or deport them to Germany to be sure.

And that all sounded awful. I wanted them here. They belonged.

"Time."

I inhaled sharply, nerves getting the better of me. "And?"

Mr. Anderson dropped his arms to his sides. "Nothing. I'm cured!"

I grabbed Caleb's hand. "Are you sure?"

"*I'm* sure," Dr. Elwyn said. "I pulled out all the stops. Only the best for my Herbie." She threw her arms around Mr. Anderson's neck and laid one hell of a kiss on him in a move that shocked me nearly as much as the yellow notice on the door had.

I turned sharply to see if Caleb was as stunned as I was and found him—wait—grinning?

"You knew?" I whispered.

He winked in reply.

"Acupuncture, herbal teas, and a lavender-oil massage were

all I needed!" Mr. Anderson announced, his face beaming with delight.

I murmured to Caleb, "Lavender-oil massage, huh?"

He shrugged with that silly grin on his face.

"It was written in the stars," Dr. Elwyn said, her arms still firmly around his neck. "We knew instantly that we were as meant to be as he was meant to overcome his suffering."

"And you," Mr. Anderson picked up, looking at me, "are welcome to keep the cats."

Tears rose before I could stop them. "Oh, Mr. Anderson. Thank you!"

He cleared his throat. "Just clean up after them, huh?" I could tell he felt he had to make some kind of remark after all the trouble he'd given me. But as long as I got to keep my babies, I couldn't care less.

"Yes, sir. You bet."

"Then I think our work here is done." Dr. Elwyn put her clipboard away. "We still have time to get away for the weekend. What do you say, Herbie?"

"Nothing would please me more, Elwynnie."

Herbie? Elwynnie? Holy shit, we were through the looking glass.

I saw them to the door, intending to wave goodbye, but they only had eyes for each other. Dr. Elwyn gave Mr. Anderson's butt a squeeze as they passed the threshold. *Will wonders never cease?*

Only Caleb and I, plus the cats, were left in the store.

"You played a part in that, didn't you?" It was a question that wasn't a question because the impish grin on his face told me everything.

"It wasn't predestined, but it was ideal for both of them. And

207

look what we got out of it." The Bookish Cat, with its towers of books and warm pools of lamp light, felt suddenly intimate. "I needed you to have this win." I sensed an energy pulsating between us, like the hum of a power line, both thrilling and terrifying.

Ever since that mad, beautiful kiss, and his subsequent golden glow, I hadn't been able to get him out of my mind. It was more than a kiss; it was an admission, a confession—something binding.

A promise. The memory of his lips against mine, the feel of his arms around me, the way the world had momentarily ceased to exist, kept playing on a loop. But I couldn't put a name to what it was. It was an emotion that didn't fit within the narrow parameters of language, it was simply too vast, too overwhelming.

Every time I closed my eyes, I relived that moment, and each time, it felt as though it ended too abruptly. The sweet, intoxicating taste of him lingered on my tongue, a haunting reminder of what we had and what we could have been.

And what we might still become.

"Hiya, kids!" Barb burst into the shop like a hurricane, dispelling the intensity between us.

It was perhaps for the best.

"Should I take it from your goofy smiles that the cats are here to stay?"

"Yes!" I declared and wrapped my arms around Barb. "Thank goodness for you, Barb. So level-headed and helpful."

"Ew, can't I be adventurous and dangerous instead? You kids go have fun. I'll do some tidying up now that we're here to stay. Where's that exacto knife?" She dropped her satchel on the countertop and searched for the pen knife we kept on the shelf below. It shouldn't have been an issue and wouldn't have been if she hadn't shoved a particular pile of papers aside.

Because the leather-bound journal fell out, onto the floor, in plain sight behind the counter. Caleb's journal. The one I shouldn't have had.

"Oops!" I thrust myself behind the counter, intentionally knocking down the stack of order forms that I kept beside the register. Huge thanks to gravity, for they landed over the journal, effectively hiding it from view. "Look at me, butterfingers!"

My pulse pounded between my ears. Had Caleb seen it? Could he feel it?

"Need a hand?" He bent over the counter.

"Nope." I covered his view with my body. "I've got it. Why don't you grab my bag from the back, and we can find a park bench to discuss that last, um, *bookshelf* you want to arrange."

He cocked his head. "Bookshelf?"

Couldn't he just play along? Barb was standing *right there*.

"Yeah, you know how I helped you with your other two bookshelves, and there's only one left now."

"Oh, *oh*... yes, the bookshelf. I'll grab your bag." He disappeared into the back room.

Barb cleared her throat and mumbled in my ear, "So, *bookshelf* is what kids are calling it these days, huh?"

TWENTY-SIX
Caleb

I DON'T KNOW WHAT POSSESSED ME TO TAKE JOSIE TO Rocksmith Café, only that it felt as natural as breathing. It was like my feet just led us there of their own accord, and it didn't click where we were until we were settling down at my favorite table. And maybe, deep down, I wanted to see her here, in my favorite haunt, to see how she fit.

I wasn't the least bit surprised that she fit beautifully, warmly greeting Victory and settling into the second chair at my table like she'd been there with me all along. Victory took our drink orders with a smile, shooting me a knowing eyebrow waggle over Josie's head before hurrying off to get the drinks.

"So, do you come here a lot?" Josie asked, looking curiously over the patio, the strange assortment of patrons, and the people flowing by in a constant stream. Everything felt fresh and bright, as if I were seeing it through her eyes.

"Yes, I do. This is the only place in Seattle where I'm a regular."

The corner of her mouth quirked up at that. "Is that so? What's so special about this place?"

"Well, they have the best lemonade in Seattle, for one. The service is always good, for another. But the truth is…" I leaned forward, lowering my voice to a conspiratorial whisper, even as I was careful not to touch her, "this is a café for supernaturals."

Her eyes widened, her lips dropping into a shocked "O."

"Are you saying that *everyone* here is something… like you?"

"Sort of. They aren't angels, but all supernatural beings are welcome here. The owner is dwarven, and he's very set that everyone is safe under his roof. It's a hospitality thing with dwarves."

I allowed my senses to scan the room, a cupid habit, to see if there were any unmated supes awaiting their fate. Nothing unusual came to me—a happy witch with a fae, a dwarf not yet ready for his match, and then… a hum. I turned to see where it was coming from. The sound blocked me from sensing the supe's status, and that *never* happened. I found a man, broad shouldered with nothing but muscle on him. He was dehydrated and dark circles were under his eyes as the hum emanated from the place where he sat.

A lone wolf.

The hair rose on the back of my neck as I inspected his condition more closely. He must have sensed it, because he looked up from his hands to meet my gaze.

The pain in his heart struck me like a knife.

He looked back down, and I allowed the hum to roll back through me, assessing it again with my powers. Something was horribly wrong with his aura, but I couldn't address it with Josie sitting across from me.

Her eyes were wide as she looked closer at the other occupied tables on the patio. "So… they don't care that I'm here? And why have I never noticed this place before now?"

"It's glamoured. You wouldn't see it unless you already knew it was here or you were a supernatural being."

"So, you guys can just... hide whole *buildings* from humans?"

"Supernatural species can do a lot more than you'd think."

"*Clearly.*" Josie stared wide-eyed at Victory as she set the drinks down in front of us and handed us each a menu.

As Josie studied the menu, I turned to look at the wolf shifter again. I had never experienced this sensation before— like his future had been veiled from me. His head was back in his hands, the hum ever present, but after a moment or two of concentrating, I realized that the hum wasn't coming from him, it had been cast *upon* him. A curse.

He caught me looking at him again and was out of the café like a shot. My heart was heavy as I watched him go. He had a very complicated fate. A fate even I couldn't begin to disentangle, because whatever curse he'd found himself under was not the purview of cupids.

I turned my attention back to Josie who was stuck on the menu as if that decision was going to make or break her.

"Want to try the club? It's divine." I shot her a wink to break the tension, and she snorted in laughter, then slapped both hands over her mouth, as if embarrassed it escaped.

"Yes. Yes, a club sounds, uh, great." She half-choked out the last word.

"All right, two usuals, coming up." Victory clicked her pen a few times as she walked off, shooting curious glances at us over her shoulder.

"What is our waitress? She seems so normal," Josie whispered.

"She mostly is. Best I can tell, Victory had a werewolf

ancestor a few generations back. For all intents and purposes, she's human."

"Oh, well, that's kind of a letdown."

I chuckled. "There are plenty of mixed-species people in Seattle. Not to mention, many supes can pass as human, even without a glamour." I waved up and down at myself, to illustrate the point.

"This is blowing my mind. But it's *not* why we're here." She cleared her throat to change the subject. "Let's talk about your third couple. What are their names?"

She pulled a legal pad out of her messenger bag, along with a pink gel pen of her own.

"Marigold and Axel." Their names were hard to get out, and gloom reared up inside me at the idea that this was the *last couple* we would match together before whatever came next.

"Ooh." She leaned forward on her elbows. "Interesting names. Tell me about them. What makes them tick? Why are they so hard to match?"

I took a long pull of my lemonade to give me a second to regain my composure. I couldn't focus on *my* problems right now. I had to get my job done, and then I would deal with the aftermath and what it meant for me—to be restored to the Host.

"They are very different people. The main binding thread is that they're both environmentalists—they really care about Mother Earth and preserving the planet. But they have wildly different backgrounds, and all of my attempts to match them in the past have ended... fiery."

"Fiery?"

"With them arguing, not kissing. They are practically enemies at this point."

"Ooh, I love a good enemies-to-lovers!" She practically

vibrated in her seat, and I had to chuckle at her genuine excitement.

"A what, now?"

"Enemies-to-lovers. You know, the romance book trope?"

I stared at her blankly.

"Caleb, you're not *seriously* telling me that you're *a cupid*"—she dropped her voice low, even though she now knew everyone else there was in on the secret—"and haven't ever read a romance novel? They're the very epitome of love always winning. Very on-brand for a cupid. No matter how messed up the characters may be, they always come together in the end. Surely, you know the old saying—love conquers all."

Love conquers all. It was one of the five core beliefs of a cupid. She made it sound so simple; yet how could it be, when she and I were what we were and could never cross the divide between us? If love couldn't conquer the barrier we faced, how could I believe it conquered *all*?

The realization disturbed me. Had I fallen further from my cupid calling than I realized? If the five core beliefs were no longer true—

"Earth to Caleb!" Josie interrupted my dismayed train of thought with a grin on her face. "I know it's a thing that men don't like romance novels, but come on, you're a cupid! Have you read one, or not?"

"Er, no? I've never needed to before. Do you think it would be helpful?"

"We have so much work to do. I don't even know where to begin with your book-ducation. I mean, paranormal seems like a good fit, given what you are. Except you're matching regular people, right?"

I nodded.

"So, contemporary. Enemies-to-lovers, for sure. I'm

guessing we could find something else that fits them that could give you some ideas. Tell me more about them, and then after we finish our sandwiches, we can get right back to the shop!"

"Okay, well, they've known each other now for more than seven years, but the first time I matched them, I did it all wrong. They're eco-warriors, and I decided to match them through a fender bender."

"A fender bender?" She wrinkled her nose adorably.

"I know, okay? I realize now that it only drove a wedge between them. He was driving a luxury car, she was riding a city bus... He tapped the back of the bus, and ever since then, she thinks he doesn't, and I quote, 'put his money where his mouth is' because he drives a gas vehicle and doesn't take the bus."

"Oh, this is too good! Okay, so, we need to draw them together on the ways they're alike instead of different. Show them that they were wrong about each other. We can definitely work with that. Hmm... tell me what else you've tried."

"There was a Lovers of Mother Earth conference two years ago, and I made them seatmates. That went over like a lead balloon. Then last year, I sent him to surf at her favorite beach. I thought with all the early morning sunlight and him in a wet suit instead of a *business* suit, maybe she'd see another side of him. Nope. Then—"

"Here you go, guys. Let me know if you need anything else." Victory dropped off our sandwiches, stopping me mid-rant.

"You get the idea," I said after she left, taking the first bite of my favorite double-bacon club, though I hardly tasted it. The love-conquers-all thing had left me rattled. It was starting to feel like I was missing something. Things had gotten so complicated, when my life used to be simple. Follow the five core beliefs, match my assigned couples, always bet on love, and don't get distracted by a human stealing my heart.

Being a cupid was not a confusing job.

So why couldn't I be with Josie? If love always wins in the end, *why couldn't I have the woman I loved?*

"I do," Josie continued while I tried to silence the tortuous back-and-forth in my mind. "You get points for creativity, but now that it's this bad, it's going to take a real grand gesture to get them over their past differences. But it's okay. When in doubt, we go to the books! Right after lunch, I'm going to show you around the part of the Bookish Cat that applies."

Go to the books. I was jolted out of my train of thought with the reminder from Gabriel, about the book of angelic seals. I'd gotten so caught up in her issues with her landlord that I'd never followed up and asked Josie if she could help me find it.

"Speaking of books, I have a favor to ask."

"For you? Anything." The way she smiled at me froze the breath in my lungs. I couldn't deny that I loved her, that I wanted her, that I wanted her *as my Chosen*. She was everything good and bright and beautiful about this world, in one perfect, curvy package.

But a quick glance around the packed patio was enough to put me off telling her that right now. For someone who was divinely driven to bring people together, I had terrible timing. Meanwhile, she was eagerly waiting to hear the favor I was about to ask.

"Okay, part of the reason I got into my predicament seven years ago was more than just making some mistakes matching my couples. I lost something, an angelic artifact, and it occurred to me that you might be able to help me find it."

"O-kay..." She dragged the word out, looking confused.

"It's a book. Leather cover, embossed with a feather,

216

though I don't know if a human would be able to make out the insignia. There's nothing terribly unusual about it to the naked eye, though it holds a lot of power. The inside would look blank, actually, because only someone with angelic blood can read the angelic seals. And it has to be in the state because it can't have gone far from where it was lost."

Her eyes grew wide. "You lost an *angelic book* on Earth?"

"Yes, unfortunately. Makes your tax mishap not look so bad, huh?"

"What if it's just gone? Stolen? Destroyed."

"Ahh, good question." She tilted her head, weighing the idea. "But the fact is, it has a kind of magnetism to me. It's not lost forever, but it isn't found either. I suspect a rare-books collector would be exactly the type of person it might find itself with. And that is now right in your wheelhouse. Do you think you could ask around, see if anyone has it in their collection, or maybe in a museum?"

She grew still, wiping her hands on her napkin thoughtfully. Her aura was an interesting shade. Confusion and... guilt? Strange.

"If it looks like a blank journal, how would someone *know* they'd found it? Journals are a dime a dozen, even old leatherbound ones. It's a needle in a haystack."

I drummed my fingers on the table, thinking. How would she know if she'd found it? "Well, I could obviously tell, if you were able to bring it to me. If not, you'd have to open it under the moonlight. Even though you wouldn't be able to see what's written on the pages of the book, there's an inscription on the inside of the back cover, marking it for what it is. May I?"

I gestured to her notepad, and she passed it over. I quickly sketched out the sealing sigil on a blank page and slid it back across the table to her.

"I've never seen a journal with this in it, but I've also never made a point to look at one under the *moonlight*. I'll keep an eye out and see if I can help you find it." She took a big bite of the sandwich and scrunched up her face.

"You don't like it?"

She set the sandwich down and looked out across the busy street. "I think I've lost my appetite."

TWENTY-SEVEN

Josie

THE REST OF THE DAY FELT LIKE YEARS.

All I wanted to do was get that book home and hold it open under the moonlight, but there was no hurrying the moon.

I watched the minutes tick by, first at the shop where I got to help a sweet group of third graders pick out girl-power stories and an older gentleman find a book on overcoming grief. His hands shook, and my heart went out to him as he thanked me with glassy eyes.

And then it was time to go home.

I held the mysterious journal in the palm of my hand as I walked to my reading nook, where the sleeping cats immediately woke and scattered. They knew something was up. Cats always knew, and these in particular had their own special connection to other worlds that I couldn't understand.

The large window in my reading nook had a perfect view of the moon.

Slowly, cautiously, I lowered myself onto the cushion, placing the book on my lap. In the worn leather, I could just about make out the embossing, which could very well have been a feather... but maybe not. Maybe it was just an artistic symbol, not at all what Caleb described. Maybe I could convince myself this wasn't what Caleb was looking for, and, therefore, I could keep him in this world a little longer. Or forever.

One thing was for sure: the sensation the book gave me was electric in a way it had never been before, like the time Fred made me touch my tongue to both tips of a nine-volt battery.

"That's still not proof," I said to the closed cover. The blank pages inside seemed to mock my feeble attempt to explain away its strangeness. The fact that I couldn't read angelic seals was neither here nor there; if it were any old blank journal, there'd be nothing to read either.

The leather felt oddly warm, alive under my touch. *That* was a bit awkward. I took a deep breath, mentally preparing myself for the next step.

My hands trembled as I turned off the light, then pulled back the curtain and allowed the moonlight to fill the room. Thank God for a cloudless sky.

Nothing is going to happen, I told myself again, *so chill the fuck out and open the damn book.* I counted to three, then turned it over and slowly lifted open the back cover.

And then I was blind.

An intense golden light burst from the page, so brilliant I had to squeeze my eyes shut. The book slipped from my hands, landing with a thud, but the light remained, unwavering.

As I batted my eyes open, a beam shone up into the ceiling, and even though I could see my ceiling was perfectly intact, I could also see something else.

Something beyond the ceiling. Beyond the skies.

Into the great beyond.

I picked up the book from the floor, my eyes having adjusted to the wash of illumination. Even if I didn't *want* to see what was happening in the pages of the journal, my body reacted independently from my head. Blood surged through my veins as the weight of the book settled in my hands, a dizzying rush overtaking me.

My vision sharpened, revealing what had been hidden only moments before. The pages, covered in ancient scrawl, flickered between invisible and glowing, as if I were seeing through someone else's eyes.

The eyes of an angel.

My heart swelled with Caleb's undeniable presence—he was here, inside me, woven into my soul, whether he knew it or not.

I slammed the book closed, not daring another second with it. The sensation I'd felt when I brushed my fingers over the cover paled in comparison to the raw power I had just experienced.

There was not a shred of doubt that this was Caleb's angel book.

And possibly my last chance to keep him with me on Earth.

I WAS HUNCHED over the counter the next morning, intentionally buried under paperwork Fred sent me so that I could pretend for a little longer that I didn't have something I was keeping from Caleb. But a curious sound broke the silence. Music, vibrant and peppy, and undoubtedly out of place. I picked this location for the Bookish Cat specifically because it was quiet, but just off one of the main drags.

I set aside the application for a new-business tax break because whatever was going on sounded like it was worth seeing.

Music from the eighties filled the air as I opened the door, and my first thought was that a flash mob in costume had come to the neighborhood. I loved a good flash mob, and the shop was currently empty, so I stepped out the door.

Before me, the sidewalk had transformed into a spontaneous dance floor with a flurry of movement, fingers jazz-handing in the air. A group of women in matching velour tracksuits shuffled and swayed, their silver wigs catching in the sunlight. Except...

Wait, those aren't wigs. And those aren't costumes.

A crowd of elderly ladies were cutting the rug to the sounds of an eighties heartthrob, and they were heading my way.

In the midst of them all, one woman stood out. With a mini boombox perched on her shoulder, she led the brigade of dancers with a spryness that contradicted her age.

The way the woman tossed her head left and right reminded me so much of—

"Nana Geraldine?" I blurted in surprise.

Nana Geraldine, clad in bright-purple leggings and a sweat-band around her forehead, was front and center. She kicked high for her age, bent low, and twirled, her arms windmilling wildly in the air. She was both graceful and unpredictable, with facial expressions that belonged on a commercial for a cruise ship.

Behind her, the ladies mimicked her moves with varying levels of success. One particularly enthusiastic lady, wearing oversized sunglasses, did almost a full split, though her friend yanked her back up.

As the music hit the final chord, the group struck a pose, hands on hips, elbows out, in full diva stance. I could now attest that a crowd of eighty-year-old-plus ladies in Lycra was far less frightening than I would have imagined.

Nana scuttled right over to me, grinning widely. "Do we know how to make an entrance or what!"

Next thing I knew, Nana Geraldine and her dancercise troop stormed the Bookish Cat like a pack of lively flamingos. The silence of my bookshop was shattered by their energetic chatter, interspersed with the occasional whoop.

They flocked toward the romance section, huddling close around the shelves.

"Here's what we're looking for, girls!" one of the ladies shouted.

Oh, my word. Steamy Highlander romance, of all things?

I could feel the blush creeping up my neck as Nana Geraldine held up one of the books, its cover flaunting a bare-chested hunk with flowing hair.

"Look at this one, ladies!" she squealed, pointing at the book. "Those biceps could crack walnuts!"

"Good gracious!" One of the ladies gasped, running to check it out.

I had to hide my eyes, suddenly feeling like I was an embarrassed teenager who just caught her parents making out.

"Don't mind us, dear," Nana patted me on the shoulder. "Just a bunch of old ladies having a bit of fun. Carry on with whatever you were doing and pretend we're not even here."

The ladies chattered among themselves, and as much as I tried to turn my attention to online order forms, it just wasn't possible. The women fawned over the bodice-ripping tales, giggling and whispering.

"Oh, Betty, look at this one!" Nana Geraldine held up a

book with a Highlander in a kilt, his chest gleaming under the painted sunlight. "Isn't he a handsome brute?"

Betty, a petite woman with hair as white as snow, squinted at the book before she gave a sharp nod. "Handsome, yes, but nothing compared to the hunk on *A Highlander's Promise*. Now *that's* a man."

"Nana," I half-whispered, "what's the deal with the enthusiasm for Highlanders?"

"It's the kilts," she quipped. "So much... mystery."

Another round of laughter burst from the shelves, louder this time. Nana Geraldine looked at me, a gleam in her eye. "So, dear, do you have a favorite?"

"Highlander?"

"Uh-huh."

My face grew hot, but I took the teasing in stride. "I can't say I have a favorite, Nana. I... appreciate all the... erm, covers."

Nana Geraldine winked at me. "That's my girl!"

I shook my head, smiling despite my mortification. The giggling group of dancercising, steamy Highlander-loving ladies had turned my bookstore into a lively mess, and I didn't mind it one bit.

As the women continued on, Nana laid a soft, wrinkled hand on my arm and gave it a gentle squeeze. "You know, my girl," she said, her voice soft and full of warmth, "I'm proud of you. Proud of you for taking a dream and turning it into this... this wonder."

"Thank you, Nana." My voice broke. I knew she was proud, but it meant a lot to hear her say it, and most of all I was grateful that the woman who had been my cheerleader my whole life was still there to see it. "You know a lot of it is thanks to you."

"Let's not battle with feelings now, sweetie pie." She

winked. "You have other joyful topics, like your own High-lander romance." She must have seen the question on my face because she added, "You know, that tall, handsome drink of holy water."

"Nana!"

"What? It's not blasphemy if it's true." She huddled up close. "It can't be easy for you to wrap your head around what he is. Wrapping your arms, however—"

"Nana, I am not going there with you."

"Okay, then stick with the topic at hand. What's the deal with the angel? Are you his Chosen?"

I bit my lip. "I don't think such a thing is possible, Nana."

She set her hands on her hips. "You think love is held back by any human sense of possibility?"

It didn't feel right to expose everything Caleb had told me about angel-human relations. I knew that Nana only wanted to put me at ease, and that nothing would make her happier than knowing I was going to be okay. Given her brush with the supernatural already, it seemed best that I steer the conversation into safer territory. But there was something she could help with...

"Regardless of what I think, I know that he's doing everything he can to get back into the heavens. And with only one more couple to match, he's already got one foot out the door."

"And where's his other foot?"

I beckoned with a finger for Nana to come behind the counter, where I covertly pulled the journal out, just enough so that she could see it.

"It's his?" she asked, wide-eyed.

I nodded.

"And I suppose he doesn't know you have it?"

"I've had it for seven years. And he just told me yesterday that he needs it in order to go back to the Host."

"Oh." She bit her lip. "Then you're in a predicament indeed. Keep the book and keep the man—"

"Exactly."

"—or give the book back and *keep* the man."

"You see—wait, what?"

Nana crossed her arms the way she used to do when I was a girl and asked when the cookies would be finished baking. Her answer was always the same: when they're done.

"Dear, no matter what, that book must return to him. If you keep it, you'll never know if he's staying for you or if he's stuck on some divine tether. If you are his Chosen, then the heavens will find a way for you to be together."

"And if I'm not?"

She caressed my cheek. "Then you have to let him go."

Nana's eyes held mine, a glimmer of tears on her lashes.

"Is that what happened to you, Nana?"

"Something like that."

A fire alarm went off. Fire and books were the worst possible combination, swiftly followed by water and books, so I flew into action.

"Everyone out! Clear the shop! I'm going for the extinguisher!"

"Hold up!" a lady called out. "That's just my phone. It's the ringtone for my nephew."

"Anita!" Nana shouted. "You nearly gave us all heart attacks!"

"He's a firefighter." Anita shrugged. "And I'm half deaf."

"So *that's* why you never get the kick-ball-change in rhythm." Nana shook her head dismissively.

"Look what he just found!" Anita held up the phone.

"Strolling along the tidal end of Alki beach. It's an orca! Poor thing is washed up on the rocks. He's gone to alert the authorities."

A beached orca... help not yet on the way...

"Your gears are turning," Nana whispered.

Axel and Marigold's grand gesture. I turned back to Nana. "They are. And I've got to go." I grabbed my phone and dialed Caleb, who answered on the first ring.

"Josie? What's—"

"No time, listen up. I know how to get your couple together."

TWENTY-EIGHT

Caleb

My ears were ringing. Why were my ears ringing?

"Caleb, are you listening to me? I said there's a beached orca on Alki Beach! This is perfect! We can get both of your eco-lovers over there and help them save the whale together. But we've got to move quickly. Barb can watch the store, and I can meet you there, but it'll be—"

"I'm coming to get you. Stay at the shop, and we'll go together."

"Okay, okay. I'll get my things together, but hurry!"

She hung up the phone without saying goodbye, leaving me alone with the tinny ring.

The Host was calling. The same thing had happened the last time, when I'd been called up for correction.

Not yet. I can't leave her now. I still have to figure out if I've started the Chosen seal on her!

I swiped my keys off the hook and jogged to my car, the '87 Buick Grand National, which purred like a kitten when I cranked it up, as always. But even the rumble of my classic car couldn't bring a smile to my face. Not when the ringing in my ears meant that I was nearly done with my task, and any minute, I'd be called back to stand before the heavenly Host.

Plus, I still hadn't found the book. How could I be so close to completing my mission without it? It didn't make sense.

I whipped out of the parking lot more quickly than I should have and forced myself to suck some deep breaths through my nose as I made the short drive to the Bookish Cat. My hands were steady if a bit white-knuckled on the wheel when I parked next to the curb, jumping out to tell Josie I was there.

I hadn't made it through the front door when a wolf-whistle cut through the usually quiet bookshop.

"Well, look at you, Mr. Hot-to-trot! I like your car. The eighties were my jam." An elderly woman in neon Lycra sidled up next to me. Her hair was sprayed into a flare of riotous curls, and was she wearing a pearl necklace and earrings with her... was that workout gear? I blinked, trying to figure out what was going on, as a peppy eighties song played over the sound system I didn't know the shop had.

"Josie?" I called, opting to go straight to the source. Maybe she had planned some sort of eighties theme day, and I missed the memo.

"Caleb! There you are." She plucked her messenger bag from behind the counter and walked quickly toward me. But she didn't make it all the way to my side before I heard a familiar voice.

"There he is, ladies! That's my great-granddaughter's new beau! Isn't he a doll?" Nana Geraldine crowed with delight.

Coos of, "Oh, he's so handsome!" and "He'd be a perfect cover model for *Highlander Escape*" had me backing toward the front door like a deer surrounded by a dozen hunters. More and more of Nana's friends came pouring out of the stacks, several of them with towering piles of books adorned with bare-chested men in kilts. All of them wore fluorescent Lycra and leg warmers.

"This has been great, ladies." Josie tried to save us. "Unfortunately, we must be going. We've got an urgent—"

Someone poked me in the backside, so I grabbed Josie's arm and bolted for the door, not waiting for the rest of her goodbye.

She laughed at my panic as she slid into the passenger seat. Before I pulled away from the curb, I saw a dozen ladies, all with their noses pressed against the glass door.

"What is wrong with you? Surely, you're not afraid of Nana Geraldine's friends. They're sweet as can be."

"Maybe to *you*. Did you see how they were looking at me? I felt like they had x-ray goggles. And I'm pretty sure one of them pinched my butt. That's when I bolted."

She stifled her hysterical laughter with a hand over her mouth, but there was unbridled glee in her eyes.

"Laugh all you want. I'm going to get us safely to the beach."

"I'm sorry! It's just too cute. Here you are, an angel with all this divine power, and yet... you're scared off by a bunch of elderly ladies in their dancercise gear." She tittered again, and it was like a dam burst inside me. All of a sudden, I was laughing, and then she was laughing louder, and we were just cackling like loons as I drove us down the highway.

We made good time, and I worked on pulling both Marigold and Axel to the beach as we crossed the city. While I usually would have used some vague suggestion, this time I opted for an anonymous text to both of their cell phones.

They both responded back in the affirmative, and twenty minutes later when we arrived, I could feel their auras rapidly approaching.

"What do we do now?" Josie asked as we climbed out of the car. I saw she'd left her messenger bag behind. I paused, staring at the bag for a second. The ringing in my ears was intensifying, but that made no sense. Marigold was coming from the other direction, and Axel was already on the beach. What about that bag was causing the Host to call me home more quickly?

"Caleb, are you okay?" she asked again, concern stealing over her beautiful features.

"Sorry, yes. I'm fine. *Now*, we find an unobtrusive spot to watch and pull strings if necessary." I tugged on my ear, willing the distracting noise to quit so I could finish this match well. It was one of my deepest regrets that I'd thrown these couples off track for their fate; today was my chance to finally rectify that.

"Okay, I kind of thought we could go help them save the orca."

"That's also an option." I shot her a smile.

She tugged me by the elbow, not the least bit put off by the clinging sand. She quickly charged ahead, undeterred by the throngs of beachgoers. I followed, struggling with disorientation from the persistent ringing. It was growing steadily louder as the crowd thinned, and the ground beneath our feet shifted from sand to pebbles.

"Can we just—hang on, I need a second." I stopped, dropping my hands to my knees. I shook my head, trying desperately to clear it.

"What's wrong?" She laid a hand tenderly on my back, and I closed my eyes at the touch. She was drawn to me, and the more time we spent together, the stronger the seal between us would grow if it truly had started.

How many more of those little touches did I have left? Not many.

Dread curdled in my stomach at the thought of losing her. Today, tomorrow? The ringing would only intensify until the clarion call came, and I would be pulled back to the heavens to face the Host.

The ringing steadied, and I slowly straightened.

"I don't have much time left," I admitted. I owed it to her to be honest, after leaving so abruptly last time. So many mistakes piled up around me like a brick wall, separating me from the life I was supposed to have. The phantom flutter of my wings made me want to weep at how far I'd fallen from grace.

"What do you mean? Much time left for what?" Her brow furrowed, the excited energy of making a match together and saving a whale drained away from her like someone put a pinprick in the balloon of her happiness.

"The call, it's starting. It means I'm nearly done with my mission, and the Host is about to call me back." I pointed up to the sky, and her eyes widened.

"What happens then?" She swallowed hard. "Will you... will you be able to come back?"

"I don't know." The words were hoarse, and she closed her eyes as if I'd smacked her.

It felt like I'd been punched, too.

After a few long moments, she opened her eyes again, a new determination in them. "That means we're on the right track, and we don't have time to waste. Let's get this couple together." She looped her arm through mine, by my side, despite the fact that I was about to leave her, *again*.

In that moment, I knew that it wasn't possible for me to love this woman one speck more than I already did. She'd consumed me, filled up every place in my heart that used to feel so empty. Whenever she was near, everything clicked into place. With Josie, I felt *whole*.

And I didn't know how, or why, or what it would take to make it work.

But I knew it to the very depths of my soul that she was mine, and I was hers. But how could I make the Host see that even though she was human, she was *mine*?

We crossed the pebbly shore, and after one more twist in the coastline, we saw the shape of the beached orca, people crowding around it. One of them was pointing and shouting orders, trying to get people into place, while a few others had buckets and were dumping water over it, keeping its skin wet.

"Oh, Caleb, it's really stuck. How in the world are we going to get it out of here?" Josie asked, immediately focused on the orca's plight instead of our own rapidly dwindling time together.

The gathered crowd was attempting to get it onto its belly instead of on its side, where it was currently. That was when Marigold arrived. The spark of recognition between her and Axel tipped me off, and I homed in on the two of them.

"They're here." I nodded toward the two would-be lovers, exchanging words we were too far away to hear.

"How do they seem? You can tell from a distance, right?"

"They're okay, both focused on the orca, right now."

"Right. Let's get over there and pitch in." She set her jaw in determination, and we crossed the last of the distance.

It was breathtaking and sad, seeing one of God's creatures

up close. Breathtaking because the orca was magnificent—a male, not quite full-grown. But sad because I could sense his distress. I sent a wave of soothing calm over the animal while simultaneously sending a tendril of power down, down, down, to start funneling out a deeper channel beneath him, urging the water to come up more quickly than it would on its own.

Can I change the tide?

I'd never tried something of that magnitude; never needed to. I reached out tentatively with my power and pulled, urging the water to hurry. If it worked or not, I couldn't say. Only time would tell, but at least there wasn't any push back. With the way my power had become unstable around Josie, I wasn't sure what else it might refuse to do.

"Everybody to this side! We need to get him back onto his belly before the water starts coming back in." To my surprise, it was Axel, button-down shirt sleeves rolled up past his elbows, water and grit stuck to his otherwise fine clothing, who was directing the rescue efforts.

Josie and I circled the orca and lent our muscle to the efforts to get the creature righted. He panicked and thrashed his tail when everyone started pushing on him, but I urged him back to calm, pressing the suggestion that we were all there to help. He stilled, and moving as one, all of the volunteers heaved along his side, trying to roll him.

Water lapped at our ankles as our first attempt failed.

"Take a breather, and we'll go again! Bucket brigade, let's do another run. We can't let him dry out!"

Marigold took a bucket from a flagging volunteer and sprinted to the deeper water. She ran with practiced ease in the uneven terrain, making four laps before Axel called out for everyone to push again.

"Now!" Axel called.

Josie grunted as she put her shoulder into the whale's black and white hide, putting everything she had into the effort. We all heaved again, but this time, while everyone pushed, I exerted my angelic might, moving the pebbles beneath the orca so he could roll to his belly.

"Oh my goodness, I didn't think we were going to budge him." Josie turned to me, eyes questioning as she swiped her hair out of her face, leaving a trail of sand and seawater across her forehead.

"I may have helped a little," I answered quietly.

I stumbled back a step as the ringing in my ears took on a strange, doubled quality. It was a sound like when two speakers were too close together, and I couldn't help but grab my ears. It felt like my head was going to crack in two. I had to see this through, and quickly, or else I would be too incapacitated to help anyone.

"Caleb? Caleb! You're scaring me. Tell me what I can do." Josie held my shoulders, her worried face peering up at mine.

"It's nearly time. I've got to get this whale back to sea, so they can—" I swayed on my feet and Josie held me tightly, not letting me pitch over.

"Come here. Back out of the way, and sit down. You don't have to be touching the whale to help, and if you fall you might get crushed." The water was nearly to our knees now, coming in much more rapidly than usual.

Was that why I was having trouble? Had I used too much power, trying to call the tide?

I didn't know, but what was done was done.

"Everyone to the front! The stretcher is here. Let's see if we can get it under him, and get him off these rocks!" Axel bellowed, and volunteers darted this way and that, everyone trying to grab a section of the thick orange fabric. Josie guided me to a drier area, away from the rising tide, and looped her arm around my waist as we watched the people work.

Marigold and Axel were side by side, shoulder to shoulder as they helped tug and maneuvered the stretcher alongside the team that brought it. Watching them work like a well-oiled machine brought a smile to my face, despite how terrible I felt.

The water was coming in faster now, already lapping at our toes even though we'd come a long way up the beach. I felt a siphoning sensation, as if something was draining out of my chest, and I realized with a start that I was still calling the tide. I didn't know how to stop it, nor if I could, until the whale was back out to sea. The volunteers continued working the stretcher underneath him, but I had to speed things along.

Closing my eyes, I blocked out everything else. Everything except the salty ocean breeze and the feel of Josie's arms around my waist. And I *pushed*.

Reaching down deep, to the core of my being, I tapped into the fount of golden divinity that resided inside of me. I leaned into Josie, pressing my cheek to her forehead, and the skin-to-skin contact made my power swell, eager under my direction. Forming it into a scoop-like shape, I urged it under and *up*, easing the way for the humans working to save the orca.

Shouts of encouragement rose from the beach, but the tin ringing in my ears grew to drown them out, reaching higher and higher.

I felt more than heard Josie gasp at my side, and then she was shaking me. "Caleb! It's done! Caleb, open your eyes! Shit, you're glowing again. But I don't think anyone's paying attention, they're all watching the orca."

I did as she suggested and smiled at the sight of a black dorsal fin disappearing under the surf, the orca already speeding away from land, back to deeper waters where it belonged. The volunteers were all cheering, many hugging, as a few of them dragged the stretcher back out of the water.

But that wasn't what my eyes focused on. No, it was Axel, arms curled possessively around Marigold, the two of them locked in an earth-shattering kiss.

"We did it," I mumbled the words as exhaustion threatened to take me under. I felt when the power I'd been calling snapped free, letting the tide go back to its usual rhythms.

"We sure did," Josie murmured, pressing her lips to my cheek in a soft kiss.

The ringing changed in resonance, arcing toward a crescendo, and I must have closed my eyes again because Josie was shaking me. Yelling for me to open them back up.

"Come on, we've got to get back to the car."

"I'm out of time, Josie. I'm sorry. I'm so sorry."

"No! Caleb, *now*. It's urgent!" She dragged me to my feet, and I stumbled after her. But I knew deep down, even if we made it to the car, I would only have moments after that before I was taken.

Taken back to the heavens and out of her life. Possibly for good, if I couldn't convince the Host that she was my Chosen.

TWENTY-NINE

Josie

THE SALT AIR HAD NEVER FELT SO HEAVY. CALEB leaned against me, his energy ebbing away as pain gripped him. My heart broke, but I was charged with a strength beyond my own, helping him stay upright as we headed for the car. Every step we took was an ordeal.

"Nearly there, Caleb," I murmured, doing my best to keep my voice steady. I refused to believe that he was being taken away from me. It wasn't denial, it was a pure and unadulterated belief to the core of my being that he was *meant* to stay.

I managed to guide his weight into the sleek black classic car. His skin was ashen, eyes clouded, though I felt a radiance rolling off of him. As I let him go, the glow dimmed and he gripped his head.

I closed the door, the solid click echoing ominously. For a moment, I leaned against the cool metal of the car, watching the scene of new love between Marigold and Axel. Jealousy burned in my chest.

Why shouldn't I get my man? Why was I the one who had

to give him his last remaining artifact, the one that would send him off, possibly never to return.

Never. It was too much—too dark, too deep of a word.

But I had already made my choice.

I loved him too much to keep him.

This was not like seven years ago. Seven years ago he disappeared and I was torn in two. Incapable of facing another day. I was nobody without him, or so I had thought.

Now I knew who I was and I *knew* I loved him. Body and soul, with all of my heart, and forever. Maybe I would never love again. That was fine, because I already had the love of a lifetime; it didn't get any better than this.

And I couldn't be the one responsible for him facing an eternity of torment. It was worth having my heart broken in two if that meant he would be okay. He would forever be my great love.

My gaze dropped to my bag in the car's back seat. It all came down to a book, and the irony wasn't lost on me. Seven years to build my bookshop, and our love story was going to end with a book that held the power to send him back to a world beyond what my eyes would ever see. A tool of salvation and a harbinger of our end.

It was his, yet it felt like it was mine, too.

I opened the driver's side door and slipped in beside him. My hand trembled as I reached into my bag, the cool, embossed leather of the journal meeting my fingertips and instantly heating up. A shiver ran down my spine, the sensation eerily similar to the very first time Caleb had grazed his fingers against mine. With a deep breath, I pulled the book out. It felt heavier than it should, every ounce loaded with the weight of longing, regret, and acceptance.

I met Caleb's eyes. His features were drawn, the usual spark of life subdued. I knew there was only one thing I could do to make it better. And in that moment, I could deny him nothing.

"This belongs to you," I said, my voice a hushed whisper in the car's confines. As the words left my lips, it felt like a piece of my heart had been torn away.

The journal left my hands, moving to Caleb's. Our fingers brushed in a bittersweet farewell.

The moment the leather binding met his skin, the pallor left his face. A glow began at the top of his head, cascading downward over his body in a ripple of golden shimmer. His eyes widened, surprise quickly giving way to a profound relief, leaving only stunned silence.

The faintest of smiles danced on his lips. "You found it."

"I... had it. All this time. When it fell as you ran from me, all I wanted was to keep a part of you." A blush rose up my neck. "Do you hold it against me?"

"I never could." The corners of his eyes crinkled. "This is exactly where it was meant to be."

In that instant, everything around us stilled. Time came to a halt, a perfect frozen snapshot of life as we knew it. The laughter and chatter of beachgoers, the distant honking of cars, even the soothing crash of the Pacific waves against the shore— all was held suspended.

The world had taken a collective breath, waiting, watching, as if it knew the significance of this singular moment.

In that surreal bubble, it was just Caleb and me.

He was right—this was how it was meant to be. This was the right thing. We were a part of something larger than ourselves, a narrative spun by the hands of fate, and now, our page was being turned.

"My Caleb," I said, knowing that any word I said could be the last I'd ever get to say to him. "It's my turn to tell you what you told me seven years ago. Those words changed my life and brought you back into it."

"Josie..." Anguish in his eyes, his voice, the tilt of his head.

"The future you seek is already seeking you."

The distant toll of a bell cut through the silence, though I knew no churches were around here. As the sound echoed, winding its way through the frozen tableau of the world, Caleb turned to face me. His eyes held a world of emotions—fear, determination, and underpinning it all, a love so profound it left me breathless.

"I love you, Caleb," I managed between silent sobs. "You can go now."

He leaned toward me, his hands cradling my face as the world waited. His breath ghosted over my lips, a soft brush in the stillness.

And then, he was gone.

The warmth disappeared and his touch faded, leaving the passenger seat empty. Empty like the hope inside me that faded the instant he was gone.

The world continued as it had been. The orca volunteers laughed, cars zoomed by, and waves crashed against the shore.

And I was alone.

I stared at the place he'd been, the lingering traces of his presence still tangible. I touched my lips, still tingling from his kiss. It was the right thing. He was where he needed to be.

Slumped against the steering wheel as volunteers outside cheered for the rescued orca, I cried until there were no tears left.

THIRTY

Caleb

I BLINKED AT MY SURROUNDINGS, TRYING TO
remember where I was and what was going on. Everything was
white. There was no defined floor, or ceiling, or walls. Just...
white. The white of a blank page, of empty air, of clouds.

The Host.

The sensations of Earth still rested on my skin. Josie's
words telling me I could go hummed in my ears though that
world was already far behind me.

I'd been drawn into the antechamber. But why wasn't I
inside? I looked down and realized I was still clutching the
book of angelic seals, Josie's last gift to me. I held it to my heart,
tears beading at the corners of my eyes as I thought of her
pressing it into my hand. Her love as evident as the book in my
hands. She knew my destiny, and through her love, she helped
me fulfill it. Even though it hurt her, she'd still let me go.

And yet here I was, waiting in the antechamber.
Completely and wholly unwilling to let *her* go.

Was I supposed to keep waiting or go inside? I didn't know.

There was no visible doorway, so waiting seemed right. But for what?

My ears popped as the air pressure changed next to me, signaling that I had company. I turned to find Gabriel studying me with a serious frown.

"Welcome to the celestial waiting room. Seems you have a decision to make."

"Me? I need the Host to decide if I've done enough to earn my wings back."

He smiled, the expression gentler than I was used to from my archangel friend as he lay a hand on my shoulder.

"Caleb, I've been trying to steer you for quite a while, but I think the time for subtlety has passed, or you wouldn't be stuck in limbo."

In limbo.

The words struck an ancient fear into my heart. If I hadn't successfully regained my place as a cupid, I'd be cast out, unable to ever return to the Host. Unable to ever get my wings back, or claim my Chosen. A broken destiny, never to be repaired. There would be nothing left to save me from falling.

But if I had earned my place back, did that mean leaving Josie behind? This thing between us was unprecedented, but I knew deep down that it was right.

There has to be a way.

"A decision." I swallowed though my throat was drier than the Sahara. "I'm listening."

"You have to decide if you want to claim Josie as your Chosen."

I rocked back on my heels in shock.

"I really thought that kiss to prove her parents wrong would have done it," he continued with a sigh, "but I guess even *I'm* wrong some of the time. All that fantastic meddling, and you're still stuck. It's rude, really." He sniffed dramatically.

"Wait, *you* were the one pushing her parents to disbelieve our relationship?"

"Guilty as charged."

My feet were suddenly entangled, and I looked down to find three divine felines weaving between my legs.

"Them too." Gabriel crossed his arms. "Their progress reports, however, just continued to illuminate how clueless you were. I used every trick in the book to push you two together. Hell, I even sent her *Nana* to tell her she was meant to be with you. But damn, you two were convinced that the fact you'd tried and failed once before was the end of it. I thought by now you'd know that a case of bad timing doesn't mean something isn't written in the stars."

He rubbed a hand over the back of his neck as he studied me for a reaction. But I was so shocked, it felt like my brain had short-circuited.

Was he telling me I was *free* to claim Josie as my Chosen, or that I had to choose her or the Host?

"What did any of this have to do with you, anyway? Why meddle?" It was barely the tip of the iceberg, but the longer I stayed in the antechamber, the more disembodied I started to feel. I had to choose, and quickly, so I could get out of here.

"The power between you two surpassed even angelic projections." He scratched the back of his head and looked away. "Your time to be together was always now, but seven years ago..." He shrugged. "You jumped the gun."

"You knew even then?" My head swirled with questions but all my beating heart could say was *Josie-Josie-Josie*.

"You weren't the only one to make mistakes." He leaned

forward. "The Host was *not* pleased with me, but the draw between you was too strong to keep you apart. You had your matches to make, and I had mine. But at last, your time has come. The moment of decision is *now*. If you wait any longer, the window will have closed on your and Josie's chance. I let her find the book, you ignored the signs. I led you to the bookstore, you figured it was to help you match couples. You are no easy mark, Caleb. Just like Marigold and Axel, yesterday was the final day for you two to decide before setting off repercussions that span generations. Frankly, I didn't think you'd cut it so close to the line, but you're stubborn. That's unusual for a cupid. And yet another trait you and Josie have in common." He winked at me. "So, *cupid*, do you believe that love truly conquers all?"

I gaped at him, jaw slack, completely flabbergasted.

I get to choose. An angel has never before had a human Chosen, yet they are letting me choose.

All the rest faded to background noise. I was here, in the antechamber, to decide if I was going to claim Josie as my Chosen or reclaim my birthright and my wings. Of course, I wanted her. I wanted her with every fiber of my being, every molecule yearned to complete the bond—and yes, I could feel it now that we were on the incorporeal plane—the golden tendrils that transcended time and space, fragile as silk thread and yet connecting us. Binding our souls.

Such small beginnings, but it meant that the seal had begun to weave us together. My power hadn't been on the fritz at all. It knew what I'd been too stubborn to see all along—Josie was my Chosen.

Relief flooded me, just like the water rushing back on Alki beach. *She's mine.*

Everything else felt less catastrophic, less overwhelming, now that I knew I wasn't losing it.

But what would happen with the Host if I claimed her as my Chosen? Would I be cast down, sealing my fate as fallen from grace and hers as bound to a being who would only grow darker as my angelic light faded for good?

I couldn't condemn her to that fate. It would be worse than death, for a beautiful spirit such as hers to be bound to ever-deepening darkness. One day the change would be complete, and she'd find herself bound for eternity to a demon.

But... if I didn't choose her, didn't complete the seal, she'd be alone forever. She'd have her bookshop, her friends, and her cats. Even her family would be by her side; I truly believed that now. But companionship? A spouse, children? She wouldn't have any of that.

And I wouldn't be able to go back to her. I saw that now, saw it laid out in Gabriel's somber words that our window was about to close, permanently.

What would she want me to choose? It felt wrong to take that decision from her, but I'd missed my chances to ask her. *Fuck*.

I'd never really explained. My head had been so far up my ass that I'd never sat her down and told her what she was to me. How precious. Granted, I didn't know it was *possible*, not even to the bitter end.

I never even told her the truth, that I loved her too. Could I leave her alone forever without telling her that? What a depressing fate, to never know how deeply you were loved.

"It's time, Caleb. The Host grows impatient."

I looked up, letting my fingers trace over the cover of the book that she'd kept safe for me for seven long, lonely years. The faintest whiff of her essence still clung to it.

246

And suddenly, I knew. There was only one choice.

"I'm ready."

He nodded, looking grave.

We stepped forward, side by side, into a doorway of light.

THIRTY-ONE

Josie

As I approached the base of Mount Rainier, a quiet melancholy welled up in my chest. The towering mass of stone and snow loomed above me, but it was mine for the taking. Caleb and I had said we'd do it together, all those years ago, but I had to make my own way now.

He'd been gone for three weeks, and though there were moments I thought I felt his presence, his watchful eye upon me, I knew it had to be from afar.

The air was crisp and clean, filling my lungs with an invigorating chill as I shouldered my gear, the weight comfortable and grounding. I ignored the voice inside me that said I was like Frodo leaving the Shire, because I was not in the mood to confront any wizards, warlocks, or witches on this trip. Especially since I knew now more than ever that it was a real possibility.

Each tiny detail of the world around me seemed magnified, the crunch of gravel underfoot, the sweet, sap-filled scent of the pine trees, the cool touch of the early morning wind against my skin. I was alone, yet I felt an inexplicable connection to everything around me—to the mountain, to the sky, to the air I breathed.

I had decided to undertake this expedition alone, equipped with only my backpack and the grief that fueled my heart. I didn't want the distraction of a trekking group, the chatter, and the constant companionship. I needed solitude—a chance to clear my mind and my soul, to face my own thoughts and fears without the noise of the world interfering.

I knew it was foolish, but a tiny seed of hope had taken root within me. If I could just reach the top of this mountain, to see alone what Caleb and I had planned to do together, I might find a way to start over.

Perhaps on the summit of Mount Rainier, I could begin the next phase of my life without Caleb.

The whistle of a gentle wind made the vast expanse feel even more lonely.

... until I heard a purr.

"Now what on earth are you doing here?"

There was no point in asking, for Gatsby, Matilda, and Heathcliff were never going to be the domesticated felines who puttered about the house. I wouldn't have pegged them as hiking companions either, but there they were, ready to go.

"Well," I murmured. "Looks like it's just the four of us, then."

With a deep breath, I straightened up, casting one last glance at the world below before turning to face the path. As I headed forward, the cats fell into step beside me, their little bodies weaving around my legs as we ventured onward.

By the end of the day, my body was wiped, but the sense of accomplishment overtook any aching muscles. I found a flat, grassy area nestled against a cluster of boulders, perfectly sheltered from the wind. The snow-covered peaks reflected the fading light, casting a soft, silvery glow over my little hideaway. It wasn't exactly cozy like a warm bed, but up here, surrounded by nature's raw beauty, it felt just right. I wrestled the tent into submission and crawled inside with Gatsby, Heathcliff, and Matilda right behind me.

They had taken every step at my side, stopping with me to nibble or when tears welled in my eyes so badly that I risked missing the path. With their little bodies curled up against my tired legs and their purring filling the quiet night, I drifted into a deep, comforting sleep.

Until the tent flapped in what must have been a freak windstorm.

The cats pawed at the tent door and swiftly rushed out as I opened it, probably seeking shelter in something that wasn't about to blow away. I, however, had no other choice.

I hunkered down and waited as the morning was a forbidding bluster of hail and wild gusts, turning my tent into a pitiful excuse of a fortress.

None of this had been in the forecast. It was like the mountain had turned on me overnight.

"Why? Why is this happening *now*?" I screamed at the wind as it whipped against the tent, hoping that oh-so-powerful Host up there heard me, too. "Why can't I catch one single break? Isn't it bad enough that I was left behind? Now, the one thing I'm trying to do to heal myself has to go wrong."

The storm outside wasn't half as bad as the one in my head. I was *mad*. Mad at myself, mad at the weather, mad at the heavens, just a little bit mad at Caleb for having to go. The tent was too small to contain my raging emotions, so even though the gusts threatened to tear it away, I scrambled out of it.

"Is this all you got?" I yelled at the sky. "Don't you want to throw me off the side of the mountain? Or maybe break my leg so that I have to crawl back down, leaving my dignity behind?"

My voice was getting hoarse, but I couldn't stop myself.

"It's not fair! None of this! All I wanted was to find my future. Is this it? Is this the future that's seeking me, a freak storm with runaway cats, and the love of my life leaving me behind? It's not right!"

The wind tore the tears from my face.

"Caleb! Can you even hear me anymore?" My screams turned to anguished whispers as I poured it all out into the storm's onslaught. "Why? Why did it have to be like this when everything around us, everything inside us knew that we were meant to be together? Caleb!" My voice broke on his name, the sobs racking me too much to contain.

The world went dark, and I choked with terror.

I was enveloped in warmth, the winds instantly muffled, and I was in an enclosure, a cocoon that protected me, though it was stifling me, too. With my arms tucked against my chest, I had no room to move. I could hardly breathe.

Am I dying?

And then there was light. I was right where I had been, on the side of the mountain, but everything had changed. No more wind, no more squall. Only a few fluffy clouds were in the sky, which I was sure was a shade of blue I had never seen before.

Beside me stood Caleb. But not the same Caleb I knew.

Vast and luminous, his wings filled the space around us, and I studied them with awe. Silken and mesmerizing, each feather shimmered in the colors of champagne, blushing rose petals, and the occasional deep red among the others. They were the color of love itself. Fanned out, they were majestic and otherworldly. As if they could only be half-present in this plane of existence.

His muscles tensed as he tucked his wings behind him and brushed my cheek with the back of his fingers.

I shook my head, but he was still there. In jeans and a fitted linen shirt, he was not an apparition and not a dream. I squinted up, his ethereal figure towering over me. Feathers fluttered gently in the light breeze that had been an icy tempest just a moment before.

"That storm," I started, my voice quiet. "That was you."

It was part accusation, part awe, part sheer delight that I didn't dare let myself feel.

Caleb's response was a grin, boyish and cheeky, his eyes gleaming with mischief. *That* was the Caleb I knew.

"Want to go for a ride?" he asked, extending a hand. The instant I nodded, he swept me up, one arm securely around me, and we were off. It wasn't just that his reappearance was unbelievable, it was that I didn't know what it *meant*. After all Caleb and I had gone through, I wasn't able to let go of the idea that this might be a divine ending to our incredible story.

Ascending through the crisp air, everything felt unreal. His divine energy wrapped around me, warm and protective. "Are you afraid?" he asked, his arms holding me firmly but not tightly, the muscle from his shoulders and biceps a comfort that only he could give.

"I've never felt safer." I held his gaze, reveling in the fact that *he'd come back*.

I ran my fingers along the curve of his jaw, a thrum inside me demanding I take those luscious lips with mine. While I might have doubts about the significance of seeing Caleb on the side of a mountain, my body knew exactly how it felt. It asked no questions, entertained no doubt. It needed to have

Caleb closer than he'd ever been, to be filled by him. To feel his breath on every curve, to feel his tongue on my most sensitive places, to surround his cock inch by glorious inch.

As if he could hear my thoughts, he pulled me tighter, his hand caressing the small of my back as we flew, then reaching down to grab hold of my ass and press me tighter to him. The thickness of his cock was stiff against my stomach, and a small gasp escaped my lips at the sensation. Caleb looked at me, his eyes hungry as a different kind of smile spread across his face.

"That's my needy girl," he whispered, sending another jolt of awareness through me. "But first, I have a question for you."

I playfully slapped his chest. "You couldn't have asked me on the ground?"

His eyes crinkled and he relaxed. "I could have, but the view's better up here."

"Are you about to start singing that song from *Aladdin*?"

"What?"

Oh, Caleb and his angelic lack of pop culture references. "Not important. What's the question?" My tone was light, but a lump began to form in my throat. Whatever this question was, I didn't know that I wanted to answer.

"Just you wait. When we reach the top, I think it will all be clear."

He landed on the summit of Mt. Rainier, the world sprawled below us, a vast expanse of beauty that took my breath away. It was the sort of sight that put everything into perspective, the sort of sight that made you believe in the magic of life again.

He held my hands so I wouldn't slip as a wing encircled me.

The world unfurled around us like a masterpiece painted by the hands of the divine. The vibrant green of the valleys sprawled below, adorned with wildflowers that bloomed like a palette of summer's colors—vivid yellow, burning orange, and soft lavender, which I still swore I caught the scent of, despite the distance.

We were somewhere between heaven and Earth, a magical bubble of our own making.

That thought interrupted the intensity of the moment, and I couldn't pretend it didn't scare me. Was this his last goodbye?

"Caleb—" I lost my footing, which would have brought a rocky end to our rocky relationship before I even had the answer I needed.

"I've got you." He had a hold of my wrist, and with a pull, I was right back in front of him. His hands steadied me, running down my sides until they settled on my hips. He stepped closer so I had no choice but to look up at him, despite the nervous energy that made me want to fidget. His chest rose and fell with a steadying breath before he started to speak.

"Josie," he started, and I closed my eyes at the sound of my name on his lips.

Just a little longer. I wanted—no, *needed*—to stay in a place where he and I could be together. I might have been delusional, in denial, but whatever it was, I had to have him a little longer. If he was about to say goodbye forever, I needed to savor this last moment of delicious possibility, his heat and strength and scent surrounding me, making me feel whole.

"Caleb..." I pressed myself against him, letting my breasts mold against the hard muscles in his chest. My nipples immediately responded, and a rush of heat flowed through me, my underwear soaked through from even that little bit of contact.

Caleb's eyes shut, a throaty groan coming from his lips

before he said, "I can feel everything that's happening to you. The desire, the lust—"

"The desperate need," I finished, taking his cheeks in my hands and making him look at me. "What I feel goes beyond sense, Caleb. I'm aching for you, like I cannot be complete without having you again. On me. Over me. Inside me."

A low rumble, possessive and fiery, told me he felt the same. There was just one thing.

"Caleb," I mustered up the courage before my aching core overtook all sense. "Is this the end?"

He put a finger to my lips, gently stopping me in my tracks, his eyes reflecting the blue of the sky above. "Oh, my Josie. Is that what you thought?" He stroked my hair with such tenderness that I melted into him. "It turns out that the future I sought was seeking me, too."

He leaned in, his lips meeting mine in a kiss that was all possession, so overwhelming I felt it down to the tips of my toes.

THIRTY-TWO

Caleb

WITH OUR LIPS STILL LOCKED, I HELD HER CLOSE TO my chest and swept us back up and into the air. She gasped against my lips, fingertips digging into the soft shirt I wore.

"It's okay, I won't let you fall."

"I trust you," she breathed the words against my neck. The close contact—the warmth of her breath—sent a surge of adrenaline through my veins that was even greater than the joy of flying again after so many years without my wings. I pushed them hard, enjoying the feel of the air flying past us as we swept above the landscape below.

"Josie, you are the heart that beats in my chest. The power that fills my spirit. The heavens have ordained our match, for now and for eternity."

Tears filled her eyes as I spoke, and she bit her bottom lip. If I couldn't sense the joy pouring off of her, I would have been a nervous wreck. Instead, I was just elated. I'd spent so much time thinking I could never have her, all that was left was euphoria at how wrong I'd been.

She's mine.

"As you know, there is a special bond that an angel can bestow on only one other being, for the whole of their existence." I spoke slowly, watching her face as each and every word sank in.

She was wide-eyed, digging her nails into my pectoral muscles through my shirt without realizing it. I relished the bite of pain. It meant she was solid and real in my arms.

"I know. You've told me of the *Chosen*. But you told me you and I could never have that bond, because no angel has ever bonded with a human before."

"Well, I was wrong. Apparently, our match was determined years ago, but it wasn't the right time. But we overcame every obstacle we thought prevented us from being together. Sometimes, it's just meant to be, no matter the odds. *You* are the one for me, the one written in the stars since the beginning of time. Josie, will you accept your place as my Chosen, and seal this bond between us?"

"Yes!" Her voice shook with emotion, but her hands didn't when she reached up and cupped my jaw, drawing my lips back down to hers with fierce possession of her own.

How did I get so damn lucky to have her? I wasn't sure, but I was never going to question it again.

Our tongues tangled in a feverish kiss. Her fingers dug into my hair, pulling me closer. I let my wings drive down hard, lifting us up into the clouds so that we were wrapped in our own, private cocoon.

Using my power, I held her secure as I reached down and played with the hem of her shirt. It was a sensible hiking tank top, but it didn't diminish the fire I felt when I looked at her. I was determined to take it slow, make sure she enjoyed every second—but Josie was driving full steam ahead, not the least bit interested in *slow*. She reached down and peeled her top off, leaving her in a baby-pink sports bra that framed her cleavage perfectly. I sucked in a breath as I got a full view of her breasts, the perfect curve of her making me groan with need.

"Uhm, where do I put this?" She looked around, blinking slowly as she seemed to realize where we were, and that there was nowhere to put the clothes.

"Do you want me to take care of our clothes?" I asked, voice husky with desire.

"Yes." Her pupils were blown wide when she dove back into our kiss, so I plucked the top from her fingertips.

Josie wound herself around me like a vine, locking her heels behind my back. I let both of my hands roam up her back, stopping at the band of the sports bra, teasing the sensitive skin over her spine.

She tugged at my hair, impatient for me to get on with it. Between one heartbeat and the next, I had all of our clothes off of us, and deposited them in the bedroom at my house. She gasped against my lips at the feeling of all of our skin, suddenly bare. She was smooth, soft perfection from head to toe, and I let my head fall back at the sensation.

"My Chosen, my perfect Chosen." I let my hands slip down and cup the soft globes of her ass, kneading the flesh beneath my fingertips.

Now, it was her turn to moan and drop her forehead to my shoulder. I could feel the wet head of her center pressed against my abs, and I couldn't wait to taste her again.

I dropped kisses down the column of her throat. "Do you trust me?" I murmured against her collarbone.

"With my life," she answered.

I may as well have been struck by lightning, the way her words affected me. I was thrumming with need for her, and my desire to take things slow evaporated in an instant.

"Lie back. My power will hold you." She didn't even hesitate, leaning back and letting her hands skate down my sides to rest on her thighs. Her hair floated around her like a curly halo, and the sight was sheer perfection. I was harder than steel and dying to sink into her tight heat.

With all of her on display for me, I let my lips and tongue tease every bit of available skin. I cupped her breasts, teasing first one side and then the other with my tongue until she started grinding against me, using her heels to pull me tighter and tighter against her center.

"Somebody is impatient."

"I've been waiting *seven years*, Caleb. I'm still a little afraid you're going to disappear." Her eyes were closed, head dipped back in bliss, but I couldn't let that stand.

I dragged her up flush against my chest. Her nipples were hard peaks, chafing against my chest and driving me to distraction. But this was important. She had to know everything.

"Look at me, Josie."

She bit her bottom lip between her teeth and looked up at me under her eyelashes. Her aura was tinged with vulnerability, and I knew every word I said next was important.

Fuck, I never want her to stop looking at me like that.

"I'm *never* leaving you again. My power is going to bind us together permanently."

Josie nodded, but I knew that little worry line between her eyebrows was only getting erased in one way. She'd feel it when the seal locked into place, and she'd know.

I kissed her, hard and fast on the lips, and then urged her to lean back again. Once she was sprawled back out, I unlocked her feet and lifted her hips until her core was even with my face. Her thighs trembled as I hooked them over my shoulders, but she cried out in pleasure as soon as my lips met her pussy.

I feasted on her, licking and sucking and kissing straight through her screams of pleasure as first one orgasm, then another rolled through her. I didn't stop until her hands landed on mine, where I held her hips.

"Caleb, I can't take any more. Please. I need you. Please, please—" She moaned again as I pointedly worked her clit with the flat of my tongue.

And then she unraveled again, screaming her bliss and arching against my hold as her honey dripped down my chin. I held her hands as she rode out the orgasm, and then let her slowly sink back down my body.

When our foreheads were touching I held her there, wrapped in my arms. Her eyes were glazed as she pressed little kisses to my cheeks.

"Why did you stop?" she asked, wiggling her hips against me.

"Are you ready? Once we complete the binding, it can't be undone, not for any reason. It's forever."

She gripped my chin, her eyes clearing as she looked into mine. "I'm sure. No more stalling, Caleb." Without waiting for my answer, she leaned down and nipped my bottom lip.

I lowered her the last bit, the blunt head of my cock meeting her slippery folds. She arched her back, and I let her take control as she guided herself down onto me. She slowly took me, inch by inch, and my power turned golden in the air around us.

When I was fully seated inside her, she clung to me, breathing hard as she took a moment to adjust. Her palms pressed tightly against my shoulder blades, as if even now she was afraid I was going to disappear.

"Look at me, Josie," I urged as the pleasure tore through me like a living thing.

When her eyes fluttered up to mine, I began to move, slowly at first. Long strokes in and out, holding her gaze the entire time. She pumped her hips in time with mine, crashing into me faster and faster as the power spiraled higher around us, in a beautiful golden cascade.

"Are you ready?"

"Yes! Caleb, ahh—" Her channel locked into a vice grip as she orgasmed around me, and she nearly drove me over the edge before I was ready. I stilled for a second, trying to concentrate over the incredible sensation of her. When my left hand was exactly where I wanted her to wear my mark—across her upper thigh—I started moving faster, driving her higher in the midst of her release, not letting her come back down.

If I had my way, she'd never come down. We'd live in this bubble of bliss forever. But first, I had to bind us, complete the seal.

When I was on the precipice of my own release, I let the power I'd been holding so tightly go in a rush. It surged through my veins, concentrating in my palm as golden light flared between us.

She screamed, the ecstasy it added too great for her human senses to comprehend. Her body bowed, seating me even deeper inside her as my own release took me, burning down my spine in a molten wave. I shouted her name, unable to hold anything back as I filled her.

We stayed locked together until the light faded, and then I pulled her close. Our bodies were damp, with water from the clouds and sweat from our exertions.

She trembled lightly in my arms as I brushed a curl back from her forehead.

"That was... incredible. What was that, at the end?"

"That was the seal. You'll wear my mark here," I let my

fingers trail over the smooth flesh of her thigh, where a golden wing glowed under my touch. "And I'll wear yours, here." I pressed her fingertips back over my shoulder blade where she'd held me, her own matching mark permanently branded into my skin. To a human, they would look like any other tattoo. But any time a bonded angel touched their mate's mark, it glowed, the divine energy inside it proof of the sealed bond between them.

"It's really real, then. I'm your Chosen," she whispered in awe, tears glittering along her lower lids. I kissed along her cheekbones, chasing them away.

"You're my Chosen, now and forever."

THIRTY-THREE

Josie

SEVERAL MONTHS LATER

THE WARM GLOW OF THE BOOKISH CAT'S LIGHTS
spilled across the shelves, casting a romantic spell over the place.
It was twilight, my favorite time of day, when the shop
hummed softly like a contented purr—or maybe that was
Matilda. A few lingering customers thumbed through pages,
the faint scent of vanilla mixing with the aroma of books both
old and new. Scattered heart-shaped garlands hung from the
shelves, and a small bowl of chocolate truffles sat atop the
counter beside me, a delicious reminder that it was Valentine's
Day. The store was mine, my sanctuary, and tonight, it buzzed
with a touch of extra romantic magic.

Which meant it was only a matter of time before Caleb
appeared.

From somewhere behind a stack of mysteries, Heathcliff
emerged, padding gracefully across the wooden floor like the
feline royalty he believed himself to be. Gatsby followed close
behind, while Matilda was perched on a shelf in the poetry
section, tail flicking with the cadence of her own quiet

musings. I shook my head, smiling, and grateful that they hadn't left despite Gabriel dismissing them from their mission.

I felt eyes on me and turned to see Caleb wandering between the shelves, but his eyes were on me. He raised his fingers to his lips and then pointed to the individuals browsing through the new French cookbooks I got through an independent publisher.

The man and woman were oblivious to the magic swirling around them. Caleb, with his usual understated elegance, had maneuvered them into this nook of the shop with all the subtlety of a master cupid at work. The couple struck up a conversation, and their enthusiasm made me smile. Caleb had drawn them together over a shared interest in something mundane yet oddly intimate: bread-making.

Caleb's celestial powers were never flashy—more of a gentle nudge than a shove. As the couple's fingers touched over the book, I saw the faintest spark of attraction pass between them, like a flicker of a candle just waiting to burn bright.

"Do you have another copy of this?" the woman asked while keeping her fingertips on the book.

"Sorry," I shrugged as I smiled on the inside, "the translations from French were few and far between. I was lucky to get that copy at all." Warmth came over me, a wave of communication from Caleb and the right words came to me. "But you know that baking in France is an art to be shared..."

The man smiled at the woman. "I would love to buy you this book."

She smiled back, a blush growing up her neck. "Only if I can bake you the first loaf."

It was borderline cheesy, though I'd never read a line quite like it before.

I rang up the sale, the couple never taking their eyes off each other. I could have charged ten times more for the book and they'd never have been any the wiser, not that I ever would. Love born over French loaves on Valentine's Day sounded perfect for these two.

The bell above the door tinkled as they left, chatting about the benefits of homemade versus commercial sourdough starters.

Well done, my heart, Caleb communicated to me from across the shop. There were a few other folks browsing, and some words were best shared silently. *You have a gift.*

Pride bloomed in my chest. This was our life: me and my celestial matchmaker, creating new love stories in the midst of our own. I glanced at Caleb, who caught my eye and winked, my heart doing that familiar flip.

How was it that one look from him still made me feel like a girl falling in love for the first time all over again?

We held each other's eyes, desire growing like a vine that tied us together, as the last of the browsing patrons stepped outside.

No customers in the shop, I sent to him through our connection. *And you know I got a new shipment of Gaelic dictionaries in the back...*

The dim light caught the sharp angles of his face, his eyes smoldering with an affection that left me breathless. His gaze traveled over me, slow and deliberate, as if committing every inch of me to memory. I swallowed, feeling a rush of heat coil in my belly. He didn't need to say a word—his intentions were as clear as the tension building between us.

Let's celebrate another couple who have just begun their love story, he said through silent air.

Let's tear off these clothes so you can fuck me senseless, hmmm? I headed toward the storeroom, keeping my eyes on him.

He didn't reply immediately. Instead, he walked toward me with a grace that was almost predatory, each step sending little tremors through my body. My back pressed against the door, and I realized I was holding my breath. By the time he reached me, his lips curved into a small, knowing smile.

I laid my hand on his chest. "Maybe that couple will get up to some naughty stuff tonight, too."

"All in a day's work," he murmured, his voice roughened with desire, the sound vibrating straight through me. His hand came up to cup my cheek, his thumb grazing my bottom lip.

He leaned in, his lips brushing mine in a teasing, barely-there kiss that made my knees go weak. I closed my eyes, my senses sharpening, every nerve attuned to him. Heat radiated from his body as his mouth claimed mine fully then, a surge of passion that left me gasping.

My hands found their way to his hair, tangling in the softness of his curls as he deepened the kiss. His tongue stroked against mine, the taste of him heady and intoxicating. I melted into him, arching my body against his as he pressed me against the door. His hands skimmed down my sides, setting every inch of me alight, and I couldn't suppress the soft moan that escaped my lips.

"God, Josie," he breathed against my mouth, his voice thick with need. "You're everything."

I barely had time to process his words before he scooped me up into his arms, my legs wrapping instinctively around his waist. He closed the storeroom door, our lips never parting, his movements fluid and assured.

AFTER OUR STOLEN moments in the storeroom, I walked back out to the front counter, a stack of Gaelic dictionaries in my hands and Caleb's. And then...

Everything *changed*.

A surge of energy erupted within me, searing through every cell of my body. I gasped, the force of it blinding, like molten gold flowing through my veins, so strongly I nearly dropped the books. My skin tingled, every nerve vibrating with sensations that stole my breath. The room around us blurred, bathed in a golden radiance that seemed to pour out from me.

Caleb stilled, his eyes widening as he dropped the dictionaries to look at me. "Josie..." he whispered, awe lacing his voice. "You're glowing."

I blinked up at him, dazed and exhilarated, as the light around me slowly began to dim. My vision cleared, and I could see him staring at me with wonder. A new awareness settled over me, as though the world had shifted, revealing secrets that had been hidden in plain sight. I could sense things I never had before—the pulse of emotions, the faint whispers of thoughts around us. It was as if some barrier had broken inside me, leaving me wide open to everything.

"What... what just happened?" I managed to gasp out, my voice trembling.

He smiled, his thumb tracing my cheek tenderly. "You were always extraordinary."

The world around me had shifted, and everything felt alive with an intensity I'd never experienced. Colors around the room seemed to shimmer, more vivid and vibrant than before. The dark mahogany shelves glowed with rich undertones, each spine gleaming in hues I hadn't noticed in the light's reflection. The lingering scent of paper and ink smelled sharper, almost sweet.

The air itself vibrated with a hum of emotions, layered and complex, like music, entire symphonies that hadn't even yet been written.

And Caleb. Oh, Caleb. He shone more brightly than anything else in the shop, his presence like a beacon of warmth and light that wrapped around me. His emotions washed over me in waves: awe, joy, love, and something even deeper, more profound. I felt the pulse of his heartbeat without touching him, a steady rhythm that matched my own.

"Our auras are entwined more deeply than before," Caleb said as his eyes wandered over me. He lifted his arm and extended his hand to caress my shoulder, tracing down to the place his seal lay on my thigh. The glow intensified for a moment before dimming away again. "Perhaps that's what you feel?"

I could only nod, overwhelmed by the rush of sensations. I could feel everything: his happiness, his wonder, his love for me —a love so deep, it nearly brought me to tears.

But then, just as I was beginning to wrap my mind around this new reality, I sensed something deeply *wrong* on the side-walk. A man—no, a *shifter*, I could now sense for myself—tall and powerfully built, stood on the other side of the glass door. His eyes scanned first me, then lingered knowingly on Caleb, as if they'd met before. There was a storm of emotions pouring off him, so strong it enveloped me in melancholy and loneli-ness. But before I could say a thing, he bolted. The melancholy left me as quickly as it had arrived.

Whatever had caused this newfound awareness, it was going to take some getting used to.

"That man…" I started, taking my time to find the right words, but nothing came.

"I've seen him before. At the café." Caleb sighed. "But the curse on him is beyond even my power."

The idea of a curse created more questions than it answered, but I didn't get a chance to ask anything more because at that moment, the room filled with a blinding light. I gasped, clutching Caleb's arm as he instinctively stepped in front of me, shielding me.

When the light faded, I blinked, and there, standing in the center of the Bookish Cat, was Gabriel. Only he didn't look as regal and untouchable as the times I'd seen him before. His eyes sparkled with a casual friendliness, like he was just some guy dropping by to chat.

"Well, this is cozy," Gabriel remarked, looking around the bookstore with an amused grin. "I love what you've done with the place." He smiled as his gaze landed on me. "First of all, congrats, you two." He pointed at my stomach, wiggling his eyebrows. "Little Nephilim on the way! Exciting stuff, right? The new level of sensory input when carrying an angel-child takes some getting used to, but I'm sure you're up for it."

I froze, a jolt of energy surging through me at his words. My hand instinctively flew to my abdomen, heart pounding so loudly I was sure Caleb could hear it.

Caleb wrapped his arms securely around my waist, holding me close. I pressed my forehead against his chest, feeling the steady rise and fall of his breathing as I tried to process what had just happened.

Nephilim. Angel-child.

Caleb's eyes shone as he rested his hand over mine on my stomach.

"Our child." He chuckled, the sound light and relaxed,

sending every lingering thought of the strange shifter away. "*Of course* you'd be covered by a golden aura. How do you feel?" he whispered, his voice full of concern but tinged with the joy I felt myself.

My cheeks flushed but couldn't help the smile that broke across my face as I turned to Caleb. "So… it's true?"

"It is. I would have spotted it myself, if we hadn't just been, uh, occupied." He blushed. My eternal, sexy angel *blushed*. I wanted to laugh at his expression, but I smothered it behind my palm.

Gabriel didn't seem to notice, his smile warm and genuine. "Your kid's going to be something special—a bridge between our realms, I have no doubt." He laughed softly, crossing his arms. "And let me tell you, this child will have some crazy talents, but that's for another time. Right now, enjoy the moment. This is big. The whole Host is talking."

Caleb pulled Gabriel into a big hug, clapping him on the back with a quiet, "Thank you."

As joy bubbled up within me, Gabriel rubbed his hands together with unbridled glee. Glee that made me both suspicious and a little bit nervous. "Looks like a celebration is in order! And by the way, you've got company coming in three… two…"

The door tinkled as Nana Geraldine burst through with a loud whoop, streamers in hand. "Where is she? Where is she? There she is!" She rushed at me with the sprightliness of a septuagenarian, and I swore she lifted me off the floor with her hug. "I am so, so happy for you." She kissed my cheek. "We all are."

"Surprise!" Mom squealed as she rushed in with a cake. "My baby is having a baby!"

"And look!" Dad pointed with pride. "We were even able to

get a last-minute cake! We had to make do with a Valentine's one, but we figured you would understand."

The cake was adorned with the most elaborate three-dimensional baby cupid I had ever seen. "It's perfect," I said as Caleb shook his head with a big, goofy smile on his face.

"But how did you know..." I looked at Nana.

"Let's say a little—um—birdie told us." She shimmied her shoulders in Gabriel's direction. "And of course the whole family needed to come down to celebrate with you. A baby!"

Gabriel cleared his throat and whispered to Caleb, "I'll go set up the kid's room." In that same instant, I heard a faint pop and Gabriel vanished, while my family wasn't looking.

Birdie, my ass. That Gabriel can't keep a secret to save his soul... Oh, never mind.

I was swept into a massive hug, my face smothered by red-and-blue checked flannel. "I'm so happy for you, little sis." I hugged Fred back with all my might. If anyone had told me a year ago that this was where we'd be today, I'd have told them they were high in Wonderland.

But there we were. Caleb. Mom and Dad. Fred. And Nana.

My heart swelled with feelings that weren't just my own. A new power now surged through my veins, coloring my view of everyone around me. My family—each of them lit up with a joy that shimmered, a swirl of elation and tenderness.

Then, there was Caleb. My love. His pride and quiet adoration, steady and fierce like an anchor in the storm.

And, of course, the life growing inside me—a blend of hope, awe, and the tiniest flicker of uncertainty that came from deep within myself. It was more than I'd ever dared to dream. The rush of emotions, both mine and those around me, overwhelmed me, leaving me breathless in the most wonderful way.

"You are everything to me, and this child already has my heart," he whispered, his voice raw with emotion. "I love you."

I whispered into his ear the words that had made forever a reality.

"And love conquers all."

Our intimate moment came to an abrupt end when Nana stepped in, taking me by the shoulders. "I am so proud of you, Josie." Her eyes misted over, but a grin quickly overtook her face. "And I know you know that no party would be complete without—"

"Oh, no."

"—a flashmob!" She threw her hands in the air and a parade of movement burst into the Bookish Cat. Heathcliff, Matilda, and Gatsby headed for the high shelves as we were suddenly surrounded by jazz hands, kick-ball-changes, and streamers in every color of the rainbow. "Let's show this baby some love, girls!"

Caleb pulled me into his arms and we *laughed*. My life had taken a lot of twists and turns. Some of them crazy, like Nana Geraldine's flashmobs, and others simply supernatural. But as I leaned into Caleb's chest, I was at peace. *At home.*

Just an angel and his Chosen, with a baby on the way.

Ready for More?

If you enjoyed Caleb and Josie's story, you'll love Fated to the Wolf Prince by April L. Moon. ***Great Pack Gathering. Three little words, one mandate that ruined my life.*** What happens with the prince of the shifter world gets matched with a lowly psi, the lowest rank of any pack? Find out in Fated to the Wolf Prince, free to read with Kindle Unlimited.

Grab Fated to the Wolf Prince here!

>»—♥—→

How about that dark and brooding wolf shifter, what's his story? Find out in The Cursed Wolf King by Harley Hunt! Logan is desperate to save his pack from a deadly curse. All he has to do is find the woman who spoke the curse and kill her. But when he finds her? She's his fated mate.

Grab The Cursed Wolf King here!

Pick up your steamy bonus scenes...

If you couldn't get enough of Caleb and Josie, good news!

Remember that sexy scene in the bookshop's storeroom? Get an extended version with all the spice by joining Harley Hunt's newsletter and get that scene now!

https://BookHip.com/BPJTPNP

Join April L. Moon's newsletter and get a bonus scene of Caleb and Josie taking off on an international sexy date night.

https://BookHip.com/VDSTPZW

Author Note on Marine Life

Hello, lovely readers! April and Harley here with a quick note on Chapter Twenty-Eight. When we decided to set this book in Seattle, we knew we wanted to lean into a lot of the fun local landmarks, as well as the unique geography of the area. One exceptionally beautiful thing about Seattle is the coastline, and the marine life surrounding it.

Because we included the beached orca rescue, we wanted to include some more information on how those rescues actually happen, and how you can report a stranded marine animal if ever you see one on the beach. We *wouldn't* recommend approaching stranded wildlife yourself, unless you happen to be a fallen cupid with divine powers of your own. 😊 But since we did a ton of research for our book, we thought you might find some of it as fascinating as we did, and wanted to share how the real-life heroes do the rescuing.

Happy reading!
XOXO,
April and Harley

savethewhales.org
uswhales.org
fisheries.noaa.gov/whales

Playlist

"Stay With Me"—Sam Smith
"Something Just Like This"—The Chainsmokers & Coldplay
"Good Old-Fashioned Lover Boy"—Queen
"Thunderstruck"—AC/DC
"Flowers"—Miley Cyrus
"No Light, No Light"—Florence + The Machine
"Where It Ends"—Bailey Zimmerman
"Take It Slow"—Conner Smith feat. Ryan Hurd
"New Years Day"—Taylor Swift
"Come on Get Higher"—Matt Nathanson
"Someone You Loved"—Lewis Capaldi
"Say It Right"—Nelly Furtado
"Halo"—Beyoncé

About the Authors

April L. Moon

A lover of all things paranormal, she thinks the story didn't stop at *Twilight*. April lives in Florida, with her husband and two children, and the Goldendoodle who runs the place. When she's not writing, she can be found watching *Supernatural* and *Grimm*, her two favorite shows, and eating copious amounts of chocolate. If you love fated mates with cinnamon roll alphas and smart heroines, check out April's first series, which starts with *Fated to the Wolf Prince*! It's an epic shifter romance you won't be able to put down.

Harley Hunt

Harley Hunt has always had a soft spot for dark forests, full moons, and heroes with a hint of danger. When not dreaming up steamy paranormal worlds, Harley can be found sipping wine during sunset, savoring French cheese, and spoiling a very sweet Golden Retriever (definitely not a werewolf). Harley's first book, *The Cursed Wolf King*, kicks off a gripping wolf-shifter romance series—a tale of forbidden love, fierce loyalty, and the kind of passion that bites back.

www.ingramcontent.com/pod-product-compliance
Lightning Source LLC
Chambersburg PA
CBHW020436030726
47495CB00006B/1829